Red, Green, or Murder

Books by Steven Havill

The Posadas County Mysteries
Heartshot
Bitter Recoil
Twice Buried
Before She Dies
Privileged to Kill
Prolonged Exposure
Out of Season
Dead Weight
Bag Limit
*Red, Green, or Murder**
Scavengers
A Discount for Death
Convenient Disposal
Statute of Limitations
Final Payment
The Fourth Time Is Murder

Other Novels
The Killer
The Worst Enemy
LeadFire
TimberBlood

*Although *Red, Green, or Murder* is a new addition to the Posadas County Mysteries series, it takes place immediately after the incidents recorded in *Bag Limit* and before the action in *Scavengers*.

Red, Green, or Murder

Steven F. Havill

Poisoned Pen Press

Library of Congress Catalog Card Number: 2009924489
ISBN: 978-1-59058-666-2 Large Print

Poisoned Pen Press
6962 E. First Ave. Ste. 103
Scottsdale, AZ 85251
www.poisonedpenpress.com
info@poisonedpenpress.com
Printed in the United States of America

For Kathleen

Chapter One

"Hooooowhup!" Dale Torrance bellowed, and his horse understood whatever that language was and ducked hard to the left, cutting off a calf's escape. Dale and another of the H-Bar-T hands, Pat Gabaldon, worked the herd counter-clockwise around the corral's perimeter. Every now and then a calf, all gangly and awkward like a teenager, would bolt sideways from the flow, figuring who knows what in its bovine brain.

I stood in the middle of the arena with Herb Torrance and enjoyed watching the two kids do all the hard work. Half of their efforts went into playing rodeo stars, and they were spending a good deal more time having fun than the actual task at hand demanded. But we were in no hurry—although if I dawdled much longer, I would be late for lunch. Since I had no other plans on this pleasant day, I had agreed to meet another old friend, George Payton, for a take-out burrito after I'd finished with the paperwork for the Torrances.

The late September sun baked the khaki shirt against my shoulders, and the sweet tang of New Mexico dust mixed with livestock manure, horse sweat, and leather. The notes on my clipboard reminded me that I'd hit the same count three times with this particular lot—fourteen cows, four heifers, and six calves. Patrick's blue heeler, Socks, worked the cattle with his nose close to the ground, beady little eyes unwavering.

The twenty-four H-Bar-T brands were all correct, high on the left flank. As each wide-eyed Angus paraded past us, I saw no signs of disease, no coughing or diarrhea, no runny or glazed eyes, no hitches in gait, no dings or dents. But then again, even though I'd been a livestock inspector for less than a year, I could have eyeballed any of Herb Torrance's livestock from the other side of Posadas County with my eyes closed.

"Can you imagine John Chisum doin' this?" Herb's smoke-eroded voice jarred me out of la-la land. I looked across at him, amused. I knew exactly what he meant, and he knew me well enough to know I wouldn't take offense at a gentle jibe aimed at my employers.

"He would have shot somebody, probably," I said. Well, maybe not. Maybe old John would have been enough of a gentleman not to do that. But he sure would have shaken his head in disgust at the thought of the government meddling in his affairs, demanding all kinds of penny-ante paperwork and fancy-schmancy permits.

Today, all Herb Torrance wanted to do was move this particular little herd of cattle from the pasture near his home to a section leased from the U.S. Forest Service up on the back side of Cat Mesa, north of Posadas—about forty miles as the ravens flew, maybe sixty-five by road. The grass was tall and lush there, and the cattle would fatten up for market. But bureaucracies being what they were, ranchers couldn't just move cattle anymore. They couldn't just hire a bunch of dollar-a-day cowpunchers and drive the herd here or there as John Chisum would have done back in the 1880s.

Now, the critters traveled in the modern style, sandwiched hide to hide in a stock trailer pulled behind a snorting diesel one-ton pick-up truck. And before ranchers could even do *that*, the State of New Mexico and the livestock board wanted their cut from the operation, because, after all, it's always about the money.

In this case, the tally that Herb Torrance would have to pay for a transportation permit from me included forty cents for each set of four legs, plus a five dollar service fee, plus a buck a head paid to the New Mexico Beef Council. Herb would fork over $38.60 for a state permit to truck this modest bunch from one little dry patch of New Mexico to another just a few miles away.

If I valued my time even a little bit, the money paid wouldn't cover my time and travel from Posadas to Herb's ranch. But the bureaucrats evidently felt better when the cattle trail was littered with paperwork.

As the herd circled for my inspection—and to give the boys some much-needed practice with their fancy horsemanship—the wind kicked up a little. All morning, it had been calm enough that the dust had risen from the hoof-stirred arena in a great cloud, drifting straight up. Now I felt the breeze against the back of my neck, a reminder that this was a good time to finish up before I missed my luncheon date and before the afternoon gusts made working outside a miserable chore.

As if someone else agreed, the phone in my truck chirped its imperative. I knew my phone was the culprit, since Herb's was on his belt and he made no move for it. I ignored the summons. The phone could wait. The two cowpunchers on horseback gathered the cattle for me once more, and then I waved a "good enough."

The breeze found a foam coffee cup that had been lying under one of the pickup trucks parked outside the arena and gave it a kick. I saw the flicker of white about the same time as did Dale

Torrance's sorrel gelding. Why a thousand-pound horse thought a cup was a fearsome threat, only he knew. Up until then, the horse had been handling himself with professional skill. Young Torrance was only a fair rider, more at home on a four-wheeler or motorcycle, tending to saw the gelding's reins like a pair of handlebars.

He kicked his mount toward the corral side of the herd just as the little white cup bounced and clattered under the rails, then blew between the animal's hind hooves. The gelding saw it and promptly came unglued. The critter crashed sideways into one of the railroad tie uprights, crushing the young cowboy's leg—a thousand-pound hammer with Dale caught against the hard, smelly anvil of the creosoted oak.

A heifer jostled the big gelding and doubled his panic. He danced hard to the left, losing Dale in the process. The youngster went down with a crash, a flail of arms and legs in the dust. The sorrel, brain empty, inadvertently planted a hoof squarely on Dale Torrance's right knee and then rocketed off to mix it up with the cattle. The kid's scream was shrill and chopped off abruptly.

Herb dove into motion. He raced toward his son, his own lame knee turning his sprint into an awkward, skipping shuffle. With a deft snatch, Pat Gabaldon caught the loose horse and eased him back to reality, the gelding's eyes wide and nostrils flared. The cattle drifted into a confused, milling bunch across the way. Socks, the blue heeler, yapped his excitement without a clue about what to do next.

By the time I had crossed the corral, Dale's face was a pasty gray. He had squirmed under the bottom rail of the arena and now lay flat on his back, fists clenched and beating a tattoo on the hard dirt. His breath hissed through clenched teeth, coupled with whimpers and tears. It didn't take an orthopedic surgeon to see that his right knee was a wreck, with the lower half of his leg at a grotesque angle. Another bolt of pain bent Dale at the waist, and he clawed at his leg with both hands.

"Easy now," his father said, and dropped to his knees in a fashion that any other time would have been funny, his own bad leg crabbed straight out to the side, boot heel dug in for support. "God damn, son," he observed. "That's sure as hell broke." He glanced up at me.

I looked around for options. This wasn't the sort of injury where we could just shoulder him to his feet and hop-a-long to the house for an ice pack. We had pieces of bone where they weren't supposed to be, and an orthopedist was going to have to do some reassembly.

If we tried to fold Dale into the cab of one of

the pickups, he'd have to bend the wreckage of that knee, and that wouldn't work—not for a fifty-mile ride, part of it on hopeless dirt roads. Riding in the back with all the hay, shovels, reels of barbed wire, steel posts and bags of Nutri-Steer wouldn't be a whole lot better. His mother's Chrysler was parked across the road in front of the Torrance's double-wide, and no way in hell Dale would fold into *that*. But we couldn't just stand dumb and wait while an ambulance took the better part of an hour to run all the way out from Posadas.

"Let's put him in the back of my rig," I said. "Don't move that leg, and find something to use as padding." I didn't give Herb any time to discuss it, but set off at my own version of a jog. I hadn't driven the veteran state truck that day, leaving it in the shop to have all four wheels toed around to point in the same direction. That left me driving my own late model Chevy SUV. I huffed inside, and as I set about swinging it around to drive to the arena, I found the cell phone in the clutter of the center console and thumbed the auto dial for the Posadas County Sheriff's Department.

Dispatcher Gayle Torrez picked up on the second ring, and I could hear radio traffic in the background.

"Gayle, this is Gastner," I said. "Look, I'm out at the Torrance ranch. Dale Torrance just busted his knee with a nasty fracture. I need an ambulance to meet us on 56."

"You're not going to bring him all the way in?"

"I can do that, but the sooner he has an I.V. running the better. This is a bad break, Gayle. Lots of bone chips and bleeding."

"Ten-four."

"I'm in my red SUV. I'll keep an eye out for the ambulance and flag him down. Tell the driver to pay attention."

"Yes, sir."

There are some perks that come with being a has-been. When the has-been's life includes thirty-five years as deputy, undersheriff, and finally sheriff of Posadas County, some of the county doors remain open, ready to expedite favors.

By the time I'd brought the Trail Blazer over to the arena, opened the back and flopped down the seats, they'd come up with a couple of saddle blankets and three pillows from Dale's own mobile home across the paddock.

Dale's mother, Annie Torrance, had bustled out from the house, her face grim and white but her nerves like tempered steel. She directed the operation as Herb, Pat, and I lifted Dale into the SUV. It would have been easier for Dale if he'd managed to faint, but he was a tough kid, with a string of curses colorful enough that they surprised even me. Annie Torrance was tougher yet. She didn't bat an eye.

"I have an ambulance on the way," I said. "They'll meet us down on 56. Faster that way. Herb, one of you needs to ride in back with him."

"You bring the car," Annie Torrance said to her husband. "I'll ride with Dale."

"You can finish up here?" Herb asked Pat Gabaldon, and the young man nodded.

In another minute, we were southbound on the washboards and potholes of County Road 14, the wandering dirt by-way that ran down the western side of Posadas County. Any other time, I would be ambling along on CR 14, windows rolled down, marveling at the country—the broad sweep of the dry short bunch-grass prairie, rugged mesas with rims crumpling, arroyos so deep you could effortlessly hide a herd of cattle or a tractor trailer with license plates issued in Chihuahua.

This time, I paid attention to my driving, but for every thump and bump that I avoided, three more pummeled the Chevy's stiff suspension. The cries and gasps from the back made me feel like a card-carrying member of the Inquisition. Annie did what she could, but a few hundred CC's of morphine would have been just the ticket. Behind us, Herb kept the Chrysler just far enough back that our dust cloud had time to drift off the road. In seven miles—an agonizing twenty minutes—we reached the last cattle guard that crossed CR14, and I slowed the SUV to a walk as we waddled across the steel girders. Just beyond was the intersection with New Mexico 56, and pulling onto the pavement of the state highway never felt so smooth.

"You doing okay back there?" My passengers had been too quiet.

"He's passed out," Annie said. She stroked Dale's forehead. "I guess that's the best thing." She was all scrunched up, not an easy ride for her sixty-year-old bones.

"Hang in there," I said. "We have an ambulance coming."

Just beyond the intersection, the Broken Spur Saloon marked the only pocket of civilization in the thirty-five miles between the village of Posadas at the north end and the Mexican border and the tiny hamlet of Regál down south. Traffic was nonexistent, and for three miles, we had clear sailing. Herb apparently thought that the posted fifty-five was as fast as his old Chrysler would go, and he dropped far behind as my speedometer touched eighty-five.

I felt confident enough to glance at my call record, and recognized George Payton's phone number. My Thursday lunch date was with the irascible old retired gun dealer, and I knew that he didn't call just to chit-chat. I pushed the dial option and in four or five rings, his sunshine-filled voice greeted me.

"Yeh-low?"

George and I tried to celebrate our stay on the planet over a luncheon burrito once in a while, and in the past year, we'd eaten take-out at George's place more often than not. He needed a walker to get around and refused to be seen in public with it. We missed our lunch date now and then, almost always my fault, but both of us looked forward to an occasional hour of good food and lies. We'd settled on this day, a Thursday with no particular complications on the horizon. Until the Styrofoam cup.

"George, I'm going to be late," I said, able to predict what his reaction would be. "We got a little issue going on."

"Huh," he grunted, his curiosity underwhelming. "Some other time, then. I'll have the Mexican send over something for me. He'll do that, all right." The "Mexican" was Fernando Aragon, owner of the Don Juan de Oñate restaurant, and of course the Mexican would be delighted.

"Can you give me an hour?" I said. "I was going to pick up some wine."

"Nah, you say an hour, that means two," he countered. I knew that arguing was a waste of breath. George Payton didn't do casual in his daily schedules, even though he had nowhere special to go, nothing special to do. In his world, lunch was noon, straight up. Predictable and comforting. "Look, I don't feel all that great anyway. And you got things to do, Billy," George said, the only human being on the planet who could get away with calling me that. "Catch you next time around."

"Your call," I said.

"You be careful," he said, his habitual parting shot.

The next time I glanced in the rear-view mirror, I saw sunshine wink on chrome. I paid attention to the highway as we hit the curve leading to the concrete bridge across the Rio Guigarro, a gravel arroyo that tasted running water maybe once a season. In another minute, the vehicle had caught us—and sure enough, the light bar blossomed on the roof of the sedan. I didn't slow, but reached for the phone. I think dispatcher Gayle Torrez was expecting my call. The first ring hadn't finished when she picked up.

"Hey, sweetheart. This is Gastner again. We're north on 56, looking for the ambulance, and I've managed to collect one of your young hot rods. You want to fill him in? He needs to leave us alone."

"The EMT's are on the way, sir," Gayle

laughed, and in a couple of seconds the red lights went out behind us. The Crown Victoria backed off my bumper a discreet distance. "Deputy Collins wants to know if you need an escort."

"I'm sure he has better things to do, thanks. Oh, and there's a blue Chrysler on the way as well. That's Herb Torrance. He's coming in to the hospital with us."

"Can you hang on a second, sir?"

"Sure."

I heard radio traffic in the background, and in a moment Gayle came back on the phone. "The ambulance is just coming up on Moore, sir." The remains of that little ghost town lay eight miles ahead, and at the rate the ambulance was closing with us, we'd meet in less than four minutes.

"Thanks, sweetheart."

"You bet. Who did you say owns the knee?"

"Dale Torrance. His horse stepped on him. It's a mess."

"Ouch. Well, stop in when you get a minute. Don't be such a stranger."

"You bet." I switched off and glanced in the mirror at Annie. Her expression was worried, but she caught my eye and looked heavenward, the crows-feet deepening at the corners of her eyes. "He's going to end up hobbling just like his old man," Annie said.

"Maybe not that bad," I said, not believing a word of it. Knees that pointed sideways never turned out as good as new.

Behind us, Deputy Collins had slowed and U-turned to return to his speed trap. The kid had been my last hire in the final months before Robert Torrez, dispatcher Gayle's husband, took over the sheriff's office. Like most young cops, if Collins could put three or four years' experience under his belt without making any bone-headed mistakes, he'd probably make a good deputy. But by then, he'd want to move on to some other department that paid more than a street person makes working an intersection in Albuquerque.

Far ahead, as the buttress of Salinas Mesa rose to the south, I saw the first flash of ambulance lights. Just before the bridge across Salinas arroyo, I took the turn-out and pulled to a gentle halt, turning on the flashers. By the time the EMTs pulled the heavy diesel rig to a stop, I had the SUV's doors and tailgate opened for them.

In minutes, Dale Torrance was strapped to a proper gurney, an IV started, and the mercy of morphine—or whatever magic potion they use nowadays—flowing into his arm. I stayed out of the way. In a bit, the ambulance, loaded with mother and son, took off with a wail and flash, followed by Herb Torrance in the Chrysler.

That left me standing by my SUV, in no hurry to join the parade to the hospital. There was nothing I could do now except my job. Life at the ranch would go on. Pat Gabaldon and Socks, left by themselves with a day's work still ahead, would need the transportation permit to move the cattle. The paperwork rode on my clipboard on the passenger seat.

I looked at my watch and saw that it was already coming up on noon. It would take at least another hour to finish with Patrick and then head back to town. George Payton was right. When the day starts to go to hell, it's a hard snowball to stop. I climbed back into the SUV and pulled it into gear, then planted my foot hard on the brake, jolted to a stop by another siren.

This time, Deputy Dennis Collins wasn't sparing the horses. The county car came in from the west, traveling so fast that when it shot by me I felt its bow wave rock my truck. The siren note wafted away as Collins sped north on State 56, winding through the parade of mesas.

I had no sheriff's department radio in my personal rig. Retirement was retirement, I had decided. I didn't need to be listening to all that jibber-jabber of 10-this and 10-that. Still, curiosity takes longer to retire. Hopefully EMT Matty Finnegan hadn't swerved the loaded ambulance off the highway in an effort to miss an errant steer or antelope. I reached for the phone but immediately thought better of it. With an emergency serious enough to shag a deputy in from the other end of the county, Sheriff's dispatcher Gayle Torrez would have enough to do without fielding curiosity calls.

Instead, I U-turned the SUV and headed southbound toward the ranch. After issuing the Torrance permit, the rest of my day was clear, and I relished that notion. After thirty years in the same tiny county, you might imagine that there wasn't a corner or niche that I hadn't explored. But I knew of a couple such places, and I planned to spend my afternoon in the bright sun, poking here and there like an old badger scouting out a good spot to dig another hole.

A pickup truck and two cars had stopped at the Broken Spur Saloon as I drove past. Two women, one of them carrying an infant, were just climbing out of a Volvo station wagon. I almost swung into the parking lot myself at the thought of one of Victor Sanchez's enormous, dripping Spur burgers, but disciplined myself. I had a permit to deliver. Maybe on the way back, although I had second thoughts about that, too. Ice tea was one of my passions, and as edible as the rest of his food was, Victor didn't have a clue how to brew tea leaves.

That was the magnitude of my daydreaming as

I turned off State 56, once more running the kidney jolting surface of CR 14. The wheels of the SUV rattled over the cattleguard and as if vibrated to life, my cell phone interrupted my peace and quiet.

"Gastner."

"Sir," Gayle Torrez said, "are you ten-eight?"

I laughed at the ten-code expression, an affliction I was still trying to cure. "Almost. I'm running a permit out to the Torrance ranch so that Pat can move some cattle. What's up?"

"Sir," she said, "we've just been called to an unattended death over at 1228 Ridgemont." She said it as if I knew the address, but she had forgotten my selective memory—remember meal and bed time, forget everything else. In this case, however, there was no doubt that I would remember.

I slowed for a particularly jarring section of CR14, a well of apprehension already growing in my gut. "Phil Borman called us, sir. He found Mr. Payton in the kitchen."

"Well, shit." I damn near drove off into the bar ditch.

"Estelle said you'd want to know." Gayle's voice was soft with sympathy.

"Thanks, sweetheart," I muttered, and that's about all I could think to say. The dirt road stretched out in front of me, and it seemed a little emptier.

"She said she'd like to meet with you if you're clear," Gayle added. "She's over at that address right now."

I heaved a grand sigh and pulled my senses together. Moping wasn't going to accomplish diddly. Estelle Reyes-Guzman, the county under-sheriff but to me more like an adopted daughter, wouldn't request my presence at the death scene out of sympathy. I was still fifteen minutes south of the Torrance ranch, and the time to drive there and back, with the state livestock paperwork in addition, would add another hour. Estelle hadn't asked for me to come to George Payton's home 'sometime,' or *mañana*.

"I'm on the way," I said, and found a wide spot to execute another U-turn.

Chapter Two

George Payton's dilapidated International pickup dominated the driveway at 1228 Ridgemont. I recalled one of George's pronouncements when I had suggested that he might consider something a bit smaller, agile, even lower to the ground than the mammoth green beast. Climbing into the truck was on a par with climbing the front of Cat Mesa. The suggestion was too sensible.

"Might want to carry something someday besides my walker," he'd growled, and that was that. It was likely that the truck had not moved from that spot in the last month.

Cars marked and unmarked from both the Posadas County Sheriff's Department and the dwindling Posadas Village P.D. were curbed in front, along with Linda Real's little red Honda. That the Sheriff's Department's photographer would be at the scene wasn't surprising. Any unattended death was just that—unattended. Until investigators decided otherwise, the case would stay open, and documentation was required.

On the other side of the street, where pavement blended into weeds and pasture, another jazzy SUV and a sleek Cadillac sedan added to the clot. An EMT first-responder unit dominated the street, lights pulsing.

The young deputy who'd blown by me a few moments before on State 56 stood by the curb with one of the village part-time officers, and when he saw me the deputy stepped out into the street and waved me forward. I rolled down my window.

"How about right in front of the undersheriff's unit, sir," Deputy Dennis Collins said. "We're getting a bit of a snarl here." I glanced around at the congregation of neighbors and gawkers. The scrubby front yards all showed compliance with the neighborhood policy of "let 'er grow, and when it blocks the view, set it on fire." Adept as I was at counting livestock, a quick survey came up with nine folks who should have found something better to do.

Collins patted my SUV's door sill as if reminding me where I was. He pointed ahead toward a vacant spot. "You bet," I said, and as I pulled forward I saw the undersheriff of Posadas County step out onto the front stoop of George Payton's house. Estelle Reyes-Guzman held the front door with one hand while she talked with someone inside. Estelle saw me, nodded, and started down the sidewalk to meet me.

My oldest daughter Camille was fond of referring to the undersheriff as my "fifth kid." Camille was only half-joking when she said that, and it was said with as much affection as if it were genetically true. In fact, I'd first met Estelle when she was twelve years old. A particularly interesting escapade with her great-uncle Reuben had taken me south of the border to the tiny village of Tres Santos, where the tiny, dark, sober child lived with Teresa Reyes, Reuben's niece. A fierce guardian, Teresa had arranged for Estelle to come to the United States a few years later to finish her high-school education. The child had lived with Reuben, which must have been a colorful experience.

I parked, locked the truck, and climbed out, taking time to survey the neighborhood and the gawkers before turning my attention to matters at hand. As I trudged up the sidewalk, I found myself thinking that Estelle Reyes-Guzman hadn't changed much over the years—dark olive complexion, raven hair cropped a little closer now with the added hint of steel gray here and there, full eyebrows that knit over the bridge of her nose when she was thinking hard. Her fine features reminded me of the Aztecs, not that I knew anything about that tribe beyond the fanciful paintings of their heart-rending ceremonies that I'd seen in the National Geographic.

And who knew. Estelle's stepmother, Teresa Reyes, had adopted the two year-old child from the local convent in Tres Santos. No records existed of who Estelle's parents might have been. Perhaps they had descended from a long line of Aztec heart surgeons. And keeping up the tradition, Estelle had married Dr. Francis Guzman, who'd tinkered with a heart or two in his time.

The undersheriff caught my elbow and escorted me to the front step. "I'm glad you could come over, sir," she said soberly. Sometime decades before, she had settled on "sir" as the appropriate all-purpose name for me, alternating that with *padrino* after I had agreed to be godfather to her two urchins. I could count on one hand the number of times that she'd called me "Bill," or "Mr. Gastner," or "Sheriff."

"Has Alan been here?" I asked

"Not yet."

I shook my head, muttered an expletive, and said, "I'm not ready for this." Estelle gave my arm a sympathetic squeeze. "Who found him?"

"His son-in-law," Estelle replied. I knew Phil Borman only casually, enough to greet him by name on the street.

I nodded in the direction of the Cadillac. "Maggie knows, then."

"She's inside."

"You know," I said, "George and I were all set to have lunch together today. I talked to him just…" and I looked at my watch. "An hour ago, or a little more. Right when I got tangled up with the Torrances."

"Gayle told me," the undersheriff said. "Did George call you earlier?"

"No. He might have tried," I replied, remembering the ringing phone. "I called him to tell him I'd be late, and he wasn't in the mood to wait. He said that he didn't feel all that hot."

"Ah," Estelle said, without explanation about what she was thinking. But I was used to that. I took another deep breath to fortify myself for the meeting with Maggie Payton Borman, George's daughter and only child—and one of those type AAA personalities who always made me feel tired. Now in her forties, Maggie hadn't lost any of her spunk. She ran the Posadas Realty with her new husband, Phil. I knew they enjoyed an enviable track record of convincing potential home or business buyers that the village of Posadas was poised to grow like kudzu, rather than being the dried-out desert runt that it really was.

Linda Real, the Sheriff's Department photographer, met us at the door. An inch shorter than Estelle and tending toward chubby, Linda's passion, besides Deputy Thomas Pasquale, with whom she lived, was shooting enough hard film and using enough digital bits and bytes that stock prices rose every time Posadas County reported a serious incident.

She greeted me with an affectionate half hug, the huge digital camera that hung around her neck banging against my belly. "Hi, Sheriff," she said, one of about half the county who had kept the title attached to me as an honorarium. She lowered her voice to a whisper as she said to Estelle, "I'm finished until Dr. Perrone gets here. You want me to stick around?"

"Yes," Estelle nodded. I didn't know how many pictures anyone really needed of a heart attack victim, but I'd learn long ago not to question Estelle's judgment.

I looked beyond Linda into the house. George Payton had lived simply in this little two bedroom, cinder-block bungalow. In the past decades, I'd been inside dozens of times. With my eyes closed, I could draw the floor plan—in part because nothing was out of the ordinary. The ambiance was neo-utilitarian. I knew that, when I looked inside, I'd see only one thing that would remind me of George's wife, Clara—a bright, cheerful woman. Her hand-me-down, battered upright piano would still be sitting against the east wall, a bright orange vase filled with a bouquet of plastic flowers on top.

Clara had died on daughter Maggie's eighteenth birthday. With his wife gone and Maggie headed off to college, George had sold their fancy home behind Pershing Park and pulled into himself, making do in this tiny, 950-square-foot place. He'd brought the piano and flower vase with him, even though he didn't know middle-C from Adam and never replaced the dusty, fading flowers.

The old man had always lived simply, but with a fondness for anything related to the firearms industry. His Sportsmen's Emporium had been a fixture in Posadas for almost forty years. He had an amazing inventory of stuff packed into that store, both new and historic, mass market or unique. That's where I'd first met him, and over the years we'd become good friends.

Wearying of the day-to-day grind and the bureaucracy of the Treasury Department's paperwork, George sold the business when the millennium turned. The young man who bought it streamlined the operation, cleared out a lot of the old junk, ran inventory control through a nifty new computer system, raised prices to current levels, lost two-thirds of his customers, and went out of business within the year.

An enormous cartridge collection hung on the south living room wall, its heavy walnut frame thick with dust. Each cartridge, from the tiny Kolibri cartridges designed to dispatch rabid houseflies to gargantuan shells developed to batter elephants, was labeled and mounted on a painted background depicting Cat Mesa, the mesa north of Posadas. It was an impressive collection and probably worth some money to the right buyer. Posters advertising firearms ringed the room, with paintings reminiscent of Russell or Remington painted on sheet metal—except these were all period originals, not stamped replicas.

Maggie Payton Borman was standing beside the piano, gazing out the window at the tiny side yard that grew an abundant collection of goat-heads and tumbleweeds. There wasn't much of a view, just the neighbor's unkempt car-port and a tarp-covered boat on a small trailer with flat tires. The neighbors hadn't lived there for more than a year, and the boat hadn't been in the water for twice that.

I doubt that Maggie saw any of it. Her mind was elsewhere. Off to her left, a yellow sheriff's ribbon stretched across the narrow doorway into the kitchen, the bright color a jarring intrusion on this dismal scene.

Maggie turned, saw me, and held out both arms. We met in the center of the room and she held me hard enough to make me flinch. She hung on for a long time, not saying a word. Eventually she drew back and looked me straight in the eye without saying a word.

"Maggie," I said, "what can I say." She squeezed my shoulder. A good-looking woman, tending to be stocky like her father and with the same honest, open face, Maggie was the kind of person who bustled. She bustled to arrange things, to control things, to take charge of things, even when she didn't have to. Now, she had been hauled up short, with nothing to bustle about. She had nothing to do but stay out of the way. She couldn't even go into the kitchen to fix us a sandwich.

"I was supposed to have lunch with your dad today," I said. "Herb Torrance's boy managed to break a leg, and we got hung up with that."

She shook her head sadly. "Dad told me yesterday that you two were getting together. But isn't that's the way of it," she said. "It was Dale who was hurt?"

"Yes. He'll be all right."

"Such an attractive young man," Maggie said, and then heaved an enormous sigh. "Bill, I'm just not ready for this."

"No one ever is," I said. "Had you talked to your dad this morning?"

She shook her head again, a quick little twitch. "I meant to look in on him this morning." She squeezed her eyes shut, forcing the tears back. "Meant to. And isn't *that* the way. Like I said, he told me yesterday that he was having lunch with you." She tried a brave smile. "More of that health food from the Don Juan."

One of the things I liked about Maggie, regardless of her power-brokering in the professional world, was that she tried hard to let her dad be himself. She hadn't tried to force George's habits, or clean a house he didn't want cleaned, or manicure a yard that pleased him just the way it was. "What happened, do you know?" I asked.

Maggie sighed deeply again, and I saw her eyes flick toward the yellow ribbon "As nearly as we can tell, dad sat down to lunch and then had a seizure, right there at the table." This time, her sigh had a little shake to it, the misery close to the surface. "I wish I had been there, Bill. But," and she shrugged helplessly, the kind of gesture that prompted me to rest a paternal hand on her shoulder. "The world turns, you know. I had to show a house, and *that* dragged on and on. I guess…I guess that I didn't even think about it. I didn't worry about dad. I mean, he said you were coming over and all. And then another call came in. I had folks waiting for me in the office—a family from Maryland, of all places." She reached out and held my right wrist. "Phil was going to talk to dad about maybe going over to Elephant Butte for an outing this weekend. He came by here after lunch and...and found him."

"I'm sorry that had to happen."

"I just can't believe this," Maggie continued, and she smiled wistfully at Estelle, who had crossed the living room like a dark shadow and now waited patiently, and obviously for me, by the kitchen door. Maggie dabbed at her eyes with a tiny hanky. "He's been so frail the past few weeks, and we check on him often, you know. He won't wear that alert gadget I got for him."

That was easy to imagine—on both their parts...Maggie wanting to do something protective, George refusing. Estelle ducked under the yellow tape, but went no farther into the kitchen.

"Where's Phil now?" I asked.

"He's outside," she replied. "I think he's out by the garage, if you want to talk with him."

"No, no," I said quickly. I wasn't sheriff of Posadas County. I didn't need to talk with anyone, unless George had secreted a herd of cattle somewhere out behind the house. I would pay brief respects to Phil Borman eventually, but there was nothing that either he or Maggie could tell me about George Payton that I didn't already know. I'd spend a lot of time in the next few days and weeks missing old George and his dour, often profane comments about life. The world would march on now, a little poorer for his absence.

"Let me talk with Estelle for a minute," I said, and Maggie nodded.

"Sure," she said. A hint of a smile touched her pleasant face. "She's so thoughtful, isn't she. So professional, but with such a sympathetic touch. We're so lucky to have her."

"Yes, she is," I replied. I always felt better when I was in Estelle Reyes-Guzman's presence. It was only logical that others would feel the same way.

"You go ahead," Maggie said, and turned away.

The undersheriff didn't move as I approached. I didn't need to be prepared for what was in the kitchen, she had to know that. After twenty years in the military and almost thirty-five in civilian law enforcement, I'd seen enough final moments that I was adequately armored, even when the departed was one of my oldest friends.

"I'm a little puzzled," Estelle said in that husky whisper that traveled no farther than the ears for which it was intended. She lifted the yellow tape for me.

It would have been nice if George Payton had just drifted away in his sleep—at least I *think* it would have been. After seeing too many of them, I still had reservations about final moments. I wasn't convinced that there was a good way, or a good day, to die.

George was seated on the floor, his back leaning against the cabinet door that concealed the kitchen sink's innards. His left leg was stretched out straight, his right flexed at the knee. His right hand lay on the linoleum beside his right thigh. His left hand clutched a brown paper bag to his chest, resting on his ample midriff. His head nestled in his various wrinkled chins, eyes and mouth open.

The position was one that he might have sagged into had the seizure struck just as he bent over to toss the bag into the under-sink trash. One chair was pushed away from the table. On the placemat rested a familiar glass serving dish, its plastic snap-on top placed carefully toward the center of the table. I recognized an inexpensive Styrofoam cooler over on the counter beside George's enormous pill organizer, the cooler's top askew.

I knew exactly where the serving dish and cooler came from, and knew exactly what savory aroma had wafted up when George popped off the lid—a green chile *burrito grande* from the Don Juan. "And that's not really fair," I said.

"Sir?"

"He didn't get to finish." In fact, George had barely begun. Most of the wonderful burrito remained in the dish, and of the portion that George had spooned out on his plate, all but a few bites remained.

Chapter Three

"This was a usual thing?" Estelle asked.

"What, the burrito?" I stepped closer to the table, careful not to touch anything. "Sure it was. You know that George shared my superior taste in food. Today I was supposed to have lunch with him, and I would have stopped at the Don Juan to pick up the grub." I shrugged helplessly. "Turns out that I couldn't make it. I talked to him on the phone a couple hours ago, maybe a little longer. He said he'd have the restaurant send over take-out."

"He called you, then?"

"Well, he might have. Like I said, my phone rang but I was indisposed, sweetheart. I didn't answer it. When it became clear that I was going to miss our lunch date, I called him." I pointed at the chair pushed in at the end of the table. "My spot."

"Was there a particular reason for today?"

I shook my head. "Nope. Don't think so. Just

as good a day as any. Actually, I think Thursday is soup day from the Senior Citizens. George said soup is for sissies." I thrust my hands in my pockets. "Here lately, he was getting meals-on-wheels from them, but he complained about that." I grinned at Estelle. "Gotta have something really worth living for once in a while."

She nodded at that deep, philosophical thought as if she understood perfectly. Maybe she did. But Estelle had never eaten a *burrito grande* in her entire life—I'd bet the farm on it. Not with her waist line. She wouldn't know the pure pleasure of having about a million calories settled comfortably behind the belt. When I finished one of those mammoth feeds, I felt like an old bruin who had disposed of an entire rich honey hive in one sitting, with a bushel of over-ripe, fragrant apples for dessert.

"That's a fancy take-out dish," she observed. True enough, the Pyrex casserole wasn't the usual for the Don Juan.

"The restaurant started packing up George's burrito like this a while ago," I said. "When he couldn't make it to the restaurant any more. That's one of the perks of being a thirty-year customer." I glanced around and saw George's battered walker in the corner by the refrigerator, shoved there out of contempt, but still close at hand. "Fernando couldn't bring himself to mash that work of art all together in one of those cheap take-out containers. At least not for George." I held out my hands, drawing vaguely artistic shapes in the air. "Presentation, you know."

"Not today for you, though."

"Nope. Herb Torrance was ready to move a little gaggle of cattle, and then the kid got messed up. His horse spooked."

"Dale is all right?"

"That'll depend on who the orthopedic surgeon is. The damn horse planted a shod hoof right on the side of the kid's knee and then pushed off. Crunch. The kid's thigh is pointing this way, his lower leg that way. Nasty, nasty."

"And you said that you had agreed with George earlier to pick up the food at the Don Juan?"

"Sure," I said. "I sometimes do that. *Did* that, I should say. The restaurant will deliver, of course, but what the hell. It's nothing formal…no big deal. We thought maybe we'd hit it today, but then I got busy. I rang George when we were on the way to meet the ambulance. Told him that I was likely going to be late." I glanced over at the silent corpse, hoping he'd wake up and grump at me. "He didn't like to throw off his schedule, though. He said he'd have someone from the restaurant do the honors."

"This was right around noon?"

"Just a bit before. Maybe eleven-fifty or so when I actually called him."

Her expressive eyebrows furrowed a bit. "So the restaurant delivered," she said, adding, "The dish belongs to the restaurant, then."

"Sure. George washes it—that's a production if there ever was one—and then someone takes it back. I would have done that today." I saw the fork on the floor, and moved back. A juice glass had been knocked off the table on the other side of his plate, splashing red wine across the linoleum.

Estelle watched me as I surveyed the little kitchen. "Just a bite or three," I said. "That's about what he managed, wouldn't you guess?"

"Yes," she said. "When you talked to him on the phone this morning…did he sound okay? His usual self?"

I shrugged. "He said he wasn't feeling so hot," I made a face. "But I didn't get the impression that he thought this was his last meal, if that's what you mean."

She knelt beside George Payton's body, her hands folded on her knee. "This bag is from the restaurant," Estelle said, thinking out loud, since we both knew that it was. She cocked her head, reading the inscription on the crumpled paper. I already knew what it said: *From the Don Juan de Oñate—this ain't for no doggy.*

I backed up closer to the fridge for a panorama of the whole scene. It was easy enough to imagine what had happened. George had felt the first thunder of the seizure, dropped his fork, spasmed out and knocked over the full tumbler of wine. He had missed knocking over the nearly full bottle that stood near the center of the table. Rearing to his feet, he'd staggered away, headed for nowhere. Maybe he'd already spun into the gray void when his left hand reached out and grabbed, connecting with the restaurant's delivery bag that had probably been on the kitchen counter. Then he'd slid down, coming to his final rest like an exhausted plumber working up energy to tackle the sink drain.

"Odd thing to grab," Estelle said.

I sighed. "What ever is handy, sweetheart. He might have already been unconscious by then. Just a spasm."

"I'm surprised that he didn't reach out toward the telephone," she said. The small cordless phone rested in its recharging cradle under the first cupboard beside the toaster...no more than four feet from George's left hand.

"No time," I said. "Just boom. He had time to get out of his chair, and that was just about it." A few years before, I'd been on duty—in fact, in the middle of a homicide investigation—when a coronary had flattened me, too. There had been no time to grope for the speed dial on my phone, no time to key the hand-held radio on my belt. Not even enough time to reach out a hand to prevent my face from eating gravel.

Estelle nodded, rose, and stepped back from the body. She circled toward the table, glanced out through the door toward the living room, and when she was standing immediately beside my shoulder, murmured, "I'll be interested to know what caused the heavy discharge of mucus, sir."

I hadn't knelt down to scrutinize George Payton's face, but was ready to take the undersheriff's word for it.

"Maybe the Don Juan's chile was a little hotter than usual," I said. I'd eaten my way through plenty of those servings, pausing occasionally to mop my forehead or blow my nose as the fumes from the select Hatch green chile blew out the sinuses and numbed the tongue.

I regarded Estelle, lifting my head a bit so I could bring her into bifocal focus. As usual, I was unable to read past those dark eyes. It was obvious that something was bothering her, though. When a very senior citizen with a long medical history dropped dead of circumstances that all screamed natural causes, we generally didn't string a crime scene tape and take a thousand photographs.

But typically Estelle, the undersheriff wasn't ready to voice her concerns, and I didn't push it. I trusted her to tell me as much as I needed or wanted to know, and ask for help if there was something specific I could do for her.

"How ill was he?" she asked.

"I'm no doctor, sweetheart, but I'd describe him as old, frail, and unrepentant of bad habits. I would guess he was living on about a third of his heart, and you can add to that one failed kidney and a blown prostate." I pointed out the door. "Your hubby can tell you more, but I know that George couldn't walk from here to there without running out of air. I know that he had emphysema." I turned and indicated the walker in the corner. "Those things weigh just a few ounces, but for old George, it was a chore. Everything an effort. No wind, no circulation. And you know, when he got to feeling down in the dumps, he'd have a cigar and a glass of brandy. 'It was good enough for Churchill,' he'd say. So… 'borrowed time' is the appropriate expression in his case, I would think."

I chuckled at myself. Over time, cops develop the habit of carrying on conversations in the presence of corpses as if the victims were still very much alive and ready to contribute their two cents. It wouldn't have surprised me if George had stirred a bit, muttering a string of colorful expletives aimed at the us for standing in *his* kitchen, trying to pry into *his* very private death.

Estelle mulled that over, gazing down at the table setting. I knew better than to ask what she was thinking.

"Let me know what I can do to help," I said. "I was going to take a minute and pay my respects to Phil." She nodded and accompanied me as far as the yellow tape, holding it up for me again like a gate. I exchanged a few more words of consolation with Maggie and then headed outside, more to suck in some fresh air than to talk to anyone.

I hadn't seen Phil Borman when I arrived, but now he was facing the closed garage door, leaning against the front of George's old pickup. He was off somewhere in his own musings and didn't hear me until I was just a step or two behind him. He turned then, left arm across his striped golf shirt, right arm propped on left like Jack Benny about to deliver a punch line, his cigarette a couple of inches from his mouth.

I knew that George had thought highly of his son-in-law, and that was enough of an endorsement. "Maybe Maggie will stop now and smell the goddamn roses once in a while," George had grumbled to me at the couple's wedding two years before. No such luck, unless the roses were offered for sale with a 6 percent commission. Maggie and Phil worked like dervishes to make their business a success, opening satellite offices in both Deming and Lordsburg.

Phil Borman unfolded his arms and straightened up. "Ah," he said, extending his hand. "I saw you drive up a couple of minutes ago. I was in the back yard. Estelle's got you in harness again?"

"Not a chance," I said quickly. "Phil, I'm sorry about this."

"Well," he replied, "so am I, you know?" He dropped the cigarette on George's driveway and ground it out, then promptly groped another out of his shirt pocket and lit it. I took a step so that the air moved the smoke away from me. As only an ex-smoker can, I had grown not only terribly sanctimonious about it, but was positively repulsed by the stench of cigarette smoke. "He still enjoyed life. I'm going to miss him."

"Me, too."

"You know…do you hunt?"

"Nope. Too old and fat. Easier to go to the restaurant."

He laughed that practiced, polite response that good salesmen master when a customer tells a joke. "Hunting is always something I thought I wanted to do, you know? Never had the time. Never *took* the time." He grinned, showing irregular, strong white teeth. "George took it upon himself to perform an attitude adjustment on me. Now…and you ask Maggie—she'll tell you. I sell real estate when I can manage to take some time away from my hunting." He glanced at his watch, reading the date. "I drew a tag for a special antelope hunt up north in another month. George was pretty pleased about that and promised to loan me one of his rifles."

"Good luck with that," I said. He sucked on the cigarette, then regarded it judiciously as he exhaled, as if he was trying a new brand. "You were the one who found him," I said. "Did I hear that right?"

He nodded slowly. "What a turn, Bill. Jesus. You know, the instant I saw him sitting there, I knew he was gone." He looked over at me. "I called 911, and I don't think that it was more than four minutes before the paramedics were here. There wasn't any point in trying resuscitation."

"Had you called him before you dropped by? Did you talk with him this morning at all?" And what did that matter to me, I thought as the words came out of my mouth. Old habits were sticky things.

"No. I just came over. Maggie said you two had linked up to have lunch, so I knew he'd be here. I wanted to see if he wanted to take a day trip for fishing over to the Butte. I mean, this weather we've been having, you know? Maybe give us a chance to talk some more about the hunt." Borman hunched his shoulders helplessly. "Sure as hell didn't expect something like this. You know," he said, and stopped. I waited patiently. "He felt like shit most of the time, Bill. He absolutely *hated* taking all those meds. You saw that pill organizer by the kitchen sink?"

"Sure."

"God, what a load of *stuff.* Here a few weeks ago, he just stopped taking most of it, except maybe a little Prednisone for his arthritis."

"Well, I've been known to do the same thing," I said.

Borman went for cigarette number three. "I saw him a couple days ago, when Maggie and I took him out to dinner at the Legion. He was just fine.

"Well…just fine by his standards. Chipper as all hell. He was excited about me going after antelope."

Chipper wasn't a word I would have associated with George Payton, even twenty years before. *Lugubrious, cranky, grumpy…*not chipper.

Borman snapped his fingers. "That's the way it happens a lot of times, I guess."

"If we're lucky," I turned at the sound of another vehicle and saw Dr. Alan Perrone's dark green BMW glide to a stop at the curb.

"I don't understand the procedure for all this, I guess," Phil Borman said.

"What procedure is that?"

"It has to be hard on Maggie, her dad just lying in the kitchen." He looked at his watch and grimaced. "All this time. I mean I don't know why it's taken so long to move him."

"The coroner has to earn his salary," I said.

"I suppose so. It's hard, though."

"Any time there's an unattended death like this, Phil, things slow down a little bit."

"Even when the cause of death is obvious?"

"Even when," I reached out and patted him on the elbow. Nothing I could say would make him feel any better. Alan Perrone, the assistant State Medical Examiner and county coroner, hustled up the sidewalk. I raised a hand in greeting. "Estelle's inside, doc."

He paused in mid-hustle and cocked his head. "You suspect Mad Cow disease here?" George Payton would have loved that bit of irreverence at his expense, and it was typical Perrone that the doc didn't temper his humor for Phil's sake. The physician didn't wait for a response, but disappeared inside the house.

"What'd he mean by that?" Phil Borman asked.

"Just a bad joke in a time of need," I replied.

"Doc and I and George go way, way back." I shook Phil's elbow again. "Call me if there's anything I can do, all right?"

Borman nodded, knowing damn well there was nothing for either of us to do except stay out of the way.

Chapter Four

I went back inside. Maggie Payton and Linda Real sat side-by-side on the old, deep sofa by the living room window. The Sheriff's Department photographer had a wide sympathetic streak. It wasn't unusual for deputies to keep teddy bears in their patrol units to give to children in misery. Linda's collection probably had the highest turn-over rate. With no photos to take at the moment, I wasn't surprised that she responded to Maggie's pain.

George's daughter beckoned and Linda got up to make room for me. I sank down into the cushions, knowing that actually escaping the comfort of the sofa was going to take determination and planning.

In the kitchen, Estelle Reyes-Guzman and Dr. Alan Perrone were locked in intense conversation, and that made me uneasy. Their voices were whispers and murmurs—well out of range of my sorry hearing, and apparently Maggie's, too.

"Oh, my," Maggie said wearily, and heaved a huge sigh. She reached over and patted my hand, then folded hers on her knees. "So, how have you been, Bill?" I knew exactly what she really meant, as in *are you next?*

"One day at a time," I said. "I was just out at Torrance's, counting cattle."

"How's that going for you?"

"Counting?" I smiled. "Well, as long as the numbers don't get too big, I'm okay."

She squeezed my hand. "No, I mean the whole livestock inspector's job. I was surprised when Dad told me that you'd taken that on."

I shrugged. "Actually, it's a good fit for me," I said. "Gets me out, gives me the opportunity to talk with old friends. Did it originally as a favor for Cliff Larson when he got sick, and then *he* died on me, and here I'm stuck." I shrugged. "Things are changing, though. I would guess that it's not a long-term gig for me."

"Oh? There will always be cattle," Maggie said.

"Sure enough. But the permit policy keeps getting wound up in red tape, and the solution to that is just more paperwork. They have a whole herd of new concerns with this mad cow thing, and the illegal border traffic is a real pain in the ass, if you'll pardon my French. And then I got a memo the other day saying that *we're* going to be carrying guns now." I waved a hand in disgust. "I mean, I do anyway, and have for half a century. But now there's a whole raft of training procedures and policies coming down the pike. Christ, the whole thing is ridiculous. I don't need it."

"Like everything else," Maggie said. "We live in a world of paperwork. You should see *my* desk."

"It's silly, isn't it."

"Yes, it is." She sat quietly for a moment, regarding the none-too-clean carpet. "You said you were out at the ranch. You know, I haven't seen Herb or Annie Torrance in months."

"They're fine," I said, which was more or less true.

She nodded and regarded her hands, deep in thought. "Dad thought a lot of you," she said after a while.

"It was mutual." I knew it was about time to stir. Through the open kitchen doorway, I saw Estelle stand up and nod in response to something that Alan Perrone said. She ducked under the yellow ribbon and detoured toward us.

"We're almost finished," she said. "Are you going to be all right?" Maggie had finally dived into the tissues, and was working to restore order to her face.

"We're reminiscing," Maggie said. "Can I help with anything?"

"No, ma'am. Thanks." For a moment, Estelle stood there, looking as if she wanted to ask us something, then turned away with a sympathetic little nod. She left the house with Linda Real in tow.

"What a gorgeous creature," Maggie said.

"Yes, she is," I agreed. "She's managed to cope, though." Maybe Maggie knew what I meant, maybe not.

"How's the clinic going for them? What a venture *that* is."

Estelle's husband, Francis, was opening a medical clinic in partnership with Alan Perrone. Construction was nearly complete on the hi-tech facility on property behind my house on Guadalupe Terrace, south of the interstate. Posadas Health Center included offices for three physicians and a pharmacy. I knew that plans called for another wing that would include a dental office.

"They've had their challenges," I said. "Like anything. But it's what they've wanted."

"Realtors everywhere burned you in effigy for giving away that land," Maggie said, but a soft smile told me that I'd been forgiven for not realizing that, in any venture like the clinic, the right folks needed to get rich.

"I smelled the smoke," I laughed, trying not

to let any irritation show. "I didn't need the land, and the Guzmans did. It was that simple. I didn't need to make a bundle on the deal. Anyway, I had ulterior motives, Maggie. It gets kinda lonely out there in that big old adobe of mine. This way, I wound up with just the neighbors I wanted." She nodded at the logic of that. "Kind of like your dad deciding to give that lot behind the Public Safety Building to the county for the new office wing. He didn't need it, they did..."

Maggie looked heavenward at that. "And I don't know if dad ever finished with that or not." I cocked my head quizzically at that—and not because it was new information. The county wanted more offices, for what I don't know. One of the lots involved in the expansion project was owned by George, and I had assumed long ago that the deal to transfer the land to the county had already been consummated.

She caught the expression and patted my hand again. "*Mañana* was my dad's favorite expression when it came to things like that," she said. "Lots of i's and t's to be dotted and crossed yet."

The undersheriff reappeared, lugging the large black briefcase that lived in the trunk of her county car. "May I talk with you for a few minutes, sir?" she asked me, pausing on her way to the kitchen.

"Sure. Do I have to get up?"

She smiled and stepped closer, holding out a hand. I outweighed her by an embarrassing tonnage, but she was surprisingly strong.

"I'd make some fresh coffee," Maggie offered, "but everything is in the kitchen."

"Not to worry." I followed Estelle under the tape again. To my surprise, she closed the door behind us.

"How are you doing?" Perrone asked, looking suspiciously at me. He wore thin latex gloves and didn't offer to shake hands.

"I'm fine," I said, feeling a little rise of annoyance. People needed to stop assessing my mortality. There were better things to do. Estelle knelt over by the fridge and opened her case, removing a selection of plastic evidence bags and a fine-line marker. Perrone leaned against the counter, both hands held in front of him like a freshly scrubbed surgeon, watching.

"What puzzles me," he said, and beckoned me closer. I stepped around the table so I could hear him. "What puzzles me," he repeated, "is the allergic reaction that we see here."

"The mucous that Estelle mentioned?"

"Indeed that. Anaphylactic shock is really pretty characteristic," Perrone said. "Somebody is stung by a wasp or something, and reacts? If the allergy is acute, the whole system can crash." He spread his hands apart again. "In some ways, the symptoms can mimic a massive coronary—and I suppose that the end result is the same. The system can't get air, the pulse races, things go from bad to worse."

"You're saying that George had an allergic reaction?"

"I would say so. Just from some preliminary hints. I could be wrong, of course, but, you know…"

I didn't know. "He had a bad heart," I said, as if I didn't remember that I was talking to George's personal physician.

Perrone nodded slowly. "*Bad* is an understatement, Bill. I'd say more like *wrecked.* An allergic reaction is really dangerous for someone in his condition. I could add that he was *supposed* to be on supplemental oxygen, but didn't use it most of the time. He didn't take his meds. On and on." He bent down beside George's corpse, which had been moved now so that the victim lay on his back, parallel to the sink counter. "The massive mucous discharge is consistent with an allergic reaction." He reached out and gently opened George's mouth a bit.

"The bronchial spasm makes it impossible to swallow," he explained. "The choke reflex is going to trigger all sorts of responses, including that feeling of desperation." He glanced up at me. "All of that happening in someone with George's bad health is as dangerous as a loaded gun with a hair trigger. Likely that his damaged heart couldn't take the strain."

"So you're saying that he started to choke, is that it? And that triggered the coronary?"

"Good a guess as any at this point." He resumed his examination of the victim's mouth. "There's still food in the mouth and esophagus. That's how quick and massive the whole scenario was." He leaned back, regarding the corpse for a moment, then pushed himself to his feet. "Estelle tells me that this is a meal that George ate on a regular basis?"

"Sure. More or less. I was supposed to have lunch with him today."

"Huh. Interesting fare, Bill. Nice and light, low-calorie, easy on the spices..." He shot me one of his thin-lipped smiles.

"Some things are best withheld from the authorities," I said, and Perrone grimaced with impatience.

"But we find out sooner or later, even if we have to do a *post mortem*," he said. "Did he have any food allergies that *you* know about? Ones that he 'withheld' from me?"

"Don't know. You might ask Maggie, but all

the times that I ate with George, there was never any mention of anything. He loved Mexican food the way Fernando Aragon cooks it at the Don Juan. He loved a big glass of red wine before he ate to whet his appetite, and then another with the meal." I turned and looked at the table.

"That's not exactly a conservative wine glass," Perrone said, turning to look at the juice tumbler. "Two of those?"

"Sure."

"Wonderful kick *that* must have given his kidneys."

"He's been eating this same thing for twenty years, doc. For what it's worth, he stayed clear of red chile because he said that it irritated his gut. The green didn't."

"Until today," Perrone observed. "Something sure as hell kicked his system."

Estelle slipped past me. Hands gloved in latex, she slid the glass serving dish, contents and all, into an evidence bag and sealed it. I watched as she labeled it in fine, precise penmanship.

"I can't imagine what that might be," I said. "Maybe a wasp or hornet or something got into the house." I glanced around at the floor, along the walls. "We have those damn centipedes all over the place this time of the year."

"And maybe nothing at all," Perrone added.

"I'll have to check his file, but to the best of my recollection, George never discussed allergies like that with me. I don't recall any intolerance to meds…what few he ever took, that is." He nudged the pill organizer that I'm sure Maggie had purchased and organized for her father. "Around here, juniper pollen bothers about 90 percent of the population—that and the ragweed along the highways. George could have stood in the middle of a blooming juniper grove holding a bouquet of ragweed and never offer up a sneeze."

"Maybe it was one of the meds he *didn't* take," I said.

"Unlikely. But it's something to check." He nodded at the food. "We'll take a good hard look at that and the stomach and esophageal contents. We'll look for insect bites or stings, and who knows. Maybe something will turn up." He turned a full circle. "But you know, I doubt it." He shrugged philosophically. "My impression is that it was just the moment his general system chose to say, 'enough.'" He gathered his bag. "I'll leave you to it," he said. "You want me to give the go-ahead to the EMTs?"

"Sure," Estelle said. "Thanks."

In another couple of minutes, the silent, white-sheeted figure of George Payton was packed aboard a gurney for his final ride. Estelle held the kitchen door for them, then closed it carefully and went back to work. The fork that George had been using went into a separate bag, and then she cracked open the sealed plastic wrap around a fair-sized test tube. Methodically, using a disposable spatula made out of a slip of sterile paper, she collected more red wine from the spill on the floor than I would have thought possible, sealed the tube, and labeled it. The tumbler went into its own bag. She was filling out the label when she paused and glanced up at me.

"Everything but the kitchen sink," I said.

"I checked that already, sir," she said. "The garbage can underneath the sink has a fresh liner. One empty wine bottle, one paper bag."

I tipped open the small cabinet under the sink, and saw that the blue plastic liner of the garbage can wasn't soiled by as much as a coffee ground. The sole contents were a wine bottle nosed down into the can, with a crumpled bag wedged in with it. No doubt, Estelle would empty all that into evidence bags, too. "So tell me," I said, glancing back at the table. The bottle of wine that stood open on the table was fresh, minus only the tumblerful that stained the linoleum.

"Sir?"

"Something about all this," I said. "You're thinking again, sweetheart."

"Oh, no," Estelle said in mock horror. "It's that obvious?"

"'Fraid so."

"The allergic reaction is interesting," the undersheriff said. "That's all. That and the bag from the Don Juan." That souvenir was folded into a plastic evidence bag as well.

Chapter Five

The yellow ribbon blocking the kitchen door was down, the kitchen empty, George's body gone. Just like that. Phil Borman stood out on the front step, smoking. He held onto the screen door as if the light breeze might tear it from its flimsy hinges. I heard him talking to someone out on the front step, a neighbor perhaps.

"There's something apropos in all this," Maggie Borman said. She reached out a hand to me and used my grip as leverage to rise from the sofa.

"How so?"

She held my hand in both of hers. "Dad wouldn't have wanted to wait around until he didn't have the strength to lift a fork, Bill. He said as much to me on a dozen occasions, you know. And more often here recently, after his last stroke. I think he could see what was coming." She reached out and retrieved George's unused alert button from the top of the piano. "Even this," she said. "I bought this for him." Maggie looked up at me, eyes appealing. "There it was on top of the piano, untouched. I wonder now if it could have saved his life."

"Probably not," I said. "But we'll never know. George was George, Maggie. That's all there is to it. He knew what he wanted."

"Ain't that the truth," she said. "He missed Mama so much." She turned toward the kitchen just in time to see Estelle drop the small evidence bag holding George's fork into the briefcase.

A small cooler with the Sheriff's Department logo on the lid now rested on the floor. Arranged inside, as if for a picnic, were the various items that Estelle had gathered from the kitchen—the serving dish with its plastic lid, now encased in its own plastic cocoon, the empty wine bottle and its paper bag from the trash in one evidence bag, the almost full bottle in another.

"I was going to clean all that up..." Maggie said, starting toward the kitchen. She stopped as if the yellow tape was still in place.

Estelle smiled sympathetically. "That's all right, Mrs. Borman. We'll take care of it."

"You'll need to refrigerate that," Maggie added, and I wasn't sure what she was thinking— that somehow the undersheriff wouldn't know that food spoiled?

"It's routine to run some basic lab tests,

Maggie," I said. "We'll all be just a little more comfortable when we know what triggered the episode." *We*, I heard myself say.

She looked at me, puzzled. "Well, that's certainly all right," she said. "I don't know what the procedure is. Will you see that the serving dish is returned to the restaurant?"

"You bet." I was not surprised that Maggie was concerning herself with such trivialities. It's trivia that sometimes gets us through the toughest moments. "And Maggie, if there's anything I can do," I added, resorting to the well-worn exit line, "you let me know."

She looked as if she was about to take me up on that offer, holding up a finger and taking a deep breath. Then she deflated. "Oh, there'll be lots to do, I'm sure," she said.

I helped Estelle lug her equipment out to her car. With no further spectacle to watch, most of the neighbors had gone about their business. Depressed as hell, I waited on the sidewalk as Estelle finished up.

"Sir," Estelle said, slamming down the trunk of her car, "I'll give you a call as soon as Dr. Perrone has something for me." She glanced at her watch. "I'll get this off to the lab, and then we'll see."

"Are you ready for lunch yet?"

"Better still, why don't you plan to come over

for dinner tonight? That'll give me time to ship this batch off to Albuquerque, and catch up on paperwork."

I had been thinking of a midafternoon memorial burrito, but this was too good an opportunity to pass up. I'd manage the hours before dinner somehow. "It's a deal," I said. "What can I bring?"

"Yourself, *padrino. Los dos* will be excited." That was the charm of little kids, of course. They could see me five times in a week, and still be thrilled with yet another opportunity to drag me into their world.

"I was going to wander over to the hospital for a few minutes to see how Dale Torrance is doing, and then I need to run the permit paperwork out to the ranch. Pat is standing around out there waiting on all this. Dinner will work out just right."

"Wish the Torrances well for me." Estelle opened the car door. "See you at the house, then. Anytime is fine."

I raised a hand in salute, still unmotivated to resume whatever it was that I was doing before this. Estelle was headed back to her office. Deputy Dennis Collins and Officer Beuler had left the neighborhood, no doubt already prowling the highways and school crossings. That's what the young do when someone older dies, I suppose— pause a minute or two and then get on with life.

Us older duffers reacted a little differently. Losing one of my oldest, closest friends had punched out some of my stuffing, and I wasn't ready just yet to draw a line through George Payton's name. George would have laughed at me.

I ambled back to the SUV and called the hospital, saving myself a trip of four blocks. Dale Torrance had been transferred to Las Cruces so that an orthopedic surgeon there could whack away at the lad's wrecked knee. I switched off the phone, relieved that I didn't need to visit Posadas General. Its antiseptic atmosphere wasn't good therapy for me just then, anyway. I'd be apt to glance through some door left ajar and see someone I knew, withered and old, intubated and helpless.

The sun felt good as it streamed through the Chevy's window. I sat for a few minutes, finishing Herb Torrance's livestock transportation permit. Herb and Annie had gone on to Cruces, but Pat Gabaldon could sign off just as easily. It wasn't as if a giant, bellowing herd was tramping across four states. The single, modest trailer load wouldn't even leave the county. It was the sort of mindless attention to bureaucratic detail that allowed my mind to roam free, picking at this and that, remembering this and that.

By the time I returned to the Torrance ranch, Pat had the twenty-four critters all buttoned up in the trailer, the rig turned around and ready to head out the driveway. He was leaning against the front fender of Herb's huge diesel dually one-ton pickup, cell phone pasted to his ear, and raised a hand in salute at the sound of my approach. Pat continued his conversation as he sauntered out to meet me. A short, compact kid in faded, sweat-stained denim, he ruined his cowpoke image with an Oakland A's baseball cap worn askew, brim to the rear. He shared the old trailer behind Herb and Annie's place, the modern equivalent of a bunk house, with Dale Torrance.

"Dale's still in surgery," Pat said as I rolled the Blazer to a stop. He snapped the phone closed. "Herb says they don't know how long it'll be."

"God damn nasty break," I said. I didn't explain why I had been delayed so long in town, but Pat had made good use of the time. Horses and tack were tended to and he'd trailered the cattle with just the help of Socks, the blue heeler, who now sat in the truck, tongue lolling, excited to be going someplace where he could chase things.

"I was going to head on up to the mesa," Pat said. "Didn't see any point in sitting around here." He turned and maneuvered his wad of snuff a bit so he could spit.

"There's that," I agreed. "If I can get you to sign on the dotted line, we're all set."

Pat cocked his head and looked at the paperwork. One hand strayed to his hip pocket. "I ain't got thirty-eight bucks," he said.

"Herb's good for it," I said. "Don't worry about it." Pat signed in cramped, angular printing, and I gave him Herb's copy marked "paid", which would make the state bookkeepers cringe if they knew. But they didn't need to know. I included one of my business cards as well. "I can't imagine anybody giving you grief, but if you have any problems, give me a call."

"You bet. Thanks."

With the great work of the state finished, I left the H-Bar-T ranch and drove north on County Road 14, a rough, jouncing ride that I usually avoided. But this particular day, it felt good to be out and away. The sky was touched here and there with jet trails that wafted out and turned into wispy clouds, the wind just enough to occasionally kick up a little dust and whip it around in tiny devils. I ambled along with the SUV's windows open.

A mile north, beyond Herb's last section fence, dust blew off the tops of fresh tracks that had turned off the main road. The derrick of a well-driller's rig rose above the runty piñon and juniper a few hundred yards to the east. It surprised me that someone imagined that there was still water left under that dry patch of desert. Nosy as ever, I turned and followed the tracks. The trail wound along the flank of San Patricio Mesa, dodging stands of cacti, water-stressed juniper, creosote bush, and the occasional snarl of stunted oak. Amid a growing litter of beer cans, plastic oil jugs, plastic bags and similar touches of human grace, the two-track headed up a particularly picturesque canyon. It couldn't continue in that direction for long, since the jumbled rock of the mesa edge reared up in the way.

A tawny swale of dry bunch grass had been flattened to dust by traffic, and the drill rig sat on its hydraulic feet, a flood of dried, cracked slurry paving the area around the drill hole. I parked and gazed at the rig, thinking this a damn odd place for a water well. The bulk of San Patricio Mesa protected the area from the breezes unless the wind was from the northeast, and the last time we'd had a 'downeaster' in southern New Mexico, the ice age was in control. A windmill in this spot would sit idle most of the time.

Turning in my seat, I surveyed the rimrock above me. No electric lines passed closer than those behind Herb Torrance's house, a full mile away, with the buttress of a mesa between here and there. From the drill site, the land sloped down the swale, losing another hundred feet of elevation to the prairie to the north. In the distance, I could see the brown line of CR14 snaking off toward the state highway. Bringing in electric lines would be no problem, as long as the wallet was fat.

Switching off the SUV, I unbuckled and climbed out. Except for its being picturesque, I could see little reason to be drilling for water here, unless Herb had managed to pick up this piece of land from a neighbor and planned to extend his pasturage. *That* made sense. For him, it was convenient.

Off to the west of CR 14, I could see the rise of the hills behind Reuben Fuentes' old place, long abandoned now. Estelle Reyes-Guzman's great uncle had been as colorful as they come, and he and I had shared an escapade or two on both sides of the border—but that was long before Homeland Security took all the fun out of adventures like that.

Whoever owned the drill rig hadn't painted his company name on the weathered doors, but the driver's side wasn't locked, and I helped myself. The cab reeked of oil, chewing tobacco, and diesel fuel. A broken clipboard lay on the seat with a receipt from Posadas Electrix under the clip showing that Scott Paulson had bought a new super-duty battery the day before. I didn't know Scott Paulson, and that in itself was surprising.

Since this enormous, ponderous unit drove

over the highways and bore a commercial license plate, there should have been a registration in the dash box. Should have been. I climbed down and surveyed the rig and walked around behind. The license plate was mud encrusted, torn and battered, and carried a two year-old tag. Knowing that it meant nothing to me, but still in my busybody mode, I jotted the license number down in a small pocket notebook, and then strolled back to my vehicle.

Gayle Torrez was working toward the final hours of her day shift and certainly wouldn't mind something to do.

"Gayle," I said when she answered the phone, "do you have a minute?"

"Sure," she said. "What do you need?"

"I'd like a ten-twenty-eight on New Mexico alpha bravo kilo niner one zero one, if you'll run that plate for me."

"Sure. Do I dare ask what you're up to this afternoon, sir?"

"Being nosy."

"Ah, good." She didn't pursue the matter but sounded satisfied. I could hear the tappety-tap of computer keys in the background. After another thirty seconds, Gayle came back on the line. "Alpha bravo kilo niner one zero one should appear on a 1971 gray Brockway registered to Scott Paulson,

101 Commercial Avenue, Lordsburg. No wants or warrants."

"Expired?"

"No sir. Current. Expires in October."

"He keeps the new sticky tags in his pocket, I guess," I said. "Thanks, sweetheart."

"Are you behaving yourself?"

"As much as possible," I said. "Is his nibs sleeping in his office?"

"I think he's out by the fuel pumps with Tom Mears. You want me to haul him in here?"

"No. Just ask him for me when you see him next. I should remember, but I don't. Who owns the property just north of Herb's place on 14? It looks like a long, narrow strip that runs right along the back side of San Patricio Mesa? I didn't see any boundary fences, so it goes all the way from the road back to this new well site where I'm parked at the moment. It'd be the piece immediately adjacent to Herb's."

"That's easy enough. Bobby has his cell with him, if you want to talk with him. Thirty-nine hundred."

"No, that's all right. It's not that important. If I had any gumption I'd stop at the assessor's office and do it myself. I guess I was wondering if this was one of those parcels that the BLM picked up in that land swap with George Payton."

"Bobby will know," Gayle said cheerfully.

"That's what I figured." There had been a blizzard of land titles when the feds purchased the land that included the newly discovered limestone caves not far north of Reuben's place. No Carlsbad Caverns, the discovery was still of some local interest, and there was the promise of a decent tourist attraction if anything was ever developed. When her great-uncle had died, Estelle Reyes-Guzman had missed out on inheriting something spectacular by about a thousand yards, give or take. The Bureau of Land Management had snapped up the parcel to protect it, and now plans for the feature were plodding through the federal labyrinth.

I took a few minutes to scribble a bunch of notes to myself, including the information on Scott Paulson. No livestock appeared to be involved, so none of it was any of my business. Still, sitting there and jotting log entries felt good and proper.

Chapter Six

Posadas County was split east-west by three state highways. County Road 14 ran north and south over on the west side of the county, like a wriggly noodle laced through the tines of a fork. I continued north on the county road until it intersected with NM17, the old route made obsolete by the interstate that paralleled it. Entering the village of Posadas from the west, NM17 became Bustos Avenue, and as I cruised into town, a stomach grumble reminded me that it had been altogether too long since breakfast.

Any small amount of discipline at that moment—and it was fast approaching five o'clock—would have prompted me to pull in my belt a notch and wait for dinner at the Guzmans'. But even an hour is a long time to wait. I pulled into the parking lot of the Don Juan de Oñate Restaurant, determined to have just a small jolt of coffee and wee bit of the aromatic magic for which the place was justly famous. Just an appetizer, so to speak.

There had once been a time when Fernando Aragon's restaurant would have closed between two to five each day, giving them time to prep for the dinner rush. But those days were as long gone as the copper mines and the rush of travelers, and the restaurant remained open from 6 a.m. to 9 p.m., seven days a week, working to catch any stray customer.

When I walked in that day, the place was quiet as a tomb. No *maitre d'* greeted me, and I could have slipped away with the cash register, although no doubt it didn't hold much. I headed for my favorite haunt, a booth far in the back with a view to the southwest and the San Cristóbal mountains that separated us from old Mexico.

The kitchen door opened and Aileen Aragon, Fernando's daughter, waved at me. I thought her expression was a little less cheerful than usual. A rotund woman who wore T-shirts that didn't flatter her figure, Aileen was on the down slope past forty. During the decades I'd lived in Posadas, I could count on one hand the times I'd seen Aileen anywhere but at the Don Juan. Her parents had built the place, and she would work herself to death to keep it.

"JanaLynn will be with you in a sec. Sheriff," she called, and I slid into the booth. Aileen was one of many Posadas County residents who had become so used to my tenure that they just found it easier to continue using the title rather than my name. In a moment JanaLynn Torrez pushed through the kitchen door carrying a two-foot stack of brass baskets for the tortillas and dinner rolls. The sheriff's youngest sister had worked at the Don Juan for a dozen years, and I think that I favored the place as much for her cheerful, attractive demeanor as for the food.

She stashed the baskets, filled a tall, green-tinted glass with iced tea, and as she approached, her dark, dramatic features were sympathetic. "We heard about Mr. Payton," she said, setting down the glass. She reached out both hands to take mine. "We're so sorry."

"Yes," I said. "Not the best day."

"His heart?"

"I would guess so," I sighed.

She looked down at me for a long, empathetic moment, gave my hands a final squeeze, and knowing that comfort lay with good food, asked, "What can I get for you?"

"Well, I don't know. I don't want to ruin my dinner, so I was thinking of just a piece of pie, maybe."

"Would you like to try one of the tostadas? Aileen's been prepping those, and they're going to be *really* good."

"Oh, gosh." I twisted my left arm behind my back and feigned a pained grimace. "Okay, you win."

"The plate is going to include two, but if you're having dinner soon, you might want half a serving."

"What's the world coming to," I muttered, but nodded agreement.

"And green, of course."

"Sure enough." I loved red chile, but it didn't love me—a tragedy I had shared with George Payton. If I hadn't planned to spend the evening in polite company, I might have risked it.

She bent down to give my shoulders a hug. "Back in a minute."

"No rush." The booth offered the same familiar, comfortable lumps and bumps, even the same old strap of duct tape that sutured a rip in the plastic. I settled back, arm across the back, fingers tapping on the windowsill. The iced tea was good, although almost too fresh to have any real character. JanaLynn hadn't suggested pulling the blinds, and the sun that blasted in was soothing. The restaurant's air conditioning hammered, but they could have saved the electricity as far as I was concerned. For the past week, temperatures hadn't broken eighty-five degrees during the heat of the day—a perfect September in southern New Mexico.

Five minutes of musing about nothing in particular was all I was allowed. Then Jana reappeared with an attractive little platter that featured a six-inch corn *tostada* so fragrant I could smell it despite the symphony of other goodies that blanketed it. That small tawny continent was covered with thin-sliced roast pork joined by perfect pinto beans in green chile, and a garnish of greens and diced tomatoes. Knowing my penchant for something to cool the effects of chile on a cranky gut, Aileen had remembered a touch of sour cream peaked off to one side. George Payton would have scoffed at that and called me a sissy.

JanaLynn came by to keep the iced tea filled, but otherwise left me alone with my thoughts. I wish that I could claim that those thoughts were deep and relevant, but they weren't. My mind roamed from here to there as I did justice to Aileen's artistry, and the sun and the chile consorted. A nap started to sound like a really good idea, and I figured that I'd timed this whole thing just right. I'd finish here, then dive into my badger hole for an hour before dinner.

Halfway through the meal, I was hauled up short, as if I'd chomped down on a wad of aluminum foil. I chewed thoughtfully, using my fork to take apart the remains of the *tostada*, separating the bits of perfect pork from the slender cuts of Hatch chile. I skated the beans off to one side.

I had eaten my first meal at the Don Juan de Oñate restaurant more than thirty years before. I'd commiserated with Fernando and Bea Aragon when fire had leveled the first iteration of the Don Juan in 1988, and had been one of the first customers to celebrate the phoenix from the ashes. I'd settled on the wonderful, megacalorie *burrito grande* as my signature dish after very little menu experimentation, and I could practically guess Fernando's mood by any minor changes that might add or detract from the core triumph.

Today, this *tostada* was right up there with all the rest of the Aragons' food—a menu that would have made them world-famous had the rest of the world known where the hell Posadas, New Mexico, might be. And that was what brought me up short. So short, in fact, that it prompted a sinking feeling in the pit of my stomach. I told myself that this was all my imagination working overtime, and forced myself to clean my plate.

After a final exchange of pleasantries with JanaLynn, I left a twenty-dollar bill at my plate and glanced at my watch. Gayle Torrez would still be on duty, and Estelle would likely be in the office. The undersheriff would listen to me patiently, and then tell me if I was crazy or not.

I had left the window of the SUV open so my butt wouldn't weld to the roasting vinyl when I slid inside. Approaching the truck, I could hear the cell phone's ring. With the giggling of rough roads, the phone had slid under the junk on the passenger seat. Normal folks who eschewed belt rigs often use phone clips or brackets in the vehicle, or even those nifty little wells in the center console. I knew that and still lost the damn thing more often than not. By the time I'd found it this time, the caller had established his patience.

"Gastner."

"Ah, good," Gayle Torrez said. "I just missed you at the Don Juan."

"What's up?" I asked. "I was just headed your way." Gayle wouldn't be so persistent just to chit-chat.

"Sir, Dennis is up on 43, and he says that there's a herd of cattle on the highway, headed down hill. They're about a mile up from the quarry."

I laughed. "Tell him to ask the lead cow if she has her papers with her." When a rancher decided to move his cattle, it was my business. When old Bossie elected to go awandering, that wasn't my affair, and I wasn't about to run around in the sunshine, with a fresh *tostada* settling in my stomach, shouting at livestock. "They're not called dumb animals for nothing," I added.

"Dennis says that there's a dog herding them."

"Well, crap," I said, starting the truck and

turning on the air conditioning. "Well, have him ask the dog for the papers then. Whose cattle are they?" The county was small enough that coincidence was rare. I *knew* whose cattle they were.

"I don't think he knows, sir."

"Tell young Dennis to look on the left rear hip somewhere. There'll be a brand." Apprehension reared its ugly head, and it wasn't from the *tostada.*

"Hang on, sir."

Traffic was light when I pulled out of the Don Juan's parking lot, and even though I had far, far better things to do than worry about loose cattle, I headed east on Bustos. By the time I'd covered the twelve blocks to the intersection of Bustos and Grande—the heart of Posadas—Gayle was back.

"Sir, he says that the brand has an H, and then a dash maybe, and then he thinks a T. He wonders if that's Herb Torrance. There are twenty-five or so."

"Chances are," I said. What had Patrick Gabaldon done now, I wondered. After I left the ranch, Pat would have had plenty of time to drive up on Cat Mesa, release the critters from the stock trailer, and head home, closing the gates behind him. It was no big deal. The pasturage was less than a mile beyond the intersection of County Road 43 and Forest Road 26, where the pavement turned to dirt.

It was conceivable, although as unlikely as rain, that Pat might have left open a gate, or *thought* it was secure when it really wasn't. Dumb as they were, cattle had a sort of persistent, dim curiosity about their world. If they could wander without interference, they would. If a gate yawned open, they'd drift through it.

But the *last* thing Pat would do is leave his beloved blue heeler companion alone with the cattle. The dog should have been sitting beside Pat in the pickup, tongue lolling and slobbering all over the seat and dashboard, eager for home and a plunge in an inviting stock tank. Left with the livestock, and left to his own instincts, he would herd the cattle until either they or he dropped.

"Sir, he says he can't get the dog to come to him." I nodded with appreciation. Deputy Dennis Collins might have been a city kid, but he was shrewd and had already figured out who was the trail boss of this wandering outfit.

"I don't doubt that," I said. "Tell him I'm on my way up. In the meantime, tell him that the dog's name is Socks. What Dennis needs to do is get near enough, and shout the dog's name to get his attention, then command *lie down*. He has to sound like he means it and knows what he's doing."

"Socks, lie down," Gayle said. "Yes, sir." I could hear the amusement in her tone.

"It probably won't work, but there you go. That's all the dog lingo I know. I'll head up that way. The cattle are on the highway right of way?"

"Yes, sir."

"Well, if he can get the dog to take a vacation, they'll stop. Pat Gabaldon trailered them up there a little bit ago, and he'll be on his way back to Herb's. He may even be running some errands here in town. I'll find him and let him know."

"Thanks, sir. Should I tell Dennis you're headed up the hill?"

"Yep." I pulled over and parked across from the Chevy dealership, leafing through my paperwork. Herb Torrance's cell phone rang half a dozen times, and I could imagine him sitting there in the Las Cruces hospital waiting room, trying to shut the thing up while the rest of the folks glared at him.

"Yeah, this is Herb," he said.

"Herb, Bill Gastner. How's Dale?"

"Well, I don't know yet," he said slowly. "They said it went all right. He's still in recovery. Annie's with him."

"Good deal. Look, do you have Patrick's cell number handy?"

"Well, sure. I got that." He rattled off the number. "He moved the cattle all right?"

"Oh, sure," I said. "He got 'em up there just

fine. Apparently somebody left a gate open, though, and one of the deputies found the herd walking along the highway. I'm in Posadas right now, and wanted to find Pat so he could shag 'em back to pasture."

"Well, yeah," Herb said. "Now that's a nuisance. Sorry 'bout that."

"It happens. Look, Herb, while I have you on the line…George Peyton died this morning. I thought you might like to know."

A long pause greeted that news. "Well, hell," Herb said finally. "At home, did he?"

"Yes. It looks like he just sat down to lunch, and keeled over. His son-in-law found him."

"Well, damn. You know, I'm sorry to hear that. I liked old George."

"A lot of us did." As I drove through Posadas, I kept an eye out for the H-Bar-T pickup and stock trailer—it would be hard to hide that rig. "I'll let you go, Herb. I'm headed up the hill right now, and if there's any kind of problem, I'll get back to you."

"Well, okay," Herb said doubtfully. "You could have Patrick call me, if you wanted. Or I'll try after a bit."

"I'll do that."

"Damn all to hell, I'm sorry to hear about George," he said, and I could imagine the rancher's slow shake of the head. "Hell gettin' old, ain't it."

Chapter Seven

I dialed Pat Gabaldon's number, and for a moment, it sounded as if it had connected. Then an odd click, then nothing. Three tries later, still no Pat, and I gave up.

County Road 43 wound out of Posadas northbound and in three miles intersected State 78, the main arterial that passed by Posadas Municipal Airport and then headed out of the county to the northwest. There was no reason I could imagine that Pat would have taken the state highway for the 18 miles to the intersection with CR 14, the Torrance ranch road, where the trip south on the rutted gravel would rattle Pat's teeth, truck, and trailer to pieces. He'd stick to smooth pavement, passing through the village.

Just beyond the state highway, CR43 started its meander up the flank of Cat Mesa. On the right, the fenced-in remains of the Consolidated Mining boneyard were quiet and dismal, a vast collection of junk and detritus from the hopeful decades of copper mining. There had been a time when some of the village fathers thought that Posadas was headed for grand times. I had never agreed, knowing that the influx of workers cared about copper and the money affixed to it, but not a bit about the village of Posadas or the county. The chained gate, topped now with barbed wire, was still secure. Just beyond, no tracks cut off to the east on County Road 6.

A bit beyond, off to the left, the old quarry was deserted. The Forest Service, who owned this attractive nuisance, had tried for years to fence it properly, but icy cold seep water, so deep that legends abounded about what—or maybe who—lay on the bottom, was an undeniable attraction for partying high school kids. They'd jump the fence, and no agency could baby-sit the quarry all day and all night. In the past few years, as the entire Southwest dried out, the seep had decreased, and it seemed to me that the water level was gradually dropping. If we all just stayed patient, the quarry would both cease to be a drowning threat and would reveal whatever secrets lay at the bottom.

Pat Gabaldon hadn't pulled his rig into the shade by the north rim of the quarry for a bite of lunch or a quick plunge. And it was equally inconceivable that all this time he wouldn't have missed his dog.

For another few miles, the macadam road switch-backed up the mesa, then would top out at the intersection with Forest Road 26. Sure enough, now more than a mile downhill from the county road's transition to dirt, I saw Dennis Collins' county car pulled off on the shoulder, red lights winking. Just beyond, the cattle stood in a nervous gaggle, the routine of their day interrupted, and not a brain in the bunch knowing what to do about it.

Dennis stood in the middle of the road, hands on his hips. As I approached, the deputy jabbed an index finger at a hump in the weeds by the side of the road, and I could tell that he was shouting something. The hump was the blue heeler, lying flat and poised, a furry arrow about to dart should a cow finally make a decision.

I parked off to the side behind Dennis' unit and got out.

"Socks, lie down!" Dennis shouted, no doubt for my benefit, since Socks already was.

"No sign of Pat," I said casually as I sauntered across the highway, keeping my pace relaxed. I didn't want to give Socks the notion that the humans wanted something done. The cattle were in a tidy group, wondering. Best that they remain that way. "Good job here, Dennis."

"It's nothing I did," he said.

"The gate is a mile on up the road, right by the Forest Service sign. If we can get 'em to move that way, it'd be a good thing."

"I don't know how to drive a dog," the deputy said, and shook his head in amusement.

"Neither do I, but once Socks gets the notion in his head about which way we want to go, I think he'll do most of the work. That's the theory, anyway." I turned and looked down the county road, thankfully devoid of traffic. "We can mosey along with the vehicles, and they'll move along all right. Let's get 'em moving first, so the dog knows."

Pat Gabaldon, who no doubt *did* talk dog, might have used whistles, maybe shouts, to get the job done. But, smart as he was, it took Socks only an instant to see that these two humans wanted the cattle to go back up hill. Being a dog, I don't think he was vexed by the thought that all his previous work might have been for naught. We walked forward toward the herd, and the cattle milled and drifted this way and that until we got too close, and then as a single organism the small herd turned and started back up the county road. Since the road was fenced on both sides, there wasn't much challenge. The dog shot back and forth to harass stragglers, and both Dennis and I retreated to our respective vehicles, to drive side by side up the road, easy as you please.

Socks was tired enough that the first blush of frantic joy had evaporated in the hot sun. Now he just worked, looking for the shortest distance between points. I relaxed back in the seat, letting the SUV idle along, enjoying the whole thing—sun, heat, dust, the aromas of both livestock and trampled prairie vegetation, the sharp yip of the working dog. The journey gave me time to think, looking for an easy solution to the puzzle. None presented itself.

In a half hour, we drew within sight of the cattle guard that marked the Forest Service boundary. Sure enough, the wire gate was flopped to one side. Because the county road right-of-way fence joined the pasture fence, the cattle had nowhere to go except back over the top of us, or through the gate, and even the weary Socks could figure that out.

"Make sure that damn thing is secure this time," I said to Dennis, and he wrestled the wire gate closed as the last two calves shot through the eight foot opening. Now they had a few thousand acres to explore, and Socks was out of a job. I whistled sharply and his ears went up, and with a last warning look at the nearest cow, the heeler trotted over to us, tongue dragging the ground.

"Good dog," I said, and meant it. Rummaging in the back of the SUV, I found the plastic cubitainer of water, took the cap off my Thermos, and refueled the pup. Water slopped all over through several fill-ups, and if Socks could have fitted himself bodily into the cup, he would have.

"I don't get this," Dennis said, as he watched me loop a short length of light rope through the dog's collar. "How does a guy forget his dog?"

"I'm wondering that very thing," I replied, and tried the phone again. Ten rings and no Pat Gabaldon. I tried the Torrance land line on the slim chance that Pat had driven back to the ranch and was inside the main house. "You have a phone book?"

"Sure." Dennis jogged back to his car. He returned with the book and I found the number for the Broken Spur saloon. I'd given up decades before trying to memorize all but the most important two or three phone numbers. After a while, you get enough of them rattling around in the brain, and they all exchange digits.

I dialed and the phone rang half a dozen times before a truculent voice said, "What?"

"Victor, this is Bill Gastner. Is Pat Gabaldon there, by any chance?"

"No."

I could picture Victor Sanchez standing in the kitchen of his establishment, cleaver in hand, apron a bit on the grungy side. Victor would be a bit sweaty, in no mood to be chatty-friendly with the cops…and he still considered me one of those, no doubt. He had his own dark, sad reasons, and I always let his attitude slide.

"Was he at your place earlier?"

"What do you need?"

"He just delivered a small herd of cattle up here on the mesa. They got out somehow, but I have his dog."

"So what do you want from me?"

"I'm trying to find Patrick, Victor. That's all. If you see him, will you let him know?"

"Yeah," Victor said. The line went dead.

"What a charmer he is," I said. The dog started to fidget as I walked toward the fence, but I glowered at him. "Lie down, Socks," I said, and he did. Driving a herd of cattle through a narrow gate is an effective way to ruin tracks. The gate's wire tie was drum tight, and I beckoned Dennis. "Let me in here," I said, and as the gate came down, Socks spun in a circle, wrapping himself in rope.

The fresh tracks were obvious, and it appeared that Pat had driven through the gate, then had swung the truck and trailer in a wide arc, stopping when he was facing the gate once again. A blind man could have found the spot where the cattle had disembarked, 96 hooves diving from the trailer into the rocky dirt of the pasture. It was just as easy to see boot prints here and there, especially immediately beside where the trailer's back bumper would have been, where Pat Gabaldon would have to stand to secure the tailgate.

I ambled around the area, hands in my pockets.

"He's got a girl friend?" Dennis said, and I looked up. "Kinda small feet."

Someone had planted a foot on the edge of an ant circle, those huge platters of bare ground with a mound in the center, the hub of industry for the little harvesters. I crossed to where the deputy stood, and sure enough, the shoe print was no rancher's big hoof, nor characterized by high heal or pointy toe.

I straightened up and pivoted at the waist, surveying the country. This was not the sort of place frequented by tourists, or hikers from the village, or morning power walkers. The print could have been fresh, but I was no Daniel Boone, and Dennis Collins certainly wasn't...neither one of us could be sure. Still, the most obvious explanation was that Patrick Gabaldon had not been alone for this chore.

We found no other tracks—the cattle plunging through the gate had made sure of that.

There was nothing sinister about Pat Gabaldon having company on this particular task. He was a young, good-looking cowpuncher, and a picnic with an obliging young gal up in the perfume of the piñons, junipers, and scrub oak, serenaded by the jays and ravens, sipping a cool brew while his boss was preoccupied a hundred miles away—what could be better than that? His route with a trailer-load of cattle took him right through Posadas, and picking up a friend was easy enough.

Then later, with the cattle off-loaded and the picnic over, he'd driven back down the hill. Maybe at that moment, his mind wasn't on his job. He had not made double sure that the wire gate was secure. And worse than that, he had abandoned his dog. The whole scenario was likely—but he'd left Socks behind. Nobody does that, no matter how love-smitten.

Chapter Eight

Pat Gabaldon's personal life was none of my business, unless he was a cattle thief. But all twenty-four head of Herb Torrance's cattle grazed safely now, so purloined livestock wasn't the issue. I reflected that had the cowpuncher here in question been the lad with the shattered knee, that might have been a different matter and a cause for real concern.

Young Dale Torrance wasn't long off probation after pulling a stupid stunt a year before. Desperate to win the heart of a young gal, Dale had heisted a few head of cattle from a rancher up in Newton, just over the county line. He'd driven the trailer load of steers to Oklahoma and sold them to a dealer who didn't ask questions. Dale would have blanched at hearing himself called a "rustler," an old frontier term synonymous with "hanged". He had some vague notion that he was going to repay the rancher somehow, but first he intended to buy the girl of his dreams a new truck. Perhaps in his mind, a Ford beat a diamond ring all hollow.

We recovered those cattle well-traveled but unscathed, and the rancher, Miles Waddell, decided not to press charges. The District Attorney, Judge Lester Hobart, and I conferred about the other charges that the state thought it might press against the kid. The upshot was that Dale was slapped with probation. Call us old softies. Dale's rejection by the dream girl was worse punishment, no doubt… that and the ferocious licking he'd taken from his old man, who wielded a chunk of 2x4 with mean effect.

On the other hand, Pat Gabaldon was as steady and diligent as Dale was rowdy and undisciplined. Dale would disappear without a how-do-you-do, but Pat wasn't the type. He appreciated a job and a place to live, and he liked the Torrance family. So, until an innocent explanation presented itself, my curiosity was a powerful motivator. I tried Pat's telephone half a dozen times with no result. One logical explanation was that the young man, concerned about a badly hurt buddy, had driven Herb's big rig back to the ranch, then hopped in his own pickup and headed for Las Cruces.

It was comfortable to think that the boy had done that, except for two things. He could have used the telephone to check up on Dale—I couldn't imagine Pat electing to mope for hours around a smelly hospital waiting room. Secondly, Socks fidgeted on the passenger seat of my Chevy, his head thrust out the partially open window, tongue flailing like a wet rag in the breeze.

I took a route through Posadas that allowed me to glance down ninety percent of the side streets, but the big white H-Bar-T rig wasn't parked anywhere obvious—not at any of the service stations, not at Posadas Lumber and Hardware, not at one of the four bars or the Don Juan de Oñate restaurant.

Heading south on State 56, I dialed Herb once again. This time, the phone call caught him in the hospital's coffee shop, and I could hear the clanking of dishes in the background. Without surprise, Herb accepted the news that the cattle were safely pastured, but he was as puzzled as I was that they had gotten loose in the first place, with the dog then left to his own devices.

"I have Socks in custody," I said, and Herb chuckled half-heartedly at the joke. "I'm headed back to your place," I added. "I'm thinking that Pat went home to change and is headed your way right now in his own pickup. Somehow, we just missed each other along the way."

"Might," Herb said. "Might do that. You didn't cross paths, then."

"I took north 14, daydreaming about other things," I said. "That's where the Sheriff's

Department caught up with me. Patrick would have hauled the cattle around on the state highway, and gone back that way, too."

"Huh," Herb said. "He wouldn't go off and leave the dog, though."

"I can't imagine that he would," I agreed. "And by the way, not that it's any of my business, but who's drilling the water well just north of your place? On the backside of the mesa? I saw Paulson's rig parked out there just beyond your fence line."

There was a brief silence while Herb caught up after my abrupt change of subject. "Oh, that," Herb scoffed. "Well, he ain't got much of a start yet, I don't think. He'd like to find water there, but if he does, he'll drill deep enough that it'll come out of the ground speakin' Chinese."

"Who's he drilling for?"

"That's another of Waddell's schemes," Herb said. "It's kind of a picturesque spot back in there, you know. And there's some cold air seepin' out of the rocks enough that one of the folks from the BLM thinks that maybe there's a wing of the cave under there. Hell, I don't know. Or care."

"A little speculation going on, then," I said. Miles Waddell was the Newton rancher from whom Dale Torrance had borrowed the cattle.

"Yep. I guess old Miles thinks that if he develops a well, then come time for the BLM to work a land swap with him, it'll be worth more. He's probably right."

"I didn't know that he owned that piece." It surprised me that Herb hadn't fought just a little bit to own the property himself.

"Don't think he does. Not yet, anyways. George Payton did at one time, but I don't know about now. Him and me talked about it some. Sure hated to hear about George's passing, I can tell you. Anyway," he said, sounding as if he didn't want to pursue that line of conversation any further, "are you headed down to the ranch now?"

"I thought to check on Pat," I said. "And return the dog."

"Well, yeah," Herb said, voice brightening. "We'll appreciate that. Old Socks, he's worth about three good men."

I rang off, tried Pat's number once more, and slowed as I passed the Broken Spur Saloon. No rig, no answer. The pup's front paws danced a little tattoo on my front seat as we passed the bar. He'd been there before, no doubt locked in the cab while the humans did their thing inside. A half mile farther, I turned onto the county road and headed north toward the H-Bar-T. In fifteen minutes of jouncing and dust, I had my answer.

The heeler's agitated dance increased tempo as I swung in under the modest decorative arch over the gate. By the bunk trailer, Pat's ten year-old Chevy truck was parked under a water-stressed elm. I pulled the SUV to a stop and reached out to rest a hand on the top of the heeler's head. "Give me a minute," I said, but he was ready to go. I managed to squirm out of the truck and block his exit, mindful not to slam his eager nose or sloppy tongue in the door.

Two minutes confirmed that the cattle truck wasn't parked behind the house, or over behind the boys' mobile home, or anywhere else hidden from immediate view. Herb Torrance's place was dead quiet. I stood hands on hips, thinking of the possibilities, then dialed Herb again. This time, the phone rang nearly a dozen times before he answered.

"Herb," I said, "I'm sorry to keep bugging you. How's Dale?"

"Well, they're going to keep him at least over-night," he said.

"That's standard," I said. "The surgery went all right?"

"Well, they *think* so."

"Let's hope so. Look, I'm at your place right now. Pat hasn't been here yet. His own truck is still here. Yours isn't." I reached out and patted the hood of the veteran Chevy. It was cool. "His truck hasn't been used."

"Huh," Herb said.

"Was he planning to go somewhere today with your rig? Pick up some hay, maybe? Livestock feed?"

"Hadn't planned on it."

"A load of railroad ties, maybe?"

"Nope. We was going to move the cattle, and then go on over to Bender's Canyon to replace an old boundary fence. We got about a quarter mile stretch over there that needs work. But I don't think…"

"He'd take your truck for that?"

"Well, sure. Not with the trailer, though. Can't get through the canyon trail haulin' that son-of-a-bitch."

I walked toward the white, prefab workshop on the far side of the house. The doors were open, and I could see the reels of new barbed wire and a pallet of metal posts. "The wire and posts are here in the shop," I said.

"Then there's that," Herb said. "Look, he may have had some errand of his own that he took a mind to do. He'll show up."

"He wouldn't drive your rig to Cruces, I don't think."

"Oh, hell no. That rig's a diesel-suckin' hog with that stock trailer hooked on behind. Bad enough without it. No, I don't think he'd do that. You got the dog, though?"

"I do."

"Just put him in the boys' trailer. They never lock the place, and old Socks, he'll be all right."

"I'll take care of it," I said. "My best to Annie." I switched off, and aimed an expletive at Pat Gabaldon for being so thoughtless. Despite Herb's suggestion, I wasn't about to dump the dog in the bunk house. The Torrances wouldn't be back from Cruces until who knew when. If Pat was on a fling somewhere, the abandoned heeler would take the butt end of it. On the off chance that luck would change, I tried Pat's phone again, with no response. Ambling back across the yard to my truck, I tried to come up with some stroke of genius, but drew a blank. Tearing out a page from my notebook, I jotted a message to Pat and stuck it under the windshield of his truck, then made another copy and clamped it in the screen door of the mobile home.

Socks was clearly upset, just a click on the down side of berserk, when I returned to the SUV. He wanted out of this strange cab so he could herd something. I reached back for the Thermos cap again and gave him another shot of water, but he was too distracted to enjoy it. None of this was the way his world worked, and his distress was pitiful.

As I headed out the Torrance's driveway, my

phone rang, and I snatched it off the seat, the sound and the motion setting the furry dervish off again, his tongue spray spotting the inside of the windshield, the dashboard, and my right forearm.

"Hey," Sheriff Robert Torrez said. "Gayle said you had a question."

"Hey yourself," I replied. "And yes, I do. As a matter of fact, I have several questions at the moment, Robert." Socks was headed for my lap, and I nudged him back across the center console.

"Where are you now?"

"At the moment, I'm at Herb's ranch. Just now leaving." I quickly explained about Dale Torrance's adventure, and Bobby made a little grunting sound that translated as, "Why do I need to know all this?"

"Actually, my original question that I mentioned to Gayle was about the property just north of Herb's place, but I already found out the answer to that one. That's not what's on my mind at the moment, either. Right now, I'm trying to find Pat Gabaldon," I said. "I have his dog."

"His dog?"

"Yes. His heeler." I gave the sheriff an abbreviated version of the puzzling events up on Cat Mesa, and he listened without interruption. "I can't imagine Pat being so careless, is all."

"Huh," Torrez said. "Did you check to see

if he went on down 26 to cut some firewood or something like that?" Forest Road 26 ran along the rim of Cat Mesa.

"I didn't see tracks," I said. "I also have to admit that I didn't look that way more than a glance."

"Yeah, well. He might have done that. He's still drivin' that rig of Herb's?"

"As far as I know."

"Not too easy to hide that," the sheriff reflected. "He'll turn up. You told Collins to keep an eye out?"

"Sure."

"And you're keepin' the dog?"

Concern for this fifty-pound bundle of worried muscle and slobber wasn't surprising. Heeler pups didn't come cheap in the first place, and the hours spent training them to do something constructive added to the investment. I had no illusion that Pat Gabaldon thought of Socks as a study in economics—the nineteen-year-old cowboy and the energetic heeler were simply pals. Had it been the dog who suffered a broken leg instead of Dale Torrance, Patrick's world would have come to a stop.

"I guess I am," I said. "I don't want to leave him tied up or shut in the trailer. I doubt that Herb and Ann will be back from Cruces until late tomorrow. Maybe even later."

"Well, suit yourself," Torrez said, sounding characteristically unsympathetic. "Lemme know."

"I'll do that." During the conversation, Socks had settled down, facing me with both front paws hanging over the center console. As I switched off the phone, he pushed himself back up, looking expectant. "It would be much, much easier if you would talk," I said. My eyes had started to itch from dog dander, and I was ready to give Victor Sanchez another try.

Chapter Nine

Just before six, I pulled into the parking lot of the Broken Spur Saloon. Victor's little place was a haven for local ranchers and a watering hole for folks heading north and south—the last chance to tank up before crossing the Mexican border, and the first place for northbound folks to celebrate their arrival in the United States.

Five vehicles had collected in the lot, with a sedan sporting Michigan plates pulled up to the self-serve fuel pump island that Victor had installed the year before. The rest were local trucks, and I tucked the Trail Blazer in at the end of the line beside electrician Roy Ocate's overstuffed van, leaving Socks with a view of the open prairie on his side.

I left the engine running with the air conditioning on full blast, cracked three of the windows a couple of inches, and lowered the passenger front window far enough that Socks could stick his muzzle out comfortably, but not squirm his shoulders through. I locked the door, depending on my Swiss cheese memory to recall the entry code for the door's touch pad when the time came.

A clutter of projecting ladders, pipes, vises, and whatnot sprouted from Ocate's vehicle, and I skirted those and made my way across the graveled parking lot. Victor Sanchez eschewed air conditioning, and with good reason. Even on the hottest days, his saloon was a dark, cool cave, the thick adobe walls an effective fortress against the outside world. I entered and paused for a moment, letting my eyes adjust.

"Hey, there's the Man," Gus Prescott called. The rancher was sitting with Ocate near the end of the bar, both of them enjoying a long-neck. The trouble with being a retired cop with decades of memories was that I had learned more nasty little secrets than I really needed or wanted to know. One of the reasons Gus Prescott was a marginal, hard-scrabble rancher was that he spent way too much time curled around a bottle. His daughter Christine—the target of Dale Torrance's randy infatuation that led to rustling—was working behind the bar, and that certainly put her in an interesting position with the old man. A sociologist or psychologist would have had a field day.

"Gents." I nodded at Christine, a strawberry

blonde who looked as if she should be center on a college volleyball team…lithe, muscular in a fetching way, gorgeous clear complexion that she didn't ruin with gunk, and her thick hair swept back in a ponytail. She had tried New Mexico State University in Las Cruces, but my theory was that she worried too much about her old man and chose to work at Victor's so she could be near at hand.

She nodded an affectionate greeting at me, held up the coffee urn and raised an eyebrow. "Or ice tea?"

"You bet," I said. "The coffee's fine."

I watched her pour, and as the mug slid across the bar, she glanced at me and asked, "How's your day going, sir?"

My response was automatic and not entirely truthful. "Well, fair, I guess." I didn't want to talk about George Payton, and I didn't want to talk about the dog currently panting out in my truck, since to do that I'd have to talk about Herb's cattle roaming free and then about Dale going to Cruces for surgery—I could be stuck reciting gossip all afternoon. "Has Pat Gabaldon stopped in this afternoon? I have some paperwork that I need to give him."

"Pat? I haven't seen him. He doesn't hang out here much."

"I think he's runnin' errands for Herb," Roy

Ocate offered. "I seen him headed toward town in Herb's rig a while back when I was headed for Regál." A short, rotund man in dark green work clothes, Ocate regarded his watch. "Jeez. It's been that long…"

"What time was that?" I asked.

"Oh, goin' on three, four hours now," Ocate said in wonder. He looked down the bore of his beer bottle. "I guess I need to be headin' on up the pike." He rose from the stool. "Gonna miss dinner if I don't." I already had.

"Did you happen to notice if anyone was with him?"

Ocate paused, wallet in hand. "Didn't. Nope, I sure didn't. He mighta had, but," and he shrugged. The kitchen door opened and Victor Sanchez emerged, three platters expertly balanced. He headed for the table by the window and left two plates there with the tourists, then angled across behind the bar and slid the third platter in front of Gus Prescott.

"You want anything else?" Victor said to me. He glanced at my coffee, maybe to see if I'd taken advantage of the creamer and sugar. He carried the aroma of the kitchen with him like a personal cloud but must have been in a fair mood, since he didn't just say, 'What do you want?'

"No, thanks, Victor. This is fine. I just stopped by, still looking for Patrick."

Sanchez clacked his heavy ring against the edge of the counter. "All right, then," he said, and turned to head back toward the kitchen. I hadn't asked him a direct question, so he hadn't offered an answer. The Broken Spur was as discreet as a Swiss bank.

"Herb was going to take some cattle up on the mesa," Gus Prescott said, exploring the meal in front of him. This was one of Victor's specialties, an open-face burger and a generous mound of French fries smothered under a vast sea of chile sauce, melted cheese, lettuce, onions, and tomatoes. The dish might lack the fine touch of the food from Fernando Aragon's Don Juan, but it still provided enough flavor, calories, and aftereffects to last a long day. The rancher raked a load of fries through the cheese and sauce and forked them into his mouth, chewing thoughtfully. "I was thinkin' I might apply for a lease up there next year."

Gus wouldn't, but he'd think about it. His daughter filled a mug of coffee for him without being asked, perhaps heading off another beer, and then took the coffee out to the tourists. She had perfected not listening to bar chatter unless it was directed at her and demanded a response. Watching Gus eat wasn't going to accomplish much, and I drained my coffee.

When his daughter returned, I said, "Christine,

if you happen to see Patrick, would you ask him to give me a call?"

"You bet, sir."

"Roy says that he saw Pat in the Torrances' rig earlier. Did you happen to be looking out?"

"No, I sure wasn't," she replied quickly. She'd have to either step outside, or walk into the adjoining little dining room to accomplish that. The bar itself was a windowless cave. I patted Gus on the shoulder. "Talk to you later, Gus." With professional interest, I glanced at Gus' plate and saw that Victor's chile had a heavy scattering of seeds, par for the diced stuff that comes from a big #10 can from the food vendors—hot enough to fry the inside of the mouth, the seeds guaranteed to light up unsuspecting diverticuli.

And that stopped me short. Earlier in the day, an idea had crossed my path, and then just as promptly had been forgotten.

Leaving the saloon, I'm sure I carried the cacophony of aromas with me, because Socks launched into another dance, his piercing bark greeting me as I opened the door of the SUV. He would have enjoyed a beef burrito, hold the cheese, sauce, and garnish.

Before leaving the parking lot, I jotted a quick note to myself so I wouldn't forget again, then called Herb Torrance. The rancher sounded weary when he picked up, and even more so when I reported that I hadn't crossed paths with his employee—or his truck and trailer.

"Look," he said, "I'm headin' back this evening. Annie's staying the night here with her cousin, so that works all right. I was hopin' that I could depend on Pat to feed the horses and such, but if he ain't showed up…"

"Haven't seen him," I said. "I left notes for him both on his door and on his truck. Socks is still with me." I reached out and stroked the dog's smooth head.

"Well, look, I'll pick him up when I get to town," Herb said. "You going to be home?"

"Probably at the Guzmans'," I said. "Give me a call and I'll meet you wherever it's convenient. How about the sheriff's department parking lot?"

"That'll do it. Thanks, Bill. I appreciate it. Did Pat pay you for the permit?"

"No. I figured you're good for it."

Herb rasped something that might have been a chuckle. "'Preciate it. I'll square up with you when I get in."

"Give my best to Annie. And the boy."

"I'll do that."

I thumbed in Estelle's number and waited through six rings before her quiet voice came on the line. "Did I catch you at a bad time?" I asked.

"Not a bad time at all, *padrino,*" she said. "I heard you were chasing cattle."

"No more," I said. "We need to award your deputy the Cowpuncher's Silver Spur award, though. He did a good job for me."

"I'm glad to hear that. You're still coming for dinner, we hope."

"Indeed, if Irma hasn't given up on us. But I need to see something first. You'll be in the office for a bit longer?"

"Yes."

"I need to look at some of Linda's pictures. See, I had this brainstorm, and I want to know what you think."

"Easy enough," the undersheriff said.

"I'm inbound from the Broken Spur. See you in about twenty minutes." I switched off and saw that I was driving far too fast. I forced myself to slow down to the speed limit, straight-arming the steering wheel and taking deep breaths to help me think.

Chapter Ten

"I didn't want to leave him out in the truck," I said. Sheriff Robert Torrez had stopped by the dispatcher's island where I stood at the moment, rope leash in hand. He regarded Socks with cool detachment. The heeler managed to look miserable, his belly sinking even closer to the polished tile floor, tail low but not quite tucked between his legs, eyes darting this way and that. "Pat Gabaldon's dog," I added.

"So the kid hasn't shown up yet."

"No. Herb is coming back from Cruces later this afternoon, though. I'll dog-sit until then."

"So what's goin' on?" The sheriff glanced down the hall as Estelle Reyes-Guzman came out of her office.

"Your guess is as good as mine," I said. "Dennis found Herb's cattle wandering down 43, with Socks here keeping them tight and moving. We turned them around and drove them back to pasture."

"How far?"

"They'd covered about a mile, maybe a little more."

"An hour or so to do that?"

"I suppose."

"Huh." Torrez frowned at the dog. "Why would Pat do that?"

"That's the question," I said.

"Nobody saw him?"

"Not that I've found. I stopped by the Broken Spur on a long shot." I shook my head. "Nobody saw him. Well, I take that back. Roy Ocate claims that just as he was pulling into the saloon parking lot, he saw Herb's rig northbound on 56. He didn't take any particular notice of it, beyond just seeing it. He claims Pat was driving."

Socks looked expectantly at Estelle, who knelt and stroked his pointy little head. She ran a hand under his collar to smooth his neck ruffles, and then rubbed the underside of his jaw. He responded by shuffling closer, hoping the attention would continue.

"That's like leaving a member of the family behind," she said.

"Well, we know that happens on occasion, too," I said. "Mom and Dad forget that little Johnny is in the truck-stop restroom, and drive off and leave him. At least they *claim* they forget.

They don't often admit that their kid is a little rodent who deserves to be left behind, inflicted on somebody else."

Estelle straightened up. "He looks good on you, sir. You should get yourself a dog."

"Please. Besides, he makes my eyes itch." I extended the lead rope toward her. "You want him?"

"Thanks for the offer, sir. Francisco and Carlos would be ecstatic."

"That's exactly what I was thinking."

"We can hope that Herb or Pat picks him up before dinner." She smiled at me. "You wanted to see some photos?"

"Yep. I had a thought that damn near put me into the bar-ditch."

"Oh? What do you want to see?"

"You said most of Linda's photos from George's kitchen are on the computer? Let's start there."

"Everybody's keepin' their eyes open," Torrez said as he turned away toward his office. "For Patrick, I mean. State's watchin' the interstate." He turned to look toward the two of us. "I'm going out here in a little bit. I was going to check down toward María." He shrugged. "You never know."

Socks watched him until he disappeared into the office as if there might be an opportunity of some sort there. But now that the heeler was on strange turf—turf that obviously wasn't his—he behaved as if he'd had a lobotomy, staying close to my feet and not the least bit interested in extending the length of his leash. As we entered Estelle's comfortable office, the undersheriff gestured toward her chair. "Take the computer, *padrino.*" I settled in the chair, and the heeler dived under the desk. Estelle reached past my shoulder, keying the computer to do its thing. In a moment, the thumbnail index including photos of George Payton's kitchen appeared.

"I want the close-ups of the table," I said, and she scrolled across the index. The first shot showed the table as a whole, and I reached out to tap the screen. "Just that." I didn't need to ask if Linda Real had taken any particular photos—the young lady didn't miss a thing. Sure enough, a crystal clear portrait of the casserole dish popped up. The lid was in place, and the photo didn't show me what I wanted to know. "How about the plate itself?"

That portrait appeared, and then expanded to fill the screen from border to border. The instant I saw it, I knew I was right, and I thumped the desk top with my fist. That didn't make me feel any better. Reaching out for a pencil, I leaned one elbow on the edge of the desk and touched the screen with the eraser. And again, and again.

"Yes, sir," Estelle said without surprise, and I

turned to crank my neck around so I could look up at her. She rested one hand on my shoulder as she reached past me to select another photo. This one was the serving dish as a whole, with the glass cover removed.

I nodded and touched the image half a dozen times with the pencil eraser. "Damn it, are we chasing our imaginations here?" I asked. "This sure as hell is chopped green chile—and I'll bet right out of a can. I saw the same thing on Gus Prescott's plate down at the Broken Spur, and that got me to thinking. At the Don Juan, Fernando slices his into thin strips. I'm sure of it. Lord knows I've eaten enough of the stuff." I tapped the screen again. "We need answers for this."

"I wanted to wait for you before talking to Mr. Aragon," Estelle said.

That surprised me, since the undersheriff certainly didn't need to wait for anyone, least of all me. It didn't surprise me that she'd obviously shared my suspicions…she was always miles ahead of me. "What did you request from the lab?"

"A full profile, sir. I pulled in a favor or two, and they're asking for some help from the university labs as well. We're looking at a weekend coming up, and that'll put a damper on anything they might find."

"So late today, maybe. More likely tomorrow,"

I said. "They move fast, but usually not *that* fast."

"Well, like I said, I asked a favor or two."

I sat back in the chair, staring at the photo of the partial burrito. "We may be nuts," I said.

"Maybe."

"I thought about it this morning—the old bolt from the blue thing. Then I got distracted. Here a few minutes ago, I was down at the Broken Spur, standing at the bar beside Gus Prescott. He was eating one of Victor's creations, and that's what set me off. The whole thing was spread with diced green chile."

"That raises some interesting questions, *padrino.*"

"Indeed. You can print this for me?"

"Of course."

"Did you talk with Bobby about this?"

"I did, as a matter of fact. He's pulling in some favors of his own. He sent Tony Abeyta to Albuquerque to deliver the evidence."

"Does *he* think we're nuts?" Most folks pondered about things, often out loud, often bouncing ideas off other folks. Bobby Torrez took taciturn to new heights, and I reflected with amusement that when we combined the sheriff and the inscrutable undersheriff, we'd be a good repository for the most sensitive super-spy information.

"That's impossible to say, sir." That reply

didn't surprise me. Estelle handed me the photo as it came out of the color printer, and I glanced at the clock.

"You have time to go right now?"

"Sure," she said. "What about White Fang, here?" Socks looked up at her as if he'd recognized his real name.

"He'll just have to rough it and stay in the truck," I said. "You want to ride with me?"

"Ah," and Estelle looked around the room as if she'd forgotten something. "Let me follow you down. That way if there's a call, I'll have my office with me."

I laughed. "Gee, you mean the full power and authority of the Livestock Board isn't enough?"

"I'm sure it would be," she said diplomatically. Twelve blocks later, we parked nose to tail on Twelfth Street, in the shade of the Don Juan de Oñate. Turning on his best hang-dog expression of resignation, Socks didn't bother this time with the dervish dance of impatience. He accepted two sloppy tongue-fulls of water, then settled on his seat with a great sigh. "You hungry?" I asked, then amended that. "Stupid question. You're a dog. I'll see what I can find."

Swinging into the dinner hour, it wsn't the best time to descend on the Don Juan for anything other than food. The place was surprisingly quiet, though, and JanaLynn Torrez greeted us with a sunny smile.

"We need to talk with Fernando, sweetheart," I said.

"You go right on back," she said. "Maybe you'll cheer him up some." She lowered her voice. "He's in a *rotten* mood after hearing about Mr. Payton, sir."

"It's probably going to get rottener," I said. Ever diplomatic, JanaLynn didn't ask me what I meant, and Estelle and I headed for the swinging doors of the kitchen.

Chapter Eleven

When Estelle and I pushed our way through the swinging door to the kitchen of the Don Juan de Oñate restaurant, the chef was standing with his arms folded across his chest, leaning a hip against one of the butcher block prep tables. Fernando Aragon looked every one of his sixty-five years. He appeared to be contemplating the floor tiles. His fleshy nose was bright red and dark circles made his dark eyes appear both huge and deep.

On a cutting board on the table, a modest-sized pork roast awaited processing. I knew where the thin-sliced meat was headed, and the thought made my stomach growl in anticipation. Fernando's daughter Aileen stood at one of the large stainless steel prep sinks, washing and sorting a mound of vegetables. She saw us first, and raised her head in greeting. "Dad," she called, and Fernando eased out of his fog, turned, and saw us.

"Look at this!" he exclaimed, and drew out the

word *this* as if it had about five i's and at least that
many s's. His speech had the music of Chihuahua,
the state of his birth—a nice, rich accent that the
years hadn't diluted a bit. He wiped his hands on
his apron and then locked mine in a double-handed
grip. "Bill, *mija* said you were here earlier. I'm sorry
I missed you. I don't know where my mind is today.
I'm thinking a lot about George, I guess. You know
how that goes."

"'Fraid so," I said.

"It was his heart?"

"Most likely."

He frowned and looked askance at me, then
at Estelle. His gaze dropped to the manila envelope that she was carrying, and he waited for us
to drop whatever bombshell we'd brought into his
kitchen.

"We have a question or two, Fernando," I
said.

His eyebrows arched in surprise. "About the
food, you mean? Was something wrong…"

I held up a hand. "Everything is preliminary…
just a goddamn mess, is what it is. Look, we're starting to think that George had an allergic reaction
to something."

"An *allergic* reaction? How…"

"It looks as if he passed away just after he sat
down at the kitchen table to eat his lunch. A couple

of bites, and something came apart." I rested a hand on my own chest at that thought. "So it's natural that we would have some questions." I glanced at Estelle, wondering if she'd noticed how effortlessly I managed to slip back into the *we* business. But as usual, her lovely face gave no hints about what might be going on in that inscrutable mind.

"An *allergic* reaction?" Fernando repeated. The notion obviously didn't compute. "Tell me what that means, Bill."

I knew that he understood the word just fine—it was the context that puzzled. "Just that," I said. "You know how some folks are super-allergic to something that doesn't bother another person one bit, like a bee sting. Or pollen. Or juniper. It gets one person, and not another."

"So George..."

"There's some reason to believe that he reacted strongly to *something*, Fernando. To something. We don't know what. I don't know if a wasp flew in the kitchen and stung him, or what. It may turn out to be as simple as that."

"A *bee* sting?" he said in disbelief, and he looked to Estelle for corroboration. "¿Y usted, señora?" he asked. Estelle had remained watchful but silent, simply a presence that I knew could make a person nervous.

"What I'd like to find out from you, Fernando,"

she said, "is a list of ingredients. George had a take-out…"

"The *burrito grande,*" Fernando finished for her. "Almost every week, that's what he has." He laid a hand on his own chest. "By *arreglo especial.*" He grinned and pointed a stubby index finger at me. "And sometime he shares the festivities with a special friend, am I right?"

"Absolutely," I agreed. "Today was one of those days. Didn't work out."

Estelle rested a small note pad on the stainless table, pen poised. "Let's start with that," she said. "Just the ingredients."

"You want…" Fernando began, then shook his head, his patience under the test. "You know, such a dish is a combination of so many things. And George, he's been eating with us for *years, agente.* Why should something suddenly," and he waved a hand in the air helplessly. "All of a sudden, as you say?"

"I'm looking for changes," Estelle said. "So it will be helpful to know the ingredients. Especially if you have made a change recently."

"There has been no change," Fernando said vehemently. "That is part of the secret. But," and he took a deep breath of resignation. "If you want a list, you want a list, *¿verdad?*"

"*Cada uno y todo,*" Estelle said.

"*Híjole,* where do I begin with a thing like this," he muttered, and he glanced over at the large wall clock by the door. "*Mija,* can you?" and he gestured at the waiting roast.

"Just take one part at a time," Estelle said. "Begin with this, perhaps?" She pointed at the pork.

"That's good," Fernando agreed. "I oven-roast the pork, you know. The old fashioned way. Let me show you." He strode to the large walk-in freezer and reappeared in a moment with another three or four pound package bundled in white butcher's paper. "Little ones like this," he said. "You know, most people don't know what's involved."

"Me, for one," I said. "You never know how many customers you're going to have, do you? Or what they're going to order."

"That's *exactly* right," Fernando said. "One can never know." He held up his left index finger. "There is an *idea,* but it cannot be exact. With small roasts, there is not so much waste. And the quality is better. That is always, what do I want to say, at the *heart* of what we do. Each ingredient must be quality, or the final result is not. Simple, *¿no?*"

"May I have the label?" Estelle asked.

"Of course." He peeled off the sticker and handed it to her. "This is not the same roast, you know."

She stuck it neatly on the page of her notebook. "From the same vendor?"

"Yes, of course. But if you ask me what the pigs eat, I can't tell you," Fernando said. He crossed quickly to the stove, opened the oven, and removed a flat pan covered with aluminum foil cover, revealing a small quantity of sliced pork. "This is the remains from the roast used for George," he said. "You want a sample?"

Estelle nodded and extended a small plastic bag to him, and he selected a forkful or two. An evidence bag wasn't what the chef had in mind when he offered the sample, but he didn't question her. "Is this enough?" She nodded again. "This comes from Aguirre's Meats, of course," he added. "In Deming. They are the best. They can tell you just what the pigs ate, if you are curious." He pushed the pan back in the oven. "There's no telling what is in meats these days. I won't pay for the organic label—I don't trust them, either." His eyes twinkled. "What's an organic pig, can you tell me that?" He put the frozen package back in the freezer. "I roast the meat, keeping it just a touch *raro, ¿verdad?* It's going to be cooked again, you know."

Aileen had left the sink, and was engaged with the finished roast, a large catch pan positioned at the outfeed side of a spotless stainless steel slicer.

The gadget's motor was an innocent, soft buzz, but that spinning blade captured my respect. I had visions of thin slices of fingers spraying out the back.

"We slice *very* thin, Bill." Fernando stood at Aileen's elbow and watched the preparations. "Very, very thin," he said again as Aileen fed the first pass. "That's one of the secrets. Like paper, eh?" He jerked his chin at me. "*You* know, don't you. It's best that way." He held out his hand and caught a slice. As he folded it, he inspected it judiciously, then tore it in half, handing half to me and popping the rest into his mouth. How could I refuse?

"Seasoning on the meat?" Estelle prompted.

Fernando ticked them off on his fingers as his daughter continued to work. "Salt, pepper, maybe a touch of garlic. A little bit of sage. A *tiny* trace of chipotle, for the smoky quality. With good meat, you know, not so much is necessary." He made a volcanic gesture with his fingers. "You want the pork to come through," he said, and his hands settled. "You need some of each?"

"Probably not," I said, and realized I might be stepping on my own tongue. I didn't know *what* Estelle wanted. I did know that it hadn't been long since I'd finished eating my afternoon snack, but already my stomach rumbled in anticipation of further samples.

Fernando was patient and pre-dinner traffic slow, and Aileen adept at covering the orders that trickled in. He took us through the construction of a *Burrito Grande* step by step.

"And you know," he said at one point in the tour, "some people think that the *chile* is the heart of Mexican cooking, but it is *not*. It is *not*. You cannot save bad food with good chile. *That's* what most people forget. Use chile that is hot enough, and you might conceal some mistakes. But that's all." He held up an admonishing finger again. "The roast, whether it is pork, or chicken, or beef, must be the best. Some will prepare the dish with these enormous chunks of meat, you know, full of gristle and fat," and he grimaced. "Like something dipped out of an old stew. And to make matters worse, they soak everything in some kind of soup until the meat is unrecognizable." He shivered in mock horror. "That is not the way. The meat must be the best. Even if it's but lowly ground beef, it should be the *best.*"

"Makes sense," I said, marveling at how wonderfully detached and disciplined Estelle Reyes-Guzman could remain through this gustatory seminar right at dinner time, jotting her clinical notes without drooling.

"Now, the tortillas need to be as only my wonderful wife can make them—not like some of those things that stick to the roof of your mouth, they are so thick and gummy."

He walked over to another cooler and opened the door to reveal shelves full of small, neatly wrapped packages. He slipped one out and opened it for inspection. The flour tortillas were generous in size, remarkably uniform in thickness and texture. Again he ticked off the ingredients for Estelle. He shrugged expressively. "Nothing has changed in the recipe for two hundred years."

He watched Estelle jot notes and then slid the package back in the cooler, selecting a smaller one in its place. "If you use cheap, bulk cheese," he said, "that's what your dish tastes like." He peeled off a label, handing it to Estelle. "This is made by the Costillo dairy in Mesilla. It is a sharp cheddar that has some *life*. I have been buying my cheese from them for twenty years. Never a change. Never."

He tossed the block of cheese into the cooler, then maneuvering around Aileen, advanced on the sink where she had been working. "If you use tired, frost-burned lettuce, or tomatoes that are hard and tasteless, then, well, you know…then the chile can't save them. But," and he shrugged, holding his shoulders up for a long moment. "If everything is good, and the chile is fresh and the best…*then* you have something worth eating, ¿*verdad?*"

"*Verdad,*" I said, risking just about the full extent of my knowledge of Spanish.

Estelle rested against the sink, eyebrows locked together, examining her notes. "When you prepped either yesterday or this morning, did you do any-thing differently, Fernando?"

"No, nothing. Maybe this morning a *little* more care than usual in the presentation for him. I know…*we* know…that George is, how do you say it, *delicado?*"

"Frail," Estelle added.

"That's it. He has not been so good, you know. That's why the meal comes to him, not him to the meal."

"Was there any ingredient that came from a fresh batch of something?" I asked. "Something that was just delivered, maybe?"

"It is *always* fresh," Fernando said, trying not to sound hurt.

"But you know what I mean," I said. "In the ebb and flow of all this, there must *sometimes* be a little glitch, or a new batch of *something* that is maybe just a little different. Not of lesser quality, but just *different* in some way."

Fernando's face scrunched up in thought. "I can not imagine what that would be," he said. "You know, there are some…*places,*" and he said it as if he were deliberately sidestepping naming names, "who accept what vendors try to deliver." He held up a hand that halted the process. "They just take what the truck delivers, without question. I will not do that. I accept what I *want* to accept, and the vendors all know that."

"What about the chile itself?" Estelle asked.

Fernando frowned and returned to one of the coolers. He selected a plastic bag, perhaps two or three pounds, of green chile. I could see the pods were nicely cleaned, split in half or thirds lengthwise, with very few seeds. "This is today," he said. "And yesterday, it was another small bag, but from the same batch."

I leaned against the table, regarding the bag of chile. "How do you prep this?"

Now totally resigned to our probing, Fernando sighed with good-humored patience. "Now you are asking for secrets," he chuckled. He selected a long knife from the block, wiped the blade on a clean towel, and nudged a couple of chile pods out of the bag. "It must be this way." With amazingly rapid, expert chatterings of the knife, he reduced the chile into elegant little strips, like miniature French cut string beans. I looked at Estelle thoughtfully as she held a plastic bag to accept a sample.

"Do some folks like it cubed?" she asked. "Or maybe *diced* is the word?"

"The way Victor fixes it," I added, and

Fernando grunted something I didn't catch. He didn't bother feigning politeness by asking, 'Victor who?'

"'Fixes it' directly from a can," he said. No love lost there, but then again, Victor Sanchez brought it on himself with his continual imitation of an annoyed rattlesnake. "That is not the way I will do it."

"You've never run out of chile and had to resort to the can?" I knew I was on thin ice with that one. He didn't grab a cleaver, though.

"You only run out if you don't plan ahead," Fernando said flatly.

I nodded at the shelves clearly visible in the roomy pantry beyond the coolers. The fat #10 cans marched in rows on the upper shelves, and the distinctive labels of the canned chile were easy to spot.

"Ah," Fernando said, and ducked his head just a touch, embarrassed at being caught out. "I use the canned chile when I make...what do you call it...the stock for the sauce." He straightened his shoulders. "There are some who use soup, you know."

"Awful," I added.

"Yes. I pureé the canned chile as a stock, then add more of this," and he touched the plastic bag of sliced pods. "Just this." His eyes narrowed as he regarded first me and then Estelle, both hands resting flat on the butcher block, knife at the ready. "You're not telling me everything," he said. He jerked his chin at the envelope in Estelle's hand. "What do you have there? You brought me something."

For whatever reason, Estelle wasn't yet ready to share the photos with Fernando, and I didn't run interference for him. The diced chile so obvious in the photograph indicated Fernando leaned on the canned goods a little more than he cared to admit. We didn't want him slamming up his defenses.

"Did you know that Mr. Payton usually drank a glass of red wine with his meal?" she side-stepped.

"Now there," Fernando said, wagging a finger, "is something to investigate," and he leaned on each of the four syllables for emphasis. "If George could find a bottle of wine for three dollars, why pay four? You see?" He frowned again. "There's a word for that poison that he favors."

"Rot gut?" I offered.

"Exactly. It makes my mouth hurt just to think about it. Maybe the problem lies there."

"That's a possibility," Estelle said. "Tell me again what time you prepared his meal?"

Fernando crossed his arms across his apron. "Aileen, what time did George call yesterday?"

"Sometime after ten, maybe," she said, not breaking rhythm with the meat slicer. The roast had been reduced to the size of a baseball.

"So...sometime between eleven-thirty and twelve? That's when it was delivered?" Estelle asked.

He nodded. "You have picked up the food from time to time, have you not?" he said to me. "This time, he asked if we would deliver. Sometimes, his daughter does the honors, but she was busy this day."

"Who drove the food over?"

Fernando turned to look at Aileen. "It was Ricardo, no?" Aileen nodded. "Ricardo Mondragon," Fernando said, and waved a hand toward the swinging door to the dining room.

Ricardo was forty-five years old going on ten, but steady and dependable. He took great pride, it always seemed to me, in keeping the Don Juan polished and spiffy, despite a strip or two of duct tape on the booth cushions. The dishes in the waitress islands were always stacked just so. At the moment, I could see his stooped, pudgy figure out in the dining room, putting a final polish on table tops.

"We packed it *most* carefully," Fernando said. He pointed overhead to a broad shelf above the sink. A row of cheap Styrofoam coolers rested there, the kind stout enough for a single picnic or fishing trip, the mates of the one that we'd seen resting on

George Payton's kitchen counter. Estelle nodded absently, as if her thoughts were elsewhere. "First in the glass dish with the cover, then in a paper bag, then in the cooler. Do you need to talk with Ricardo?"

"We may need to, but not right now," Estelle said. We took another five minutes, poking into this and that, but the undersheriff had closed her notebook. I knew that any moment, Fernando would offer us something to take the edge off, and sure enough, he slid a oval plate off the rack and held it toward me.

"Let me…" he started to say, but I held up a hand abruptly, an amazing show of self-restraint.

"Fernando, thanks, but we need to be on our way," I said. "We've taken enough of your time."

"You come back," he said, and then extended his hand to Estelle. "I hope you find out," he added. "You know I will help any way I can."

On the way out through the dining room, I saw that JanaLynn was discussing something with Ricardo Mondragon, who nodded soberly. He reached out and straightened the stack of roll baskets. Estelle came up behind the older man and placed a light hand on his shoulder. He startled as if she'd used a cattle prod.

"Ricardo, may I talk with you for a few minutes?" the undersheriff asked. I think that JanaLynn could guess the subject matter, since the expression on her face was sympathetic. "Maybe we can go outside for a few minutes."

Mondragon's big, wide face turned toward the kitchen, as if he needed permission from Fernando for such a venture. JanaLynn came to the rescue. "I'll take care of this," she said, one hand on the counter. She didn't explain what the 'this' was, but Ricardo appeared satisfied. He followed Estelle toward the door.

"Thanks, sweetheart," I said. JanaLynn reached out and gave me a brief hug, one arm around my shoulders.

Chapter Twelve

Outside, I saw that Estelle and Ricardo Mondragon had skirted the corner of the building and were standing behind the bulk of my SUV. I joined them, and Ricardo was too worried by this strange change of pace in his day to manage a greeting. He eyed Socks, who was slobbering all over the door and window, trying to force his tough little body through the narrow opening. I'd broken my promise to the heeler, bringing nothing from the kitchen but aromas.

"Ricardo," Estelle said, "Fernando tells me that earlier today, you took a meal over to Mr. Payton's house on Ridgemont." He nodded and thrust his hands in his pockets. A burly guy with unruly curly hair that lined his forehead in neat ringlets, Ricardo would have looked right at home in one of those commercials for an Italian restaurant where the chef punches, pats, and flings the pizza dough with an expression of contented pride—except

Ricardo Mondragon's face was empty of anything except apprehension.

"Was Mr. Payton all by himself when you saw him?" Estelle asked.

"He was all by himself," Ricardo replied. His speech was without accent, but cadenced with a great deal of care, as if the words were slippery and elusive. "Is that your dog?"

"Sort of," I said, and let it go at that.

"You spoke with Mr. Payton?" Estelle prompted.

"Him and me talked a little. I took the cooler out to the kitchen for him." He pulled out a large handkerchief and massaged his broad nose. "They said that he died."

"Yes, he did. Sometime after you left, Ricardo."

"He was a good guy. Everybody gets old and sick." Ricardo Mondragon still lived with aging parents, and although he might not ponder his future when they passed on, everyone else who knew him probably did.

"Yes, he was a good guy. Did he take the casserole out of the cooler, or did you?"

"I guess he did, 'cause I didn't. I put the cooler on the counter."

"When you left, he was all by himself?"

"Yes, ma'am. He said he didn't need no help."

"Did you open the wine bottle for him?" That question out of left field startled me but didn't jolt Ricardo's passive expression. He gazed at Estelle, then at my truck, then at the sidewalk.

"I saw that."

"You saw the wine bottle?"

"I saw that, yeah. It was on the table. He had a big glass of wine all poured. He had some, 'cause I could smell it." Ricardo frowned and shook his head. "I asked him if I could throw it away for him."

"Throw the wine away?"

"The empty bottle," Ricardo corrected. An empty container on the dinner table would prompt that response from the fastidious busboy, I supposed.

"Did you offer to open the new bottle then?"

"I didn't see no new bottle."

"Ah." Estelle opened her small notebook and rustled through several pages. "Do you happen to know what time it was when you left Mr. Payton's house, Ricardo?"

"It was eleven fifty-two." The precision of the response amused me, but not a trace of humor touched Ricardo's face.

"Did Mr. Payton say anything about bringing

the dish back to the restaurant when he was finished?"

"He always does that. Somebody does."

"And you didn't see anyone else at Mr. Payton's house? No one called, no one came by? You didn't see anyone coming down the street as you drove away?"

He shook his head slowly. "How come you gots to know all this stuff?"

"That's just what we do, Ricardo. We appreciate you taking the time to talk to us."

"You got to know anything else?"

"I may have to talk with you again, if that's okay." Estelle made it sound as if Ricardo Mondragon actually had a choice.

"That's okay." He looked for a long moment at his watch, and I could see his lips moving. "You should come in for dinner."

"We'd like to, but it's going to have to be some other time," the undersheriff said. "Thanks for talking to us, Ricardo."

"Dr. Gray and his wife are coming for dinner," he said, and nodded off toward the parking lot. I hadn't seen the county commissioner's gray Lincoln slide into the lot, but Ricardo Mondragon had. "I'd better go."

"Thanks again," Estelle said. We watched him hustle off, and Estelle sighed. "Would that all witnesses were like that," she said, and reached out to touch my arm. "Let me show you." I ambled over to her car, and that prompted a flurry of pathetic yips from my captive. By the time I'd grunted into the passenger seat of the undersheriff's Crown Vic, she'd selected several eight-by-ten digital photos from the envelope that she had never offered to Fernando Aragon.

Linda Real must have scrunched into the corner by the fridge to take the portrait of George's kitchen caught in the first photo. I examined it for a long moment, then accepted the second one she offered, this time a close-up of the glass casserole dish. It was the same photo I'd looked at on the computer screen.

"I don't like this," I muttered.

Linda's photos were in flawless focus, once I'd figured out which portion of my trifocals to use. In the photo of the casserole, the garnish of tomatoes and lettuce couldn't hide the little pieces of diced green chile. After a long moment of scrutiny, I looked up at Estelle. "Diced, not sliced," I said. "Fernando said he uses the canned chile for sauce base. He got a little carried away this time. Or Aileen."

I looked in the rearview mirror and watched my little spotted prisoner in the SUV behind us. His tongue dangled so far out of his mouth that

I thought it might have become unhooked at the back. "So," I said, and Estelle tapped the photos on the steering wheel.

"I need to go to Albuquerque," she said quietly.

"And what can you do up there that Tony Abeyta can't?" I said. "One question's been answered," and I nodded toward the office. "We know who delivered lunch. If there was a question about the chile, I think we have our answer. Pride is a powerful motivator here. Chefs, you know." I turned to rest my hip. "He says he never uses canned chile, but obviously he does. Are we hung up on that because there's nothing else?" I asked. My cell phone buzzed and I fished it out of my pocket. "Hold on a minute," I said into it without bothering to find out who it might be, then pressed it against my thigh to give us some privacy as I waited for Estelle's reply.

"Do *you* think it was a heart attack?"

"I do, but then again, I'm no doctor, sweetheart. Now, maybe it wasn't your usual garden variety coronary that warns a guy to change his lifestyle. It obviously was one of those massive infarcts that drops a person in his tracks. If you remember my performance a few years ago, you'll recall that I managed what, a step and a half before I fell on my face? Now, I admit there are a few things here that need to be explained. You start talking about allergies and reactions, and it's a whole new game."

"And that's what's bothering me," Estelle sighed. "I'm not saying that I think something is wrong, *padrino*. I'm just saying that something happened that I don't understand. If Alan Perrone says that George suffered an allergic reaction to something fierce enough to trigger a heart attack, then I want to know what the cause of that reaction was. That's all."

"Fair enough. If it was in the food, the lab will be able to tell us," I said. "Or a spider bite, or anything like that."

"Your phone, sir," Estelle said, and I realized that I'd forgotten all about it.

"Gastner," I said into the little black gadget, surprised I wasn't talking to empty ether.

"Bill, I'm comin' up to the exit, and wondered where you're at," Herb Torrance said. "You got a minute?"

"Sure do. I have a critter in custody here for you. How about the motel right there at the exit ramp?"

"If that works for you," Herb said. "I'm comin' up on it right now."

"Then give me five minutes."

"Don't forget dinner," Estelle said when I snapped the phone closed. "We'll see what we know."

"I'm not likely to forget. Starve, maybe."

She nodded. "I'll tell Tony exactly what I'm looking for." Her dark face broke into a wide smile and she nodded toward the center mirror. "Look at this."

I turned and saw that Socks was now standing with front paws on the dash board, face against the glass, tongue dripping rivers. His eyes and ears were locked on us as if he'd been eavesdropping on the phone call.

"Okay, then," I said, and laughed. "I need to get him back to Herb before he leaves his marker all over my cab." I turned back to Estelle. "And if *you* happen to catch sight of young Mister Gabaldon in the next few minutes, give me a call."

I struggled out of the car and turned, one hand on the roof and one on the door. "There's a simple answer to all of this," I said. "That's the way these things work."

"*Nos vemos,*" Estelle said.

As I drove south through town, Socks could sense change in the air. He couldn't sit still, and as I pulled into the parking lot of the American Owned, American Operated Posadas Inn near the Interstate exchange, he started to huff little whimpers. The Torrances' blue Chrysler was parked in the center of an empty parking lot. Socks recognized it, I suppose, since every nerve and muscle in his compact little body started to twang. Herb stepped out of the car and I thought the dog was going through the window. I made sure the short rope was secure before I opened my door, and Socks used me as a springboard, scrambling down and heading for Herb. The rancher said something and the dog dropped as if he'd been shot, adoring eyes locked on the Herb's face.

"He and I were headed out to dinner." I handed the rancher the end of the lead rope. "I promised him something to eat."

"Don't need that," Herb said. He popped off the rope, gestured with one hand and the dog shot through the Chrysler's open door. "I owe you something for the permit," he said, and I consulted my paperwork, finding the receipt I'd already made out in his name.

"Fair and square," I said, taking the money he offered and tucking it in the small bank bag. "Dale's coming home tomorrow?"

"Suppose so, maybe," Herb sighed. "Hell of a deal. Just about the last thing we need right now. Last thing *he* needs. If that kid didn't have bad luck, he wouldn't have no luck at all, seems like." He surveyed the empty parking lot. "I'd best get home and see what Pat's got to say for himself."

"Let me know," I said.

"Damnedest thing, " the rancher said.

"Thanks for takin' care of the damn dog," He slid down into the sedan's low seat, pushing the heeler away from his lap.

"You bet." I didn't tack on the customary "any time."

Chapter Thirteen

The two beasts were busy at the kitchen table when I arrived at the Guzmans' modest home on Twelfth Street. So engaged that they didn't hear me drive up, their preoccupation gave me a tactical edge. The oldest boy, Francisco, just five and already having his own struggles with kindergarten, appeared to be coloring a large map of the United States.

Even at his tender age, he'd had some experience with geography after living in various parts of New Mexico and Minnesota, but why a kindergarten student needed geography studies beyond his own sandbox was a mystery to me. His younger brother Carlos, mercifully spared the harness of school, was coloring an identical map, and the states would probably go to war over the new boundaries his clenched hand was inflicting.

Both boys abandoned their art when they saw me peering through the front screen door. It wasn't that I was interested in *them*, mind you. The aroma of something in the oven had curled outside to my tender nose.

"*Padrino!*" they shouted in unison, diving away from the kitchen table amid a welter of scattered Crayons. They charged the door, and I opened it quickly to save the screen, dropping to one knee and using my generous belly to bumper them back inside.

Dr. Francis Guzman came to my rescue. Knowing just where and what to grab, he spun both little boys under his arms like two bags of sand. "Back in your cages," he commanded amid the cackles, screeches, and whatever it is that little kids babble faster than old ears can hear. I heaved myself back to my feet.

"Has your day improved any?" I saw Francis' gaze flick over my features in a quick physical. He had stuck plenty of needles in me over the years, and tried to convince me to control this and that ailment with a vast pharmacopoeia that I generally ignored. He argued gently but in vain about my life-style. I knew his question was more than just polite gab.

"Well, I'm working on it," I replied. "But whatever I'm smelling is bound to improve matters." I saw Estelle's mother, comfortable in her rocker over by the fireplace, swathed in an Afghan and supporting a heavy book with her fancy reading pillow. I headed her way from the foyer. Dr. Guzman let the boys slide to the floor head-first, and when little Francisco appeared to be winding up again, he clamped the top of the boy's head with one hand, like a basketball player palming the ball.

"*Mira, mijo,*" he said, and the switch to Spanish, the language of discipline, caught the boy's attention. "You guys need to clean up the mess now."

"Such a mess," Teresa Reyes said severely. "Those two." But she couldn't hide her pride and affection for the two dervishes. She presented a cheek for a kiss. With one hand locked on the back of her chair and another braced on one arm, I managed a courtly greeting. "It's always so nice when you come over," she said. "*¡Ahora!*" she snapped, wagging a finger. Little Francisco had started into the living room toward me again, but he stopped, spun around with a giggle, and disappeared into the kitchen.

Dr. Guzman sauntered back to the living room, watching the boys over his shoulder. "Estelle's freshening up," he said. "There's some coffee left over from last week that's still hot. You want some?"

"Actually, that would be perfect," I said. "Join me?" I said to Teresa, but she waved a dismissive hand.

"I don't drink that stuff," she said. "You go ahead."

As I followed Estelle's husband back to the kitchen, little Francisco held up his map for my inspection. "Do you know these?" he chirped.

"I can name all fifty-two and their capitals," I replied.

"Guam and Puerto Rico aren't states yet," the youngster said without skipping a beat and with the tone of heavy authority that he used with dense adults. Fortunately I didn't have a mouthful of coffee when he came up with that one. I glanced at the boy's father, since in my world, five-year-olds just don't know that sort of trivia, no matter how precocious they might be.

"Actually, we were talking about that very thing earlier," Dr. Francis said. "And *that* was part of a wide-ranging discussion about building vast suspension bridges." He held up both hands in surrender. "You would have to be there to make sense of it."

"If at all," I said. Francis filled a mug for me, then held it up so I would notice the design. Deep blue lettering announced the *Posadas Medical Center,* and the architect's rendering of the new clinic spread across the enamel.

"Take that with you," he said. "About a gross of them arrived today."

"I'm impressed," I said. I'd seen the blueprints

and artist's sketches for the clinic, of course, and walked the four acres of property a dozen times with Francis and Alan Perrone before and after I'd donated the land behind my adobe on Guadalupe Terrace. On occasions now, the back-up beeping of construction machinery awakened me as the land was prepared for the impressive building and the surrounding, landscaped parking lot.

The coffee tasted way too fresh, like something offered at a deli for three bucks a cup. I settled with a sigh in a chair by the kitchen table as Francis shooed away the boys and their fistfuls of paper-work and pencils.

"I had an interesting talk with Alan," he said. "Not now," he added, directed at his eldest son, who was homing in on me again. His tone of voice was just right—the little boy stopped as if he'd run into a glass wall.

I rested my arms on the table, cradling the cup with both hands. "And what's he say?"

"George's preliminary autopsy showed an aortic rupture just north of the heart," the physician said. "I didn't know if he had told you or not, but George had the makings of an aneurysm."

"He wouldn't mention that," I said. "I can hear him now," and I lowered my voice, trying to imitate my friend's raspy growl. "When it goes, it goes."

Dr. Francis shrugged. "You're spot on," he said. "George refused surgery for it, of course. Alan's opinion was that it wasn't an acute defect, at least not yet. One of those things that you gamble with, especially with a geriatric patient who doesn't want the surgery anyway. Take a watchful wait-and-see approach."

"We get stubborn in our old age," I said, and heard soft footsteps behind me. Two hands settled lightly on my shoulders as Estelle joined us. I patted the back of her left hand with my own by way of greeting, but her husband still had my attention.

"I think...and Alan does too...that the chain of events began with the acute allergic reaction... whatever that was, that's the key," he said. "With the spike in blood pressure triggered by that, the weak link gave out. We're following that theory at the moment because we're seeing other tell-tale markers of a sudden spike."

I craned my head around and nodded at Estelle. "That fits the scenario, doesn't it," I said. "He has the attack, whatever it was, right there at the table, and starts to get up, maybe headed for a glass of water or something to put out the fire. He makes it over to the counter when the aorta lets go, and *that* drops him in his tracks."

"It fits at the moment," she agreed.

"Except he didn't grab a glass for water," I

amended. "He grabbed the delivery bag from the restaurant. I'd sure enough like to replay the tape and see why he did that."

"I spent a long time on the phone with Tony Abeyta, sir. He's passed along everything we have to the state lab, and he's camping out with them. I had hoped that they'd bring in some of the university facilities, and it looks like they're going to do that. Tony is staying upstate until he has something concrete for us. They all understand the urgency."

"It could still be days," I said.

"Well, hopefully not. As I said, I pulled in some favors, and so did Bobby. They're thinking allergies now, and if we're all on the same track, they might be able to pull up something. The whole affair intrigued one of the med techs there. He's willing to work the hours."

"It's bound to be something simple," I said. "Some little thing that we're just not seeing."

Estelle patted my shoulder again when she saw me glance, probably a bit wistfully, toward the stove. "Irma made lasagna," she said. "You haven't just eaten, I hope."

"No, but what difference would that make, sweetheart?" I chided. "And I'm sorry I missed Irma." The Guzman's *nana* spoiled the family in all the best ways, but my waistline appeared to be the only one that suffered.

"She's helping her fiancé celebrate his birthday," Francis said. "If she takes another hour off this year, we're going to have to seriously rethink the arrangement."

I laughed. "Wait until she ties the knot," I said. "Then you'll really be cast adrift." Irma's long-suffering boyfriend, a math teacher at the middle school, somehow was able to rationalize sharing his beloved with the Guzman corporation. Even though she was paid handsomely to be on call, I would bet the farm that Irma didn't do it for the money.

"Good for her, tragedy for us," Estelle said.

In a few moments the table was set, I refused wine in favor of more coffee, and the lasagna, salad, and fruit compote arrived in front of me, along with a long loaf of hot Italian bread generously slathered with butter and garlic. The two little boys could hardly sit still, fidgeting with anticipation. I had six more decades of practice in honing my own steely resolve. I sat between them, an arrangement that the boys' parents okayed as long as I didn't serve as a bad influence. Estelle's mother sat across the table, a good strategic spot—her black eyes could flash warnings at the urchins at the least provocation.

A telephone buzzed over on the kitchen counter, and Estelle sighed, glancing at her watch out of habit.

"That thing," Teresa scoffed. "The world used to be a peaceful place."

"*Con permiso,*" Estelle said, rising from the table to pull the little cell phone out of its holster. "Guzman," she greeted, and then listened intently for a moment. "No, he's right here," she said, glancing my way. "Ah," she added, and listened some more. "Why don't I have you talk with him, then. Hang on." She held the phone out to me, and I pushed myself away from the table, using the top of little Francisco's head for support. "It's Bobby," the undersheriff said.

That in itself was a surprise. The taciturn sheriff of Posadas County didn't chit-chat on the phone with anyone—not with his wife, not with his colleagues, not even with his long-time hunting buddies. I could feel my pulse kick up a notch, and it wasn't from the coffee.

"I can run but I can't hide," I said into the phone.

"Nope," Torrez's quiet voice said, and that ended his version of casual conversation. "The truck's gone south."

"The truck," I said, left behind.

"Herb's Torrance's rig," he added. "Truck and trailer both."

I digested that for a second or two, but my

silence didn't prompt anything further from the sheriff. "Who reported that?"

"Doyle Armijo saw it go through the crossing. Two occupants, one male, one female."

"Armijo knows the Torrances?" That seemed odd, since although I didn't know much about the young Border Patrol agent, I did know that he'd been in the area for just a few weeks. I didn't bother to ask why the rookie hadn't stopped the truck because I knew why. Who cares who *leaves* the country, after all. But the Mexican side hadn't stopped them upon entering, apparently. My guess was that Mexican agents reasoned that adding a shiny new truck and stock trailer to the Mexican economy couldn't be a bad thing.

"Don't think he does know Herb," Torrez said. "He just remembers the truck and trailer, and the female who was driving."

"Well, shit," I said. The *female.* I couldn't think of a single innocent reason why Pat Gabaldon would let a girlfriend of the moment drive Herb Torrance's rig to Mexico. "Did Armijo recognize the girl?"

"Says not."

"But her passenger was Pat?"

"He doesn't know the Gabaldon kid. It could've been. Anyway, I just thought you'd want to know that we got that much now to go on. You want to be the one to tell Herb?"

"Sure. I can do that. Did you talk to the other side yet?" While officers on the U.S. side might not ask exit questions, Mexican officers were usually curious about who was coming into their country, and with what—a cynic would say that they needed to make sure that the proper hands were greased.

"I'm about to," the sheriff said without elaboration. "You going to be there for a while?"

"I had planned to be. You're in Regál?"

"Headin' north. See you in a bit, then," he said, and that was that.

I switched off the phone and turned to look at Estelle. "Pat Gabaldon is your problem now." Still mystified, I told her what Sheriff Torrez had reported. "I don't know him all that well," I added, "but Pat always seemed like a level-headed kid to me. I'd have bet that he was content working for the Torrances. I'd have to think this is a real kick in the teeth for old Herb."

"But Armijo couldn't say for sure that the passenger in the truck was Pat, right?" Estelle asked. "Those two had probably never met."

I shook my head. "Armijo was just pulling in to park for his shift, and it wasn't any of his affair to stop the truck. Nothing suspicious caught his eye, except maybe the pretty girl who was driving."

"And he's sure about that…a girl at the wheel, not Pat?"

"Nope, not Pat. And—" I took a minute and refilled my coffee cup—the way things were shaping up, there was no telling when I'd find the next one.

"There are other possibilities," Estelle said.

"And none of them particularly attractive."

Chapter Fourteen

There was time for about five forkfuls of lasagna before the sheriff's Expedition pulled up behind my Blazer at the Guzmans', and he waited with the engine running. I could see no point in dragging Estelle away from *her* dinner with the family, but she insisted, and followed me outside.

"Anything from the medical examiner yet?" Bobby asked.

"Hurry up and wait," Estelle replied. The sheriff reached across, holding out a slip of paper toward me.

"Marcario Diaz was on the stick," he said, referring to one of the Mexican officers who worked the south side of the Regál border crossing. I knew Officer Diaz in passing, enough to pick him out of a crowd but not enough to know his work habits. I fumbled out my glasses and scanned the sheriff's angular writing.

"Fifteen seventeen," I said, and frowned—not

at the military notation, but at how the timing fitted in with the rest of my day's events. The note recorded that at 4:17 p.m., Officer Diaz had recorded New Mexico license double niner two one wild life, appearing on a white 2007 Ford F-350 crew-cab pulling a CloudLiner double-axle live-stock trailer into Mexico. I looked across at Bobby. "Sure as shit that's Herb's rig."

"Diaz said that the trailer appeared to be empty." The sheriff almost smiled.

"*Appeared* to be?"

"He says he had no reason to investigate. He claims the trailer rattled like it was empty."

"Wonderful," I groused, growing angry all over again at Patrick Gabaldon, try as I might not to leap to more conclusions. "Just goddamn wonderful. And what's he say about who was driving? He saw a girl, too?"

"Yep. A young woman with shoulder-length blond hair, *muy bonita*," Torrez said. "Diaz says that her passenger was a young man in shorts and t-shirt, brown hair pulled behind his head in a pony-tail."

"Well, hell. At least Diaz stepped close enough to see all that. A man in shorts and t-shirt sure as hell isn't Patrick," I said. "For him, if it's not denim, it's not clothes. Well, *that's* helpful." I handed the paper to Estelle. "Where were they headed? And

I mean other than 'south,'" I added. "Did Diaz think to ask?"

"He says that the girl claimed they were on their way to the Hernán Domingo ranch outside of Janos. Diaz says that he didn't detain the truck because both the occupants were relaxed, and nothing fitted any wants or warrants his agency has posted. No reason to detain the two young gringos."

"Not to mention the obvious," I said wryly. "Domingo is a big fish. Unless young Officer Diaz wants to end up on a fire watch tower somewhere out in the Chihuahuan desert, he's not going to go out of his way to inconvenience *don Hernán.*"

"Something like that, maybe. Anyway, they ain't comin' back with that truck," Torrez said. "You can count on it."

I sighed and took a deep breath. Vehicles being transported south for sale in Mexico was not a new undertaking. The *burros* diligently proved that on a daily basis. The tandem vehicles heading south on the Interstate through the heart of New Mexico were a common sight, all of those vehicles long of tooth, many missing parts or with quarter panels bashed in. For the most part, the international trade was legit and served a useful purpose, too. Cars bound for the scrap heap in the United States saw a new life wheezing down the awful dirt roads of northern Mexico, where missing a headlight or two, or a bumper, or a fender was no big deal.

On the other hand, Herb's late model truck and stock trailer were many cuts more valuable than those heaps. On a dealer's lot north of the border, the whole rig, truck and trailer both, might bring $40,000. But down in Old Mexico, $15,000 would be a good haul, no questions asked in the right places. Sure, it was below book, but it was quick money, with a minimum of palms reaching out for a cut.

I could tell that my blood pressure was escalating exponentially, and it had nothing to do with rich food interrupted.

"I feel like a goddamn idiot twice over," I said. One of Sheriff Torrez's eyebrows arched up. "I want to go back up on the mesa," I said. "I need to start from the goddamn beginning on this whole sorry mess." I turned and glared at Estelle as if she would have the answers. "Look," I said, "I saw Pat out at the ranch, right around two o'clock this afternoon. Nothing was amiss. He had the cattle loaded in Herb's truck, and he was headed for the grazing allotment on Cat Mesa."

"He didn't mention to you that he was going somewhere else." It wasn't a question, but I frowned and closed my eyes for a second, trying to remember Pat Gabaldon's exact words during our brief meeting out at the ranch. "And there was no one else at the ranch at the time?" Estelle added.

"No," I said. "And no. Nobody that *I* saw. I mean, who would there be? And there was nothing about Patrick's manner that suggested he was planning something cute, either. I think he's a straight-shooting kid. If he'd been thinking of weaseling his boss with some scheme, his face would have showed a hint. Anyway, not long after I left him, maybe an hour or two, your deputy finds the cattle and dog heading back down the hill. And my *first* thought is that Pat just got careless somehow. Or that he had some goddamn chore that involved the use of Herb's rig while Herb was occupied out of town. Well, goddamn it, that earns the stupid award."

Torrez nodded slowly, gazing out through the windshield. "You think that Patrick unloaded up there on the Cat Mesa allotment, and then somehow, these other two entered the picture? Took his truck and trailer, and left the cattle behind?"

"That's what I think now, yes. *Especially* because the cattle and the dog both were left behind, Bobby. And remember..." I whacked the palm of my hand on the Expedition's door. "She left a footprint up there on the mesa. That's what we have by way of hard evidence. It's one thing to drive across the border—hell, *our* side just says,

"Don't let the slamming door smack you in the ass. Their side sees an obviously empty farm truck… so what. If it was a load of cattle, there'd be paperwork and some scrutiny. More going north rather than south, but some never the less." I took a deep breath. "And stupid again. *I* didn't think to check the border crossing. If I had, Diaz would have told me two hours ago what he just told you, Bobby. We need to turn that mesa inside out, is what we need to do. Here Pat's probably lying up there under some bush with his skull cracked open, and we're standing around with our heads up our asses." I turned and slapped the door of the sheriff's truck again.

"Unless he's in cahoots with those two," Torrez observed. "The three of them workin' together? No problem comin' up with something like this. He sells them the rig and splits. He's got family in Mexico. Maybe he headed for the big city—any big city. He's up in Albuquerque right now, havin' steak and beer."

"No," I said abruptly, but then remembered the stunt pulled by Herb Torrance's son the year before. Dale Torrance had managed his escapade with the purloined cattle all by himself, hauling the steers all the way to a willing dealer in Oklahoma. Young minds were inventive and daring. But they were also like a dog chasing a car—once the critter *caught* the car, then what? Once Patrick sold the rig—if indeed he had—*then* what? He'd be on the run for the rest of his life. Besides, I'd spent decades studying people's faces. None of that had been lurking in Patrick Gabaldon's.

Torrez pulled his seatbelt across his lap. "You want to go up now?"

"I do. We have an hour or two of daylight. And I'd like help from better eyes than mine."

"You got that," the sheriff said emphatically. "I'll spring Pasquale free, too. He'll meet us up there." The sheriff glanced at his watch. "I have a couple of quick errands, then I'll be along." I stepped back as he pulled the Expedition into gear.

"He wouldn't have left his dog," I repeated as a parting shot, and Torrez shrugged agreement with that, and releasing the brakes. I turned to Estelle. "Do you want to follow me up?"

"Ride with me," the undersheriff said, and by the time we were backing out of the driveway in her county car, I was on the phone to one of the numbers I kept in my wallet.

"*Señora Naranjo,*" a musical, alto voice said after half a dozen rings.

"Ah, Nadja," I said, grateful that she, rather than her house staff, had answered the telephone. My command of Spanish was hardly commanding, so I stayed with English. "This is Bill Gastner up in

Posadas. I hope I didn't catch you at an awkward time."

After a second or two of silence while she rummaged through her memory to recall who the hell Bill Gastner was, the *esposa* of Capitán Tomás Naranjo sounded pleased and appropriately surprised. "Well, my goodness," she said in faultless English only slightly touched with accent. "This is certainly an unexpected pleasure." I heard a thump as if she'd just set down something heavy. "Tomás is out in the garden. May I tell him that you've called?"

"If you would be so kind," I said, enjoying the odd feeling that, by speaking with Nadja Naranjo, I'd somehow slipped back into another far more genteel era.

I heard a sharp rapping sound. "It will be only a moment." I could picture her beckoning her husband through the window. "Your family is well, I trust?"

"They are," I said. "How has business been?" Nadja owned a classy gift shop in Villaneuva—her husband's travels about his state police district kept them apprised of the best work of the Mexican artisans whose work she featured.

"Ah, well...that's another matter," she said. "I've created, how does the expression go, something of a monster. Is there such a thing as *too* much business?"

"Keeping you hopping, then."

"That's most accurate. I must remember that expression. Ah, here is Tomás. You must come down and see us, Bill. Don't be such a stranger."

"I'll do it. Thanks." Another click, and the captain's voice, equally quiet and refined, came on the line.

"*Señor* Gastner, what a pleasure," Tomás Naranjo said. "This is like a fine brandy at the end of an interesting day. How have you been, my old friend?" The Mexican cop and I weren't exactly drinking buddies, and we didn't exchange Christmas or birthday cards. But I'd always had the comfortable feeling that, if I needed something on the down side of the border, Tomás Naranjo could be trusted to deliver both efficiently and discreetly. He had a positive genius for circumnavigating the avalanche of impossible Mexican paperwork.

"I've been all right," I said. "We've got an interesting problem that's brewing. I thought you should know about it."

"Ah…"

"You recall Herb Torrance? He has the H bar T ranch southwest of here."

"Not far from the Broken Spur," Naranjo supplied. His knowledge of our county always surprised me, but then again, it was easy to forget that the border was just an arbitrary, political boot heel mark kicked in the dust.

"That's it. We're pretty sure that one of his vehicles was stolen and headed into your country just a bit ago." I fumbled out the slip of paper that Torrez had given me and read off the details for Naranjo. "Officer Diaz says that the driver was a young woman and that she mentioned something about the Domingo ranch in Janos."

"Really." Naranjo sounded skeptical. "A truly small world, this. As it happens, I had lunch with Don Hernán and one of his sons but yesterday. His son is something of an artist with the welding torch."

"It may have been just a comment in passing to allay suspicions," I said. "Look, our concern at the moment is finding Torrance's hired hand, Patrick Gabaldon." I briefly recited the events of the day, and Naranjo listened without interruption.

"Would that the dog could talk," Naranjo observed dryly when I finished.

"Well, in a sense, he has," I said. "The cowboy might be careless with a livestock gate, although that's unlikely. But he would never willingly leave the dog behind. If Pat had wanted to heist the truck and trailer himself and head south of the border, he would take the dog along. He wouldn't just leave the pup out in the boonies, confused and thirsty."

"Most interesting. What else did the corporal tell you?"

"Only that he let the vehicle pass without question, and without a search. He said that the trailer appeared empty."

"I see." The two words managed to sound nonjudgmental.

I braced a hand against the dash board as Estelle pushed the county car through a tight corner on County 43. Apparently Naranjo could hear the engine in the background.

"And now? You're headed this way?" the captain asked.

"Up to Cat Mesa first," I said. "We know that Pat Gabaldon was there—at least we *think* we know that. That's where it all starts, Tomás. He unloaded the cattle up on the allotment, and then…well, and then, I'm damned if I know. They didn't waste any time. We know that if they crossed the border shortly after four, they didn't hang around thinking about it."

"And at this end, you have only the girl's mention of Don Hernán's operation. That is the place for me to start. Let me talk with him, and in addition, I will circulate the description of the vehicle. But this is a large country, with so few officers." He chuckled. "You have heard that before, of course."

"That's why I called you, Captain," I said, and if I sounded differential, I meant it. Tomás Naranjo had earned my unqualified respect over the years. Working for a bureaucracy that blew this way and that with the winds of political opportunity and sometimes corruption, Naranjo had carved out his own methods of operation, taking shortcuts with a charm and good humor that kept him in favor with his superiors.

"You are proceeding on the assumption that the truck is stolen, then," Naranjo said. "Not some other scheme concocted by these agile young minds. You don't expect to see either truck or trailer heading back across the border."

"No, I don't. And I hope I'm wrong."

Chapter Fifteen

We searched, and we searched hard. Frustration grew as we discovered nothing that I hadn't already seen: a few scuffs in the dirt, tire marks, the sudden appearance of hoof prints at the spot where the twenty-four cattle had disembarked from the stock trailer. Estelle found a single print that featured a clear heel mark, made by typical work boots such as those that Patrick Gabaldon would wear. Despite the cowboy legend, he'd taken time to slip out of his pointy-toed, high-heeled riding boots when the corral work was finished, and into the comfortable, blunt-toed, waffle-soled, lace-up Wellingtons.

I showed Estelle the smaller print that the deputy's sharp eyes had found by the ant mound, and we agreed it might be a woman's size. It wasn't clear enough to make out tread patterns, but it lacked distinctive, elevated heels. And that was it.

As the light mellowed toward twilight and the breeze swept the mesa from the northwest, we widened the search area, hoping to find signs of a scuffle or *something* that might give us a hint of what had happened on this lonely spot.

Deputy Pasquale backtracked and, as Sheriff Torrez had suggested, drove down Forest Road 128, and I could hear his vehicle clearly as he idled it along the narrow two-track that paralleled the rim of Cat Mesa. I knew that it was a long shot that Patrick would drive Herb's rig that way. For one thing, the fifth-wheel stock trailer was a monster—twenty-four feet at least. Once committed to FR 128, it would be a challenge to find a place to turn the rig around. There was no other way off the mesa rim that would be practical with a truck and trailer like that.

Sheriff Bobby Torrez stood with his hands on his hips, apparently absorbed in watching the last of the sunshine filtering through the piñons and junipers. He switched his gaze to me as I ambled up to him.

"Busy dog." He pointed a toe at a welter of dog prints near the gate. "Why would Pat let the dog out when he was *unloading* the cattle?" He waited as if I had the answers.

"I can't imagine why he would," I said. The unloaded cattle didn't need to be herded anywhere—once out of the trailer, they were free to roam and munch. They didn't need their heels nipped.

"But somebody did," the sheriff said. "And that's interesting. Why leave the dog behind?"

"Any number of reasons. He'd yap and fuss and fight, especially if Pat wasn't with him. Hell, the mutt knows me, sort of, and he and I were together most of the afternoon. But I gotta tell you, it was an uneasy truce, Bobby. And I *like* dogs, even though they plug up my sinuses. Now, you take somebody who doesn't, and the first thing they're going to do is kick the little nuisance out of the truck."

"Maybe so. Pat wouldn't let them do that, if he was still able." He leaned his back against the gate post and rocked back and forth to scratch his back.

"My point exactly," I said.

"I put all the information out," the sheriff said. "Every agency in the southwest."

"The truck's not coming back," I said. "Naranjo told me that he'd check with the rancher down in Janos, and in the meantime, he has all his officers looking in the dark corners, too."

"Both officers," Torrez quipped. "With all the problems they have, they aren't going to put much effort into looking for a pickup truck. Or a single kid." Estelle Reyes-Guzman was standing a dozen yards away near a slate-gray stump, cell phone stuck to her ear. My own phone chirped, and I dug it out of my shirt pocket, the ludicrous notion shooting through my mind that she was calling *me*.

"Bill," Herb Torrance said. "You're up on the mesa?"

"We are," I said. "Chasing our tails. There's no sign of Patrick, Herb. What have you heard?"

"Well, not a damn thing," the rancher replied.

"Look, there's one major bit of news, though, and you're not going to like it. Your rig is in Mexico. One of the Mexican cops remembers it at the crossing."

"Well, hell." He fell silent for a moment. "I don't see Patrick doin' that."

"I don't think he did. It's looking like someone took the truck. Somebody who was with him up here on the mesa. You have any ideas how that might have worked? Patrick had friends he take along on a ride like this?"

"Well, hell," he said, "I don't know about that. I wouldn't think so. But what, like somebody hijacked him, you mean? The border cops actually seen this, or what?"

"Yes, they're sure. Two people in the truck. The descriptions don't fit Pat. He sure as hell wasn't driving. Go figure that. A young couple, the Mexican cop says. He says there was a girl behind the wheel, a real looker. He remembers the long blond hair. But no sign of Patrick."

"You're kiddin'."

"No. Did you ever see Pat spending time with

someone like that? The border cop says the other one was a young man with hair back in a pony tail, wearing a black cap. Not much to go on."

"Well, I can't figure that. You know, Pat, he don't romp around much. Kind of quiet and steady." Herb almost laughed. "Not like my boys. Kind of worries me, something like this."

"You're in good company, Herb. But that's where we're at. You remember Captain Naranjo?"

"Why, sure I do."

"He's looking into it. He'll play straight with us."

"But no sign of the boy?"

"Not yet."

"I can't figure it," he said again. "He'll be all right, though." That was wishful thinking, but I didn't disillusion the rancher. I hoped he was right.

"I need to take a run up the mesa myself, I guess," Herb added.

"I can see the cattle from where I'm standing," I said. "They're in good shape." A pair of calves stood near the tree-line at the edge of the pasture, staring at us as their jaws worked in perfect unison.

"Gotta see if the water's running down at the drinker," Herb said. "You going to be up there a while?"

"Probably just a few more minutes, Herb. We're running out of light, and we're not finding much. One of the deputies is checking down Forest Road 128 to see if Pat went wood hauling or some such, but I don't hold out much hope for that."

"Can't see why he'd try to wrestle the rig down that way," Herb said. "Sure as hell, we got easier places to pick up firewood."

"I don't think that *he* did. But we have to check it out."

"Well, don't forget to close the gate."

"I'll make sure," I said. "Call me if you hear anything. You know, the odds are just as good that he'll show up back at the ranch." I didn't believe that, but it sounded good.

Estelle had approached, and she raised an eyebrow as if to say, "You first."

"That was Herb," I said. "He's coming up to check his livestock." I had entered Pat Gabaldon's cell number in the phone, and just to give my frustrations something to do, I selected the number and pushed the auto-dialer. The signals vanished out into the vapors, unanswered. "He says Pat hasn't shown up back at the ranch."

"I didn't expect that," Estelle said. She thrust both hands in the pockets of her trousers, and I saw her shoulders slump a bit.

"So what's up, then?" The sheriff directed his question at Estelle, who hadn't mentioned who she'd been on the phone with. I glanced at him with a little sympathy, since over the years we'd both become accustomed to Estelle Reyes-Guzman's reticence. It was a tribute to Bobby's tight rein on his own ego that he didn't seem to mind when folks called the undersheriff instead of him. He knew that in due time, everything flowed uphill.

"That was Tony." She let that suffice for a moment, drawing an arc in the dust with the toe of her boot. "Preliminary tests point to the wine." It was so quiet that we could hear the whisper of the early evening breeze through the piñons.

"Spiked, you mean?" Torrez prompted.

Estelle frowned at his choice of words. "There's a chemical complex in the wine that is 'unexpected,' the med tech says. But not all of the wine, either."

"Whatever that means," the sheriff said.

Estelle flashed a rare and thoroughly fetching smile. "No, what I mean is, there's a complex in the wine spilled on the floor, and from the trace remains in the glass. Nothing in the bottle. Nothing in *either* bottle. Some of the same chemical also shows up in the victim's saliva. They haven't run the tox tests on his blood yet."

"What about in the food itself?" I asked.

She shook her head. "At this point, that's all they have. But Dave Hewitt is going to work tonight to see if he can crack it." I'd seen Hewitt's name or initials on a crime lab report or two. Most of the time, the state crime lab was prompt, efficient, and accurate. But routinely, toxicology and other complex blood work—or even DNA comparisons—took days or weeks. It helped to have a young kid working there who let himself become excited by the chase…and who maybe didn't have much of a home life.

"Natural or not?" I asked. "This 'complex,' I mean."

"He can't say yet."

"Christ," I muttered. "First one thing and then another. I don't know which goddamn way to turn. First George, and now all this." I turned in a half circle, surveying the shadows. Twilight made it impossible for me to distinguish hummocks of grass from rocks until I tripped over them. In a moment, we heard the whisper of Deputy Pasquale's unit as he returned from scouting FR 128, but his report didn't help us. I hadn't expected any great discoveries. The forest road was pummeled by the tire tracks and foot prints of woodcutters, hunters, and just plain folks looking for places to dump their worn-out mattresses, chairs, and stoves.

"Are you ready to head down?" Estelle's hand touched my shoulder lightly, and I jerked awake.

"I guess." I shrugged helplessly and looked at

both Estelle and Bobby. "I'm ready to hear bright ideas."

"He sold the rig and skipped town," Tom Pasquale offered. "Simple as that."

"He wouldn't leave the dog," I said.

"Why not?" the deputy asked.

"You don't own a dog, do you?" I replied. "Especially one who works with you every hour of the day and sleeps at the foot of your bed every night. Besides, Patrick's own pickup truck is still parked down at the ranch."

"He's somewhere between here and the border," the sheriff said. "They might have chucked him in the quarry, or in one of the junk piles down by the mine, or you name it." He started toward his own truck. "But I think we're gettin' ahead of ourselves. It's only been a few hours...what, three since Diaz waved the truck through the gate? For all we know, Pat might be sittin' in the Dairy Queen in Deming, counting his money, trying to figure out what to do next."

"We could wish for that instead of the quarry," I said. "I know I sound like a broken record, but he wouldn't have left the dog behind."

Chapter Sixteen

"Swing in here a minute," I said, but the under-sheriff had already read my mind and turned off County Road 43. We jounced across a few yards of impromptu parking lot and parked facing the four-strand barbed wire fence that marked U.S. Forest Service property. Fortunately, the quarry wasn't announced by a historical marker, and couldn't actually be seen from the highway. But in the bunch grass, the well-worn trails leading to the fence and beyond suggested that there was *something* attractive over there through the trees.

I was convinced now that Patrick Gabaldon hadn't taken the rig south of the border. In fact, it seemed to me that Patrick would have done everything in his power to prevent such an episode—and that didn't bode well. The abandonment of the cattle and his dog told me that somehow, Patrick had run afoul of someone whom he'd either befriended along the highway or who had materialized out of nowhere up on the lonely mesa top. That someone had taken the rig, but no one would be fool enough to attempt a border crossing hauling a body in the back of the trailer.

If the perpetrators were familiar with Posadas County, they would know about the quarry and its dark, deep, foul waters.

For a few minutes we concentrated on the parking area, flash-lights criss-crossing the informal turn-out beaten into the weeds over the years by traffic, an area about the size of a tennis court.

In the failing light, it was difficult to distinguish one set of tire marks from another, but nothing unusual drew my attention. A big pickup pulling a long, twin-axle stock trailer would leave characteristic tracks, and I didn't see any that came close. We didn't see any blood stains, although in that light, on that terrain, it would have required a quart or two to make a visible mark.

"What do you think?" I asked, and Estelle stopped and ran her light beam along the top strand of the Forest Service fence. "I can't imagine somebody lugging a corpse all the way over to the quarry," I said. "But I can't imagine a lot of things. You up for a look?"

"We need to do that."

I used my weight to crush the fence's top wire down until I could scissors across, then with a boot on the second and tugging upward on the top wire, created a generous hole for Estelle to duck through. A moment's hike through dust-frosted scrub brought us to the east edge of the attractive nuisance that the Forest Service wished would just go away.

The quarry yawned as a sink hole approximately eighty feet across with huge limestone benches along one side that once upon a time had been damn attractive lounging spots between skinny dips. The crater had been blasted out of the side of the mesa in the 1920s, when some genius decided that there might be something really valuable in the spring-soaked limestone. There wasn't. The only remains of industry was a concrete block about the size of a Chevrolet on the west bank, with eight rusted bolts projecting from the top. I was surprised that sometime in the past an enterprising kid hadn't slapped a diving board to those block bolts. Then he could have had us dragging the waters for *his* corpse.

The spring water continued to drizzle through the years, keeping the quarry filled and probably a little less than toxic. As far as I knew, there was no outlet other than seepage and evaporation, and in the past five dry years the level of the quarry's dark, rank waters had dropped, exposing another six feet of limestone walls scarred by the blaster's drill marks.

I scanned the quarry carefully though binoculars, following the beam of my heavy flashlight. The bloated dead thing on the opposite side, nudging up against one of the benches, was too ripe to be Pat Gabaldon.

"Are we missing anyone else?" I asked, my question half in jest.

"Not to my knowledge, sir," Estelle replied soberly.

I started around the quarry, staying back from the edge, meandering around the hummocks of dry grass and weeds that were dotted here and there with runty little junipers trying to gain a foothold on the inch-thick blanket of topsoil. The quarry's water was fragrant enough and the level low enough that the randy high school kids would have to be really snoggered to enjoy soaking in what amounted to a quarter acre of spunkwater. Thinking of soaking *my* tender parts in that stuff gave me the willies.

As I made my way around the rim with Estelle close to my elbow, I paused now and then to play the light across the dark water, its surface scum an interesting admixture of various goopy things. Who knew what lay on the bottom. The Posadas Fire Department had once pumped it empty back in 1986 when the McKelvy youngster went missing. After that experience, I knew that the quarry tapered down like a rough funnel, with ledges and crevasses marking the sides, the bottom forty-one feet from the rim…a far cry from the bottomless mystery of legend. Timmy McKelvy hadn't drowned in it then, and as far as I knew, no one had since.

We reached the far side, where the contour of the hill rose sharply to the rocks and trees of the mesa flank. I could see that the mule deer hadn't been so lucky. The carcass had lost most of its fur, the hind legs entangled in rocks along the edge. An interesting soup mix. I took a deep breath of relief, but that was tempered by knowing that if the bastard—or bastards—had managed to toss Pat Gabaldon's body into the dark waters, it would be another couple of days before it bloated enough to float to the surface.

The water level was fifteen feet below the rim where we stood and on the opposite side, at least eight. I handed my binoculars to Estelle and tracked her flashlight with mine as she scanned the quarry edges again.

"No loose rocks, no fresh scuffing," she whispered, as if loath to disturb the quiet. "I don't think so, sir."

I squatted down and found a fist-sized rock,

straightened up and made sure of my balance. "Put your light out on the water," I said, and the undersheriff did so. I tossed the rock out into the center of the quarry. The splash was satisfying in the quiet of the evening, and we watched the concentric circles reach out to the quarry walls. The splash broke the surface scum in dozens of places and patterns. "How long do you suppose it would take for the scum to blend back into a uniform layer?" I asked. "I don't think anybody has been here, and sure as hell, I don't think anybody has thrown something as bulky as a body in here recently."

"Maybe not," Estelle said. She switched the light back and forth one more time. "Probably not."

"No tracks, no nothing," I repeated, as if saying it enough would make it so. "We need to get back to the car before I end up having to walk on my hands and knees." My growing apprehension wasn't because of my unstable waddle around the quarry's rim. It was akin to that of parents when their kids had missed curfew and then an hour later *still* hadn't shown their faces. That's enough time to invent all kinds of awful scenarios.

A few minutes later, as I settled in the passenger seat of Estelle's cramped county car, I closed my eyes and waited for a brainstorm. None brewed. I looked across at the undersheriff as she jotted notes on her log. As usual, I couldn't tell what was going on in that agile mind.

"I need great ideas," I prompted. She took ten seconds to finish her notes and then slid the small aluminum clipboard back into its boot. The car started with a guttural whisper. "I need to know what your intuition tells you."

"I think," she said carefully, and pulled the Crown Vic into gear, "I think that the sooner Captain Naranjo either finds the truck, or finds whoever drove it south, the better."

"That's not what I wanted to hear," I grumbled. "Hell, *I* can intuit that far ahead. That's not why we pay you the big bucks, sweetheart." That prompted a rare laugh from Estelle, and I added, "The clock's ticking."

"And we have a million square miles of desert, on both sides of the border, where he could be," Estelle added, and that didn't make me feel any better. "And *nothing* to give us a hint, or sense of direction." She held up one hand as if she were offering me a grapefruit. "We know Pat was up here, earlier this afternoon." Bracing the steering wheel briefly with her knee, she held up the other hand. "And Herb Torrance's truck was seen at the border crossing not long afterward. A couple of hours." She glanced at me. "And that's it, sir. That's it."

"Somewhere between here and there, then. Who's

got the nearest tracker dog now? Gordon?"

"Lt. Gordon, over in Cruces," Estelle affirmed. "If he's not tied up with something else." I put one hand up and braced it against the door sill as she drove down the paved road, past Consolidated Mining's bone yard. She slowed enough that a flash of the car's spotlight illuminated the secure, heavy chain-link entry gate. "And that might tell us something. If there was a struggle back up there in the pasture and they dragged Pat off into the trees somewhere beyond where we searched, then the dog will find him. If that's *not* what happened, the dog will tell us that Pat left the area—either in the truck or in some other fashion." She frowned. "If Pat was still up on the mesa, it seems to me that Socks would have stayed with him."

"I don't know about that. If the cattle are loose," I said, "his first loyalty is to work. He had the opportunity, once the cattle were back in the pasture, and work was done. I'm no dog whisperer, but he didn't give any indication that made sense to me. So, let's give Gordon a call," I said. "Get his dog up here. That's something. I can't just sit around and *hope* this thing through." I pointed at an oncoming pickup truck, an older model. "That's Herb. Stop a minute."

The light not being the best, the rancher almost didn't slow, but at the last minute he lurched the truck off the road as I hustled toward him. In the cab, Socks danced on the passenger side, tongue lolling—the news wasn't good.

He nodded. "No sign of the boy," he said. "His truck's still at the ranch."

"Well, we haven't found a damn thing," I said. "Bobby and Tom Pasquale are still nosing around up the hill. I'm going to give the Cruces P.D. a call and see if we can't get one of their search-and-rescue dogs up here. Hell, I don't know, Herb. We just don't have much to go on."

Herb groped a cigarette out of his shirt pocket and took his time lighting it. "What do you think, though?" he asked after a moment.

"Your rig is in Mexico, and I think that eventually we're going to find it. Pat's somewhere between here and there, and if I were a betting man, I'd wager that he got the worst of the deal. That's as optimistic as it comes just now."

Herb exhaled slowly. "Well, shit," he said. He stroked the top of the dog's head with his thumb. "You heard about services for George?"

For a second, I was ready to ask, "George who?" but then I caught up. "I haven't," I said, "but then again, I haven't heard much of anything from the real world this afternoon. We've been chasing shadows."

"I don't get it," Herb said, and he could have been referring to the whole day.

"You have lots of company," I said. "How's Dale?"

"He's a mess. You ought to see the x-ray of his knee." He shook his head helplessly. "They got pins goin' every which way." *And he might be the lucky one,* I thought.

"It'll turn out fine," I said instead. "He'll sit around the house for a few days until he gets the itch, and then he'll try to figure out how to ride a horse with his leg in a cast."

"It's more'n just a damn cast," Herb said. "Like walkin' around with the whole damn hardware store bolted to his leg." He shrugged philosophically, but I could imagine that his worries were growing. His son Dale and Pat Gabaldon were the sum of his ranch hands, and the work burden on his wiry old shoulders would now triple. On top of that, I couldn't imagine that Dale had any health insurance, and a new knee didn't come cheap.

"Lemme know," Herb said finally, and pulled his truck into gear.

Even as I recrossed the narrow county road, Deputy Tom Pasquale's SUV cruised down the hill, and he raised a hand in salute as he pulled to a stop. "Sheriff's hangin' out for a few minutes," he called to Estelle.

Bobby Torrez would do that, enjoying some silent time alone, mulling whatever it was that needed mulling. He'd still be there when Herb arrived, and the two of them would mull some more. Maybe something would come of it.

As if she could sense my slump, Estelle said, "We have word out to everyone. State police, Border Patrol, neighboring counties—if Pat's to be found, it'll be soon, sir."

"Sure enough," I said. "I wish I shared your optimism." I glanced at the time. "You headed back home now?"

"Yes. Are you ready to finish dinner?"

Normally, of course, that would have been a silly question. "Thanks, but I think I'll just mosey around for a while," I said.

Chapter Seventeen

I've always been thankful that few clever people turn to a life of crime. Sure, there are some successful criminal minds whose misdeeds never catch up with them—perhaps more than we would like to know. But the vast majority commit the crime when their snowball starts down the hillside, and *then* they decide to think, often too late—and that's what makes the cop's job possible.

The notion that if I could pinpoint the mistakes, that I could find the trail leading to the site of Pat Gabaldon's misadventure, fed my insomnia. Everyone else had something pressing to do. Estelle was on the phone with Albuquerque and her deputy there, trying to fit pieces into the Payton puzzle. I didn't know where Sheriff Torrez was prowling, but despite his taciturn nature, he had a good head for puzzles. He also understood that the rest of the county's activities didn't come to a stop because of a single incident or two.

I needed to stay out of the way and find something constructive to do. After retrieving my SUV from the Guzman's, I drove back out to Bustos Avenue and headed east to the intersection of Grande. Why someone would steal a fancy, almost new truck and livestock trailer was obvious—it was worth a ton of money, even south of the border where money wasn't knee-deep except for the drug cartels. Given the chance, Pat Gabaldon would have had a thing or two to say about that plan— and that was the key...*given the chance.*

I found myself parked at the intersection of Bustos and Grande, the one traffic light in town, and watched it cycle two or three times.

An infinite number of places around Posadas County would offer good sites to dump a body unseen. In some of them, weeks, even months, might pass before the cluster of ravens and vultures attracted attention. If a killer didn't want a body to be found, success didn't require rocket science. A grave only two feet deep would foil the most curious coyote.

A station wagon pulled up behind me, then swung out and passed when the light turned green and I didn't budge. The driver could have had two heads for all I noticed.

Why would the hijackers bother to haul Pat Gabaldon's carcass down off the mesa? Why not just drag him off into the trees, well away from the two-track? Somebody was being clever, I decided. But they should have taken the dog along. That was the first mistake. If the whole kit and kaboodle had gone missing—truck, driver, dog—we wouldn't have known where to start.

Herb Torrance's rig would have come down off the mesa on County Road 43. That was the only route, other than a Jeep trail or two on the west side. Then, State Highway 56 was the logical route south to the border crossing, where the rig had been spotted next. They'd certainly avoid the huge, international border crossing between El Paso and Juarez, where too many sets of keen eyes and noses guarded the gates.

But only an idiot would approach the border-crossing check point with a corpse in the vehicle, or someone tied up and gagged on the rear floor of the crewcab. If the hijackers had whacked Pat Gabaldon and heaved the body into truck or trailer, they'd grow uneasy as the border approached. The crossing at Regál was open twelve hours a day, six to six. Risking the check station in broad daylight with a corpse or captive didn't make sense.

The Mexican desert was a great dumping ground, true enough. But the risk of trying to cross was too great. Drivers never knew when a customs agent from either side would point to the parking lot, demanding a search. No. Pat Gabaldon had been dumped somewhere between Cat Mesa and Regál.

I let the SUV idle through the intersection, turning right onto Grande. If the truck thieves *knew* Posadas, there were any number of alleys and empty lots where a body could be dumped. But they were driving a big rig with an imposing twenty-four-foot long fifth wheel trailer—intimidating if they weren't used to that sort of thing. City byways and alleys wouldn't be my choice.

Several blocks south, Grande passed under the Interstate, and once out of the village, I faced almost thirty miles of rumpled country. I slouched in the seat, all four windows down, speed just fast enough that the SUV wouldn't shift down out of drive.

In the twenty-six miles between Posadas and the Broken Spur saloon, there were less than half a dozen two-tracks off into the rough country. The first was just beyond Moore, the remains of a tiny village that had folded for good in the early 1950s. I slowed and pulled off the highway. Building foundations jutted out of the bunch grass and koshia, and the Moore Mercantile loomed in my headlights, its board and batten skeleton slumping a bit more each season.

Both state police and sheriff's deputies liked

to park in the shadow of the Merc and run radar, and in the glare of my headlights and flashlight, I could see the tire prints where the cops swung in and parked.

Stopping the truck, I shut off the engine. For a minute the ticking of its guts intruded, but then the silence filled in. No ranch dogs barked in the distance, no traffic hissed on the asphalt, no aircraft moaned overhead. The silence was heavy. I found my phone, flipped it open, and touched the choice for Pat Gabaldon's number. Nothing. I closed my eyes and listened harder. Still nothing.

Snapping the phone off, I started the Chevy and idled back out to the highway. Headlights popped on the eastern horizon, and I waited, my lights off, while the westbound vehicle approached. The lights flooded over me and the large SUV braked hard. Deputy Tom Pasquale swung in so that we were door to door.

"Quiet, huh, sir." He took the opportunity to pick up his log and jot a note. No doubt, I was now officially recorded. "I was going to take a swing back down through Regál, just to see."

"That would be good."

"What are you thinking, sir?"

"You're assuming that I am, Thomas. I'd like a bolt of inspiration out of the night." I sighed. "Right now, I'm thinking that they dumped the kid's body somewhere between Cat Mesa and the border crossing. That's as brilliant as I can be at the moment."

He turned and looked at the dash clock. "It's just coming up on eight. Hasn't even been that many hours since he went missing."

"Four too many," I said. "Look, I don't have a radio in this rig, but you have my cell. Give me a buzz if you need to. I'm going to be working some of the two-tracks down this way."

"You bet." He touched his right hand to the brim of his Stetson and then swung the Expedition around in a tight circle, the fat tires loud on the gravel. I stayed parked, watching his tail lights fade down State 56 until he rounded Salinas Mesa. Long after the lights disappeared, I could hear his engine and tires, a distant complaint in the dark.

The ranch road to Gus Prescott's tired little place intersected the state highway less than a quarter mile from Moore, and I turned onto the two-track, feeling the tires nestle into the powdery dust. For a quarter mile the lane wound north across the prairie, through grass cropped to the nubbins by too many cattle over too many years. A tight left turn presented a steep grade down to the Salinas Arroyo, the graveled crossing now bone dry. I stopped on the downgrade, letting my head-lights flood the crossing. If someone had parked a big rig here, they'd done so in the middle of the road, leaving no marks on the shoulders. As I had at Moore, I shut off the engine, letting all the night sounds in. Again, I dialed Patrick's number.

I knew that he had carried the gadget in one of those nifty little leather holsters on his belt, right beside the holster for his utility knife. Those and the snuff can in his hip pocket made up the only tool kit a cowpuncher needed.

But no harsh electronic melody broke the stillness. It had occurred to me that perhaps the thugs had taken the phone, or smashed it, or any number of other possibilities. But it was worth the try. From far off to the west, a sharp wail of tires on concrete drifted to me. Tom Pasquale's heavy SUV, probably driven at his usual eighty miles an hour, had crossed the expansion joints and grooved surface of the bridge across the Rio Guijuarro. I restarted my Chevy but left the lights off, drove down into the arroyo and up the other side, bumping across another half mile of prairie until I could see the lights of Prescott's mobile home.

They didn't need company, and I didn't need conversation, so I turned around and retraced my tracks. A mile down State 56, a well traveled lane cut through BLM property, then angled up the face of Salinas Mesa.

That two-track was narrow and infrequently

used. Grass, sage, and a host of other opportunists grew in the mounded center. They brushed the bottom of my SUV, fried to aromatic perfection by the hot catalytic converter. In a hundred yards, a wide expanse of undisturbed blow sand paved the tracks. No one had driven this road in the past week. The Chevy bucked as I steered up out of the ruts, and the prairie was so dry the grass clumps crackled and turned to dust under the tires.

The evening wore on as I methodically worked my way southwest, ducking off State 56 at each opportunity, looking for tracks or scuff marks. At the bridges over the Salinas and Guijarro arroyos, I stopped and climbed out of the truck, crossed the guard rail, and then took my time sliding down beside the concrete bridge buttresses. In both cases, the arroyos were dry, and the Guijarro, much wider and inviting, was scarred by four-wheeler tracks.

For long minutes, I stood in the bottom of the Guijarro and waited as the night seeped into my bones, as if the Big Answer was going to roll down the Guijarro like a wall of storm water and engulf me. It didn't, and I wished that I had worn a heavier jacket. The tight interior of the SUV felt good when I struggled out of the arroyo and slipped inside.

I could remember instances when I'd told my deputies to be patient, to let each of the little puzzle pieces swim into place. Now, I told myself the same thing. The state highway department had begun stockpiling crusher fines in preparation for a paving project, and I swung off the highway and circled behind the uniform mountain of steel gray stone. One of the neighbors had done the same thing, then found a spot near the middle where they would be invisible from highway traffic. They had backed up tight against the pile, dropped their tailgate, and shoveled a truckful. I had no doubt that the theft would be repeated until the low spot in someone's driveway was nicely graveled.

Off in the distance, I could see the halo of the single parking lot light at the Broken Spur Saloon, the one oasis on this lonely stretch of highway that Victor Sanchez had turned into his private goldmine. Once southwest of the Spur, the highway would curve gently southward, heading up the back flank of the San Cristóbal mountains, those jutting, rugged peaks that formed our own border fence. Over the top of the mountains at Regal Pass and then down to the border crossing—and the mountains could hide countless corpses in their ravines, rock slides, and brush fields.

A mile before the saloon's parking lot, my headlights picked up the large Forest Service sign, blasted by dozens of bullet holes, that announced Borracho Springs Campground and the Borracho

Springs Trail. The campground lay more than two miles off the highway, after Forest Road 122 forked off the county two-track.

I slowed, looking for the narrow turn-off marked on each side by highway reflectors. Both markers were askew, the usual target of careless drivers. The Chevy thumped onto the rough two-track, and I jammed on the brakes, shoving the transmission into park before the tires had stopped rolling.

The flashlight was inadequate, but I didn't have one of those nifty swiveling spotlights on the SUV. Still, the marks were obvious. The first post, one of those flat things made out of tough fiber, had been caught dead center by someone who'd turned too tightly, dragging a wheel over the lip of the bar ditch and culvert. The scatter of gravel was fresh—that is, it lay on top of a myriad of other tracks. I was no Daniel Boone, but any idiot could see that.

Crossing behind the idling SUV, I inspected the other marker. It was bent and cracked, the indestructible material not so indestructible after all. The tire marks angled across the end of the culvert, dropping down into the ditch and then up and out across the marker. On the way out to the State highway, someone had not minded his turn and hooked the marker, dragging it under the axle.

That's easy to do on a narrow road, even easier to do with a trailer that didn't track immediately behind the truck during a turn. I'd done the same thing a number of times, and always felt like an idiot when I did.

Returning to the truck, I sat for a moment, letting my pulse settle a bit. There were dozens of explanations, of course. A hunter, a rancher, a tourist. In and out.

The first mile of the two-track belonged to the county, and they graded it once a year or so. I let the SUV inch along at idle, windows still open, nudging the gas only when a slight grade slowed progress. As I did so, I kept the cell phone on my lap, touching the autodial every hundred yards or so.

The intersection with Forest Road 122 appeared in the wash of my headlights. The fork to the left angled off into the prairie, ending at a windmill and cattle tank. Most of the tracks headed for the campground, and I turned that way, toward the boulder gardens at the base of the mountain.

The campground included two concrete firepits, two Port-a-Potties, and a bullet-riddled Forest Service sign that pointed off toward the rugged country, announcing *Pierce Canyon* and *Borracho Springs, ½ mile*. More important, the spot featured a donut of space large enough to swing around even the most awkward rig. I stopped, leaning forward against the steering wheel. The fresh tire cuts swung in an arc around the perimeter of the clearing.

I shut off the truck and rested back in the seat. My thumb did the little dance on the phone, but I'd tried that trick often enough that I wasn't expecting a response. When the first notes of *La Cucaracha* jangled out of the darkness, I startled so hard that I cracked my elbow on the door sill.

Lunging out of the truck, I took three steps and stopped, leaning against the hood. My hearing was by no means acute under the best circumstances, and the rock amphitheater played tricks with the sound. A dozen cycles of *Cucaracha* and I'd pinpointed what I thought was the general direction, up through several house-sized boulders. With flashlight in one hand and phone in the other, I picked my way toward the music.

Something large and energetic bolted off through the brush, and in a moment hard hooves clattered on the rocks up slope. I leaned against a buttress of limestone and gave both pulse and breath time to mellow. Switching off the phone saved some battery life and gave me time to think. The two truck-jackers would lug their victim up on the mountain? Not a chance. A mountain lion or coyote might carry off body parts, and that thought made me pause.

I dialed again, and the damn custom ring tone filled the night air, drifting down-slope from the right. The gravel was loose underfoot, and I was wearing a pair of smooth-soled boots unsuited for rock climbing. A large piñon loomed ahead, with *La Cucaracha* merry as ever, emanating from well above my head. I swept the flashlight beam through the limbs, seeing nothing but piñon needles. I grabbed a fistful, knowing I'd regret it, and shook. Sure enough, the ring tone cascaded down toward me. The phone had been flung hard enough that it should never have been found, caught high up in the piñon where it could have stayed for years.

Stretching on my tip-toes, I reached in and with a grunt of exhilaration almost grabbed the gadget. My brain clicked into gear then. I had no camera, and I'd already disturbed a crime scene. Making careful note of the phone's position, and with the night once more quiet, I found a comfortable rock and sat down.

A couple of minutes later, my breathing had slowed enough for conversation. This time, Ernie Wheeler answered my ring, and a minute after that, Deputy Tom Pasquale had been dispatched to my location.

Less than a minute after I switched off and before I'd gathered the energy to push myself off the rock, my phone came alive again.

"What do you have?" Bob Torrez's voice sounded unnaturally loud in this quiet place.

"Gabaldon's telephone. Somebody pitched it. I just found it in a goddamn tree."

That didn't prompt any gasp of wonder from the sheriff, as if he knew that phones grew on trees. "What about him?"

"Not yet."

"You think he's there?"

"Has to be," I said with more confidence than I felt. "Why would anyone drive all the way into this place just to pitch a phone?"

That prompted silence from the sheriff for a moment. "Be down in a bit," he said. "Sit tight."

I wasn't able to do that, picturesque and peaceful as my perch on the rock might have been. Instead, the notion of trajectory prompted me to point my flashlight downhill until the beam bounced off my SUV. If the hijackers had parked within a few feet of where I had, throwing the phone this far off into the trees took a strong, athletic, over-hand fastball. Why would they bother to do that? If Pat Gabaldon was still breathing, pitching his emergency link provided a little insurance. Maybe they'd been startled when they'd heard it ring—I had dialed the number a dozen times during the day.

Behind the last fire pit, a deep arroyo choked with dense scrub oak marked the perimeter of the campground, and I made my way toward it, down off the slope and back across the parking lot.

By the time I'd reached the gash eroded

through the jumble of rocks, I could hear Tom Pasquale's SUV in the distance, howling up the state highway. At the same time, a high, thin sound keened through the night, like the desperate sound a deer makes just before a mountain lion breaks its neck. It wasn't loud, but it was enough to snap my head around and freeze me in my tracks, the hair standing up on the back of my neck.

Chapter Eighteen

The cry didn't repeat itself, but I'd heard enough to pinpoint it just below my position on the arroyo lip.

"Patrick!" I shouted, probing the light through the brush. "Patrick, can you hear me?" The cry repeated, this time from the left, and I slid down the bank in a cascade of gravel. Something let out a squeak and bounded off ahead of me, and I could hear Pasquale's SUV jarring up the dirt two-track. "Patrick?" I stood in the center of the arroyo bottom, trying to find a route around a grove of scrub oak that had chosen that precarious spot.

"I can't..." somebody said, and the words were so clear, so distinct, that they were like grabbing the end of a cattle prod. Finally, my light found him, crumpled behind a Volkswagon-sized boulder, crushed up against a mass of brush. It looked as if a cloudburst's torrent raging down the arroyo had flung him into that spot, rather than a couple of thugs. The next storm would bury him.

"I heard…" he managed, but the sentence was cut short as I knelt beside him. I knew it was Pat Gabaldon by the stature and the clothing, but certainly not by the face. An enormous hematoma puffed the left side of his head, disfiguring the orbit into a purple mess. That damage hadn't been enough to satisfy his attackers. A deep, gaping slice began just in front of the ear and extended all the way to the tip of his jaw, and I could see the exposed bone.

"We're here now, Pat. Just lie still." That's all he could do. The effort to cry out had taken his last bit of strength, and I saw his shoulders sag as he slipped into unconsciousness.

Up above and behind me, a vehicle roared into the camp ground at the same time that brilliant red and blue lights pulsed across rocks and trees.

A door slammed, and I could hear the crunch of his boots as the deputy approached my vehicle.

"Thomas, over here in the arroyo!" I bellowed and waved my light so it criss-crossed the tree limbs above my head. As soon as his stocky figure appeared haloed by the revolving lights, I stood up long enough to bark a string of orders.

"We need an ambulance ASAP, and then whatever bandages you have in the unit. Big ones. Some of those big pads. And a blanket."

"You got it."

He disappeared and I knelt back down. "Just hang in there, buddy," I whispered, but there was no response. I touched the side of the young man's neck, feeling a thin, thready pulse.

Seconds later, Pasquale's light added to mine. He handed me the blanket, then bent close, keeping the beam out of Patrick's eyes. He examining the wound even as he tore open the first four inch gauze pad.

"We don't want to move his head," I said.

"This'll help," Pasquale said, and wormed a fist-sized rock out from under the young man's right cheek. I backed out of the way a bit. "Make things a little better," he said, and rested one hand on Patrick's forehead, gently, just to make a connection. "Can you hear my voice?" He reached around and lifted Pat's right eye lid as he said that, but gained no response. "He's out." The deputy ripped open two more pads and pressed them against the jaw wound. "No easy way to do this mess. How did it happen?"

"I don't know."

"Let's use that," the deputy said, and took the blanket that he'd handed me. "What other injuries, you know?"

"No idea. The hematoma on the eye, and the cut throat. That's what I know."

Pasquale ran a hand from the back of Patrick's

skull down the center of his back, then down each leg. "Everything points right." He stood back, made a quick survey for blood, then shook open the blanket and let it waft down.

The deputy unsnapped the little mike from his shoulder epaulette. "PCS, three-oh-two."

"Go ahead, three-oh-two."

"Expedite ten-fifty-five this location. One male, age nineteen, severe head injuries, significant blood loss. Pulse is weak, respiration light and ragged. Victim is unresponsive."

"Ten-four."

"And notify three-ten and three-oh-eight that we'll be inbound with the subject of their earlier complaint."

"Ten-four."

Pasquale tucked the radio back into his belt. "It's going to seem like a long, long wait," he said.

Indeed it was. Mercifully, Pat Gabaldon was unconscious for most of the forty-five minutes. A groan or two, a spasmodic twitch or jerk, and that was it. The deputy and I kept a running stream of comfort and attention, making sure that if the young man did swim back to the surface, he wasn't greeted by dismal silence.

Eventually—it seemed like hours rather than minutes—we heard the approach of the heavy diesel emergency unit as it turned onto the county two-track.

"Three-oh-two, Rescue One is just leaving the highway. You're at the campground?"

"That's affirmative. Pull beyond my unit. We're all the way in the back."

"Ten-four."

With Patrick Gabaldon's future entirely out of my hands, I stepped away, making room for the two EMTs and the bulky gurney. Matty Finnegan, half-way down the arroyo slope with her bulk of equipment, paused to look hard at me.

"Are you all right, sir?"

"I'm fine," I said, and then added to the deputy, "I'll be at my truck."

Neither Bobby Torrez nor Estelle would call me while I was in the middle of this mess, but they'd be waiting for an update. Sure enough, Estelle answered her phone after the first ring. She listened without interruption until I was finished.

"Why there, I wonder."

"Maybe they'd been there before," I said. "Maybe they saw the campground sign and figured it was their last chance before the border. I don't know."

"Patrick wasn't able to speak?"

"No. We have a long, long list of unanswered questions, sweetheart." Tom Pasquale and the two EMTs appeared at the lip of the arroyo, maneuvering the gurney to the ambulance. "They're about to pull out. I'll be inbound with 'em as soon as Tom and I secure the radio."

"That's good. Bobby and I are here at the hospital, if you'll meet us there," Estelle said. "Some interesting developments."

"I'm not sure I can stand any more interesting things." I switched off and waited for the ambulance to leave. Pasquale approached, an aluminum clipboard in hand.

"The phone, sir?"

"We need your camera and tape first," I said.

"The Sheriff wants to keep an eye on this until we have the chance to sweep the area," he said, not looking altogether enchanted with that thought. "I'll just secure the road right at the highway. Taber comes on at midnight."

"I know it's a mess," I said, "but if there's a shoe or boot print to be had, we'll want it."

Holding the idiot end of the tape measure, I made my way back to the piñon on the slope.

"Ninety-seven feet, four inches," Tom shouted.

"Not a bad toss." I waited as he rewound the tape, and in a moment he appeared at my side. I turned the light on the tree, illuminating the little phone.

"Well, hell," he said. "This is amazing. How'd you do this stunt?"

"I dialed his number," I replied. "No rocket science involved."

"Jeez."

"I want photos of it in place, and then put it in an evidence bag without touching it. I'll take it with me. The sooner we can process prints, the better."

"You're shitting me," Thomas said, still in wonder. "How'd you find it, did you say?"

"I could hear the ring tone."

"Well, damn. That's pretty neat, sir." Shaking his head, he retraced his steps to his unit and fetched the bag. A good deal taller than I, Pasquale had no trouble tipping the phone into the bag using the end of his ball-point pen.

"Why would they throw it?" the deputy asked. He handed me the sealed bag.

"That's one of the interesting questions."

The dust from the ambulance still hung in the night as I bumped my way out of the canyon back to the state highway. I ambled along in my best think mode, arm out the window, slouched against the door, letting my mind roam. There was certainly no hurry, now that Patrick was in good hands. But that forty-five minutes of deep thought during the drive back to Posadas produced no epiphanies—just more fuming and fretting.

Part of my uneasiness was worrying about Patrick's injuries. Part of it was wondering what Herb Torrance was going to do, working into the fall months without the only two ranch hands he had. I'd call him from the hospital after I'd talked with Estelle and Robert. But the dark of that night kept reminding me that we didn't know what kind of cold-blooded freak we were dealing with.

It was seeing the undersheriff's Crown Victoria parked outside of the hospital's emergency room's double doors that added another round of bleak thoughts to my mood. It seemed a year rather than eighteen hours since I'd stood in George Payton's kitchen, looking down at the end of a life and the loss of an old friend. Estelle had promised "interesting developments" in that case, and I wasn't sure whether I wanted to hear them.

I parked behind Estelle's car, making sure I was clear of the ambulance lane. Ignoring all the instructional signs that guarded the *staff only* emergency room entrance, I went inside, grimacing at the strong wall of artificially cooled and perfumed air and the bright lights that had no regard for the natural time of day.

Chapter Nineteen

The emergency room waiting area was empty, only the television entertaining itself. Just beyond the emergency room itself, before the radiology suite, the doorway of an office marked *administration* was open, and I headed for that. The room was a private lounge of sorts where medical staff could duck inside for a few private moments of consultation or snoozing. Four uncomfortable stainless steel chairs lined each wall, all upholstered in institutional orange. A small table with telephone and coffee maker graced one corner. Other than a painting that hung above the phone table, a pastel of an improbable barn located in a rolling green place like Wisconsin, the room was sterile and naked.

Sheriff Bobby Torrez sat in two of the chairs, his big frame skewed sideways so that he could prop his boots up and rest his head against the wall. He appeared to be dozing, but I knew better.

Undersheriff Estelle Reyes-Guzman sat beside

a pudgy young man who appeared unreasonably neat and well-scrubbed for the hour. Louis Herrera was the hospital's staff pharmacist, and I knew that Estelle's husband had already head-hunted him away for the new clinic.

"Ah, sir," Estelle said when she saw me. She smoothed the pages of the hefty volume that she supported in her lap and then handed the tome to Herrera. "Tomás tells us that you worked a miracle."

Torrez's eyes opened. "Hey," he said, and let it go at that.

"You found Patrick by finding his phone," Estelle said. "That's impressive, sir."

"Well, you put a call through, and the damn thing rings." I handed the evidence bag to the sheriff. He regarded the small phone critically. "Might be some interesting prints on that."

"Patrick got lucky," the sheriff murmured.

"He's not my definition of lucky." I glanced at the wall clock and saw that it was coming up on 11:30. "He was out there a good long time."

"Could still be without this," Torrez said.

"So," I said. "You mentioned some developments?"

Estelle raised a small vial and extended it toward me.

"And this is…" The vial was small, heavily

tinted, about the size of an old-fashioned ink bottle. I knew better than to open it and sniff a deep breath, but I did unscrew the top gingerly and regarded the fine white crystals inside, as unremarkable in appearance, to me at least, as sugar, salt, or cocaine. The label was beyond the powers of even my trifocals, but I squinted at it anyway.

"Histamine diphosphate," Louis Herrera said. "I was just telling the officers that it's classified as a chemical, rather than a drug. We keep it in the compounding room, normally. Don't take a taste."

"Sir," Estelle said, "Tony Abeyta is over at the university, and he called not long ago. They found substantial amounts of this chemical in the wine that was spilled on the floor, and in the portion remaining in the glass. Nothing in the bottle."

I looked at her for a long moment, completely lost. She took that opportunity to pull out a small notebook and thumb through the pages until she found what she wanted. "Here's the problem," she said. "They wanted to establish a histamine level in the body fluids. They're thinking to trace whether or not there was an allergic reaction of some sort."

"That's going to take days," Herrera said, shaking his head. "Forty-eight hours at least for blood histamines, anyway."

"And that's the trouble," Estelle said quickly. "The lab here? They have never actually *done* a quantitative histamine test, sir. It's not something that's routinely done when a battery of blood tests or urine tests is called for. They don't even have a protocol established for how to go about it."

"That's about right," Herrera agreed.

"Histamines," I said, sounding like a damn parrot. "We *are* talking about an allergic reaction here, then. Just what I've been saying."

"Not in the food, though," Torrez muttered, and his quiet voice startled me. He hadn't been snoozing.

I handed the bottle to Louis Herrera before I dropped it, and the resulting sneezing attack killed off half of Posadas County. "I don't follow any of this."

"Sir, the lab in Albuquerque found significant amounts of histamine diphosphate in the wine. Not in the burrito, not in the chile, not in the bottle of wine…but in the *spilled* wine, and in the glass," Estelle said patiently.

I looked at Herrera for confirmation. "That could do it?"

"Oh, by all means, sir." He leaned forward, staring at the little jar. "When we get stung by a wasp or have a reaction to gluten, for example… almost anything that we happen to be allergic to? The body produces a flood of histamines." He shook the bottle. "This stuff occurs naturally in the system. Not in this crystalline form, of course, but histamines are a big part of our protein chemistry. They flood the system and trigger metabolic reactions to foreign proteins. In the worst case scenario, what they trigger is anaphylactic shock."

"What if I took a spoonful of that stuff?" I asked.

"A *spoonful?* My God. You know, if they're lucky, the lab can test for this, but the results would be read in something like nanamoles per liter. That's not much. I mean, a nana-anything is one *billionth.* A bee sting is enough to kill a person who's deeply allergic to that particular protein. We're talking *tiny* amounts here, not spoonfuls."

"Nobody is going to spike food with nanamoles," I said. "What would a spoonful do?"

Herrera shrugged. "Ever been stung repeatedly by a 1,000- pound wasp?"

"Come on."

"I'm serious, sir."

"How fast does that stuff act?"

"About instantly."

I looked over at the undersheriff. "What are you thinking?"

"I'm thinking that someone put this chemical, or one like it, in the wine, sir. We'll know for certain when the blood and fluid tests are completed.

Maybe sometime late tomorrow, if we're very, very lucky. There's a lot of midnight oil being burned, but it's a whole new set of problems for the lab."

"A bunch of this stuff dumped into the wine wouldn't be noticed?" I frowned. "Hell, *I'd* notice it. Well, I think I would. Maybe not."

"Unlikely," the pharmacist said. "For one thing, histamine diphosphate is incredibly soluble." He held up the bottle again. "This is five grams, more or less, but I gotta tell ya…I could dump the whole thing in a few CC's of water, and it would dissolve immediately. No problem. One of your tablespoons in an eight-ounce glass…" He waved his hand like vapors in the air. "Dissolve right away. No taste." Then he grimaced. "Not that you'd have time to notice."

"Just dump it in, maybe swirl with a spoon."

"That would do it. Don't lick the spoon, though."

"Seriously?"

"Dead serious. The mucus membranes are the easiest route into the body's systems. Look, somebody messing with this stuff…that's scary business. For one thing, I can't imagine how anyone would be able to procure this," and he held up the bottle of chemical. "It isn't for sale. It's not on the street. At least, it *better* not be. It's not the sort of thing where a *little* bit would give a buzz." A fleeting grin touched his face. "Well, it'd be a buzz, all right. Once."

"What's the diphosphate part do?" I asked.

"That's just a chemical binder," the pharmacist said. "Something to carry the histamine radical."

"Makes it packageable?"

"Exactly so."

"So you can dump it into food, cook the stuff, and no one is the wiser."

"No...you *can't* do that, sir," Louis said quickly. "Histamine is an amino acid. Remember your biology? The old 'building blocks' of the cell?" He leaned forward, enjoying the lecture. He waggled the bottle at me. "Like all amino acids, this is *extremely* heat sensitive. Heat's the enemy. You go cooking this, it would be destroyed."

"Alcohol wouldn't destroy it?"

Herrera shrugged dubiously. "Probably not. Not the amount that's in wine, anyway. Even if some of it lost its kick, there would be plenty left over to do the job."

I looked at Estelle, but not a flicker touched her poker face. I could make a million with her as my partner in Las Vegas. I knew that she could see the little door opening, and so could Bobby Torrez. He hadn't shifted position, but now watched us like an interested cat. He moved his feet and pushed one of the chairs toward me.

Crossing my arms over my belly, I tried to make myself comfortable in the awful little chair with its hard arm rests and slippery plastic cover. "Let me give you a scenario, Louis." He looked puzzled. "What happens? Suppose I dump a tablespoon or two of this into a glass of wine. The victim drinks it. What happens?"

Louis' face screwed up in imagined pain. "Wow. This isn't a little reaction to cat hair we've got here, sir. And see, the trouble with a histaminic reaction is that so much of the body is affected." Still holding the nasty little jar a bit too casually for my liking, he jabbed the first two fingers of both hands into his neck, under his jawbone. "Like I said, the soft tissues of the mouth make a great pathway. The salivary glands kick in, the throat constricts, the pulse races, the blood vessels dilate. That's all serious stuff. But what you're suggesting with this?" He shook his head. "Spoonfuls? Kapowee."

"Kapowee," I repeated, knowing exactly what the young man meant.

"Yep," he said. "That would be one nasty ride. For a few seconds, anyway."

I glanced at Estelle, and I'm sure that she could see the anger in my eyes. She knew as well as I did that George Payton's final moments hadn't been a peaceful "passing away."

Chapter Twenty

"So," Estelle mused, "if tests confirm the presence of excessive histamines in Mr. Payton's body that match the source in the wine, we're left with some interesting questions."

"You think there's any doubt?" I paused. "Okay, after listening to Louis, I'm convinced. Either there was chemical added to the wine, or there wasn't. It's that simple, it seems to me. The questions are who…and when." I took a deep breath. "And why."

Pharmacist Louis Herrera shifted uncomfortably in his chair, as if just knowing about histamine diphosphate made him somehow guilty by association.

"Ricardo Mondragon delivered the food from the restaurant to Payton's house," Torrez said. He rested his elbows on his knees, his left hand supporting his head, and stared at the floor. "He says that when he got there, the old man was up and around, drinkin' wine."

"Ricardo isn't capable of any of this," I said. "And if someone intercepted his delivery, he would have told us."

"You think?"

"I know," I said. "For one thing, he would have no reason to hide that bit of information if he was privy to it. And regardless of what else might or might not go on in his head, Ricardo has his loyalties to the Don Juan and its customers. That job is his life."

Torrez straightened up and continued his examination of Pat Gabaldon's cell phone through the plastic bag. "Somebody stopped by Payton's after that. Enough time to distract George for a few minutes with something, enough time to spike the wine. I mean, how long would that take? A few seconds?"

"I have no brainstorms at the moment," I said, and turned to Estelle. "Do you?"

"No, sir. You were supposed to go over to his house, but didn't. From the moment Ricardo delivered the food, at about 11:50, until Phil Borman found the body around one-thirty or so gives us a considerable window of opportunity."

"And that's assuming that Phil Borman ain't lyin'," Torrez interjected.

"The histamine could have been put in the wine at any time…not even today, necessarily."

"Come on," I said, feeling miserable. "Maggie or Phil wouldn't…" and I interrupted myself, knowing I was just talking to make noise. We all knew that there was no accounting for people's motivations, no matter how affable, or good natured, or altruistic they appeared to their neighbors and business associates.

The room fell silent, and I could hear the hum of the little electric clock on the wall above the phone.

I broke the silence. "Where would I buy some of that?" I asked Louis, nodding at the histamine.

"Well, you wouldn't," he said. "Someone with an appropriate license would buy it from a pharmaceutical supplier."

"Then where would I *get* it? Where would I steal it, if I had to?"

Herrera hesitated, turning the bottle this way and that. "Well, I suppose it depends on how desperate you were. *We*…I mean here at the hospital… we store it in the compounding room behind the pharmacy. That's secure, but it isn't Fort Knox. There are times when someone could walk in. If they knew just what they were looking for, and where to look, it would only take a second to snatch the bottle."

He brightened at a memory. "In fact, I worked at a place when I was in college where a back door from the pharmacy opened right into the alley. Lots of times in the summer, they'd keep it open for the air."

"You use it often? That stuff, I mean."

"Ah, no. In all honesty, I haven't used it since I started here. That's a year and a half."

"But if you did…" I primed.

"The only use that I'm familiar with is the compound where we mix histamine diphosphate with—well, basically, caffeine. Pharmaceutical caffeine, of course." He grinned. "We don't just dump a tablespoon of this into black coffee."

"And used for what?"

"Well, it'd be helpful to talk with Doctor Guzman or Perrone, but basically it's used as a treatment for multiple sclerosis patients. The histamine-caffeine combination acts as some sort of neural trigger." He laced his fingers together around the little bottle. "That's the theory, anyway. The compound somehow establishes the neural pathway that the MS destroys." He shrugged. "I don't think anyone actually knows *how* it works, and sometimes it doesn't. But when it *does,* the results can be pretty spectacular."

"Multiple sclerosis," Estelle repeated.

"Right."

"That's all the histamine diphosphate that you have?"

"That's it." He hesitated. "Here in Posadas, I'd think that there are only two places to get this. One is here. The other is over at Posadas Pharmacy.

Gus Trombley would have some, certainly. You might want to talk with him. That's kind of an old-fashioned store, and he's an old-fashioned kind of guy." He paused, and I wasn't sure that he'd meant the comment as a compliment. "He doesn't think much of us."

"That's because you're the new kid on the block," I said. "He's had Posadas County to himself for thirty-five years."

"And he's had his way of doing things for that long, too," the young man said diplomatically. He held up both hands helplessly. "I've told you the sum total of what I know about this stuff. Like I said, I'd be happy to do some more research on it. See what I can come up with."

"We appreciate that, Louis," Estelle said. "Anything at all beyond what you've already told us."

He looked at his watch, and then heavenward. "If there's nothing else…"

Estelle reached across and extended her hand, shaking his warmly. "Thanks, Louis. Thanks for dragging out so late."

"I'll survive," he laughed. "Now that I'm here, what I should do is spend a few hours in my office. I've got a stack of inventory control forms about like this," and he held his hand two feet off the floor. "Get a head start."

"We'd appreciate your keeping all of this confidential."

He frowned at her in good-natured reproof. "You don't need to tell me that, ma'am." He shook hands with Bobby and me, and closed the lounge door behind him as he left.

"So we have the means," I said. "That's if the blood work corroborates the idea. Mix some histamine diphosphate in the wine, and there you go. That would take just a few seconds." I took a deep breath. "And that means that someone is a real opportunist."

It would be midnight by the time we reached Guy Trombley's pharmacy. He'd be grumpy but cooperative...and inquisitive at the odd hour. "Do you want to call Guy, or do I?" I said, looking first at Estelle and then at the sheriff. "Or do you want to wait for a few hours and catch him in a better mood? I don't see much point in waiting, if you're willing."

"I don't care what mood he's in," Torrez said. "There's things we need to find out."

"Absolutely," Estelle agreed. "And another thing that can't wait. If we're right about all this, there's likely a little bottle of histamine diphosphate floating around somewhere. I'd hate to see the top come off of that."

"That would put somebody's garbage-raiding mutt into orbit," I said.

"That's exactly it," Estelle said. "What do we do with an empty bottle? We toss it in the trash."

"There's not a lot we can do about that," I said. "Everything ends up in the landfill." Estelle's eyebrows puckered in a frown, and I had visions of all of us, like a flood of rats, ransacking the heaps of garbage at the landfill, looking for one tiny bottle.

"I'll call Guy," Torrez said, and pushed himself to his feet, headed for the end table where he rummaged through the phone book for a moment and then dialed. After half a dozen rings, he frowned and then looked at me with exasperation.

"Guy," he said, "this is Sheriff Torrez. Get back to me ASAP." He rattled off his cell phone number and then hung up. "Damn answering machines," he said, and mimicked a mechanical voice. 'If this is an emergency, please dial 9-1-1.'"

"You can't blame him, Bobby. I bet it gets old with all the hypochondriacs calling for aspirin in the middle of the night."

Torrez yawned and gazed thoughtfully at the clock. "I'll go over to his house and shake him out of bed," he said. "Meet you at the drug store in a few minutes?" Before either of us had a chance to answer, a knuckle rapped on the door, and Torrez stepped across and opened it.

Dr. Francis Guzman leaned against the door jamb, looking as tired as the rest of us.

"Hey, guys," he said. "We have an ambulance inbound from an accident east of here on the interstate. Before we get wound up with that, I wanted to let you know about Patrick Gabaldon." He held his hand to the left side of his head. "He was hit twice, really hard…hairline skull fractures and some subdural hematoma and brain swelling that's a worry. We have him stabilized now and are looking to airlift him to University Hospital as soon as we can."

"Is he conscious?" I asked, and Francis shook his head. "What about the neck wound?"

"He lost a lot of blood, but whoever assaulted him didn't work it just right." The doctor held his left index finger on the angle of his own jaw, then drew a line along his jaw until he touched the point of his chin. "Ran right along his jaw bone, but that protected the major vessels. Nasty, but manageable."

"So he can't talk to us," I said.

"No. Not the way we have him sedated. It's going to be touch and go. Whoever hit him really tagged him a good one. Twice. *Really* hard." Francis patted the door jamb as he pushed himself upright.

"Hit him with what? Any guesses?"

"I have no idea," Francis replied. "There were no distinguishable marks, and the wound is not really focused, the way being swatted with a lug wrench would be. You're looking for something blunt, maybe kinda flat. That's as good as it gets at the moment. Okay?"

"You bet. Thanks."

"I saw Louis out in the hallway," the physician said. "In the past ten years, I think I've treated half a dozen patients where I prescribed the H-C cocktail. It's not common, by any means. Not here, anyway."

"We need a list of those," Torrez said.

"Not even with a warrant, Bobby. We just don't do that."

The sheriff actually smiled. "I know you don't," he said affably. "I just said that was something we *needed.* Didn't say we were going to get it."

Chapter Twenty-one

I'd been inside Guy Trombley's drug store a thousand times in the past three decades. With the passing of the years, chasing various health episodes had threatened to become a major hobby of mine. I'd never considered Trombley's Posadas Pharmacy as particularly old-fashioned, any more than I thought of myself as aging—unless I looked in the mirror or started to push myself from a low-slung chair. It wasn't hard to imagine that Louis Herrera, a youthful, progressive pharmacist, might regard Posadas Pharmacy and its long-time owner as relics.

Comfortable is what the place was. All the aromas, most of them pleasant, mingled into a good, solid, dependable potpourri. I knew where I was when I walked into Guy's place, even recognized most of the teenaged counter attendants. The floor was old-fashioned, well-oiled wood that squeaked a welcome.

With construction of the Guzman/Perrone clinic, Trombley's would no longer be the only retail pharmacological game in town. I doubted that he'd deign to lower his monopolistic prices with the competition.

We stood quietly and watched while Guy fumbled with the keys for both the door and the alarm system. At one point, he stopped and twisted his tall, gangling form toward me. "I wouldn't do this for just anybody," he whispered, as if the streets had ears. He turned 180 degrees so Estelle could hear him. "Not just anybody."

"We appreciate it, sir," she said.

"I'm not even going to ask why all this can't wait until a reasonable hour," he said. His voice reminded me of a banjo. "But I'm *sure* that the sheriff has his reasons." He grinned at me as the door clicked open. "Robert isn't coming over? He was the one who called me."

"Ah, no," I said. "He decided that the two of us could handle you all right."

Trombley barked a laugh. "Well, then, here we are." He bowed and ushered us both inside. "My kingdom." He closed the door behind him, clicked the dead bolt shut, and palmed a four-switch panel for the lights. The fluorescents tinkled and blinked into life. "Now what can I do for the minions of the law?" He held up a hand before either of us had a chance to answer. "You know, nothing would taste better right now than a cup of coffee. Do you mind if I take a moment to put on a pot?"

"Oh, I never touch the stuff," I said, and Trombley guffawed again.

"Just herbal tea now, eh?" he chortled. "I know *you're* not to be tempted," he said to Estelle. "But I have Earl Grey, Oolong, and some other stuff that's mostly chopped up flower beds if you're in the mood."

"No, thank you, sir. But we really appreciate you coming down to meet us," Estelle said.

We followed him through the aisles, around a tall counter, and two steps up to the pharmacists' work counter. From this spot, Guy could look out over his domain. In a moment, he had the drip brewer hard at work, and I was beginning to think that a hot bagel with cream cheese would go nicely. He rubbed his hands in anticipation. "Now, then."

"We're interested in a particular chemical," Estelle said. Trombley tilted his head back, locking her in focus through his half glasses, his ruddy, pocked face a mask of serious interest. "Histamine diphosphate."

Trombley's head sank back down until his head rested on his chest, his eyes never leaving Estelle's face. He watched as she consulted her notebook. "Histamine diphosphate," she repeated.

His sparse eyebrows raised, and he cocked his head. "That's a little off the wall, sheriff."

"Yes," she agreed, and let her explanation go with that. "I'd appreciate whatever information you can give us."

"You've talked to your husband, or to young Herrera?" He asked the question with enough tact that it sounded more self-deprecating than anything else.

"Briefly." Estelle didn't elaborate.

"I see." Guy looked across at me, then back over his shoulder at the coffee pot. It was thinking, but hadn't produced much. "I sincerely hope that's not the new street craze, folks. If it is, you guys are going to be picking up a lot of dead bodies."

"We hope it isn't," I said.

"Well, while we're waiting for this pokey thing, let me show you where I keep ours. It's back in the compounding area. Histamine diphosphate isn't a drug, per se, you know. Your husband might have already told you all this, I suppose. It's really just a chemical that is compounded *into* a treatment. Never administered by itself."

He moved past me toward the steps. "Follow me this way," he said. "The drug you mention has been shown to be efficacious sometimes in the treatment of multiple sclerosis. That's its major claim to fame."

"It's ingested orally? The treatment, I mean?" I asked as we followed him through a narrow passageway to a tiny room in the back. Except for a touch of gray where dust touched unused flat surfaces, the place was tidy, with a gadget at one end that looked like a hi-tech bead-blasting chamber.

Trombley shook his head. "Oh, no. Through a skin patch. Like those things you wear to stop smoking."

"So the histamine diphosphate is easily absorbed through the skin, then."

"Indeed it is," Trombley said. "And that's how we can keep the dose *very* small, and *very* controlled." He ran a hand along a shelf, ticking off the jars and boxes. "It's pretty squirrelly stuff, folks. Histamine is a natural chemical in the body, as I'm sure you're aware. That's what triggers the body's response mechanism in allergies, for instance." He turned his head to cough once into his cupped hand, a loud, racking ratchet that didn't sound good.

He continued his own personal guided tour of the shelves, working his way downward through the alphabet. "Ah, here we are," he said, pulling a small bottle off the shelf. He handed it to Estelle. "Don't open it."

She twisted it this way and that, scanning the label. "This says haloperidol powder, Mr. Trombley. Is that the same thing?"

"Hardly," he replied, reaching hastily for the bottle. He squinted at it, looked heavenward, and turned around muttering, "Don't ever, ever get old, either one of you." I knew exactly what he'd done. The eyes see the target, but the hand and the attention drift a bit. I did that very thing at the supermarket, sometimes arriving home with a truly puzzling substitution for what I'd intended.

"It's too late for me," I said.

"Lest you think the wrong thing," Trombley said as he bent down to scan the inventory, "I do have a system of checks that would have prevented my mixing the wrong stuff in a batch for a patient. But…" and his voice trailed off. Estelle stood quietly in the corner, watching him.

"What's the haloperidol used for?" I asked.

"It's a heavy-duty tranquilizer," he said, still looking. "Various psychotic disorders call for it by injection. Sometimes by caplet or tablet. Wouldn't do much good in a patch. Well, damn." I heard the crack of his knee joints. "This is where the histamine diphosphate *should* be," he said, "and I don't understand why it's not." He tapped an empty spot on the shelf. He exhaled an irritated mutter, and I glanced at Estelle. Her face remained expressionless.

"Okay," Guy said, "Excuse me for a minute." He slipped past me and headed back for his work bench. "Bill, the coffee's ready."

"Perfect," I said, and wandered after him, taking in the sights. Other than dark corners, mops, utility sink, and piles of boxes, there wasn't much to see. I stepped up to his work counter. From here, he could look down on the tops of his customers' heads. I wondered if the superior position was necessary for him.

The pharmacist was bent over the keyboard, but without looking away from the computer's screen lifted a hand to point at the coffee maker. "Cups are down below. Help yourself. Pour me one, too, if you will. No additives. I like to use the green cup with the sunflowers."

"Done." As I stepped past him, I looked over his shoulder at the computer screen. He was scrolling down through what appeared to be an inventory list.

"We don't just run out of drugs," he said, rapping keys and waiting with obvious impatience. "We just don't. That's supposedly one of the great things about these damn gadgets. When I invoice out a prescription, all of the information goes in and modifies the inventory list here, right then and there. Then the *order* list is modified for restocking." He straightened up enough to take the cup I handed him. "Just like a hardware store," he added. "Just as if we were card-carrying members of the twenty-first century."

He shifted his half glasses to bring the screen into focus, adopting that characteristic scrinched up, bared teeth expression that goes with trying to read fine print.

"Huh," he grunted. "The last time I compounded *Histolatum...* that's the particular application that I use with histamine diphosphate and caffeine citrated..." He scrunched his face up some more, putting a finger on the computer screen to follow a line across. "The last time was May 10," He stood back. "In the drug business, that's ancient history."

"So it's been the better part of six months," I said.

"Does the chemical have a shelf life?" Estelle asked. She stood on the lower level, looking up at us like an expectant customer.

"Sure it does," the pharmacist replied. "Probably a couple of years. And the computer knows all about that, too. The reorder would have been automatic. This shows," and he touched the screen, "that the inventory for histamine diphosphate was virtually new in May when I compounded that prescription."

"And none since then."

"No." He beckoned. "Now, let me check again," he said. "Let's give senility its due. I might have reshelved it improperly." Once more, we trooped after him and watched while he searched the shelves. He shifted boxes and bottles this way and that, even surveying well beyond the "H" section. After a few moments, he stood up and held up both hands in surrender. "It's gone." His eyes continued to scan the shelves. "Now, I have to ask," he said. "You've come here in the middle of the night, asking for a chemical that I see now is obviously missing from my inventory." He turned to gaze at Estelle. "I've told you nothing about histamine diphosphate that your husband or Louis couldn't. So I'm assuming that you're looking into illicit use."

"Who else has access to this room, sir?"

"*Access?*" He held up his hands in puzzlement. "*I* work back here. The kids," and he waved a hand toward the front, "They never do. Other than taking trash out to the dumpsters, there's no reason for them to ever be back here." What an interesting way to describe the place as wide open, I thought.

"You have an assistant, though," I said.

"Of course. Harriet Tomlinson has worked for me for years, as you well know. But she does none of the compounding. I'm the only one who does that."

"Is this area ever unattended?" Estelle asked. The sweep of her hand indicated the pharmacist's counter including the computer, the general area of drug storage, and the small back work room.

"When we're open, either Harriet is here in the back at the prescription counter, or I am," Guy said flatly. "But *I'm* the only one who actually does any compounding back here. Harriet cleans up once in a while."

I knew that his first remark wasn't true, just as was Fernando Aragon's protestation that he would never use canned chile as part of the *burrito grande*. On many occasions here, I had dropped off a prescription to have it filled, and it had waited for half a day. Guy might be off at the links, or at a Rotary luncheon, or who the hell knows where. Harriet had her own errands. There the prescription sat, waiting for the return of one or both of them.

There were times when it would be simple enough to stroll toward the back of the store, and then, while the register attendant was dealing with another customer up front, slip around the corner to this small room.

I stepped to the compounding room's door and peered out. The door that led outside to the alley was steel, with no dents or gouges around the locks. In addition to the keyed deadbolt, it had a hefty sliding steel bar.

"Nobody has broken in," Guy said. "If they had, you or the village police would have heard about it."

He watched Estelle, who had pulled her small digital camera out of its belt holster. "Now what?"

"Sir," Estelle said, and knelt down close to the shelving. "I'd like to take a photo of this area." Even I could see what intrigued her. A jar of something had once taken up the tiny space between the haliperidol and what I could see now was labeled as hydrocortisone powder. Someone had removed that jar, leaving a nice little dust-free circle about the size of an ink bottle.

"In May," the undersheriff asked, adjusting the camera for the odd light. "You said May was the last time you compounded the histolatum?"

"Yes." Guy Trombley's answer was considerably more guarded now, his manner less casual and affable.

"Would it be a violation of privacy to ask who the patient was?" I asked.

"Of course it would be," Guy said, and coughed again. He looked at me over his half-glasses, and his fishy blue eyes were amused. "But if I can't trust you two, then the world might as well stop spinning right now. The patient has passed on, anyway. You remember Norma Scott? She passed away here a while back, first part of the summer. She was the last patient I compounded the histo-latum for. The MS didn't kill her, though. She had a massive stroke."

"Ah," I said. "I don't remember." Every once in a while, I heard about someone in Posadas whom I didn't know, and it always surprised me.

"Well, that's the last time I've prepared that particular compound. Months ago, now." He watched Estelle take several more photos of the empty spot on the shelf. "Where's this all going?"

There were a couple dozen ways I could have answered that simple question, but at this point it was convenient to remember that none of this was any of my official business. No one was injecting cattle with histamine diphosphate. "I wish I knew," I replied.

"Now wait a minute," Guy said. "If this affects me or my store—or my drugs—then I have every right to know."

"Yes, you do, sir," Estelle said, and pushed herself back to her feet. "We have evidence that histamine diphosphate was involved in an incident earlier. We'd like to know where the chemical came from."

The pharmacist regarded Estelle without expression. "And?"

"And that's all I can tell you at the moment, sir."

"What kind of 'incident', sheriff?"

I wondered how Estelle was going to side-step that question, since I couldn't imagine that she wanted to discuss George Payton's death while the investigation was so preliminary.

"At any time in the past week or two, can you recollect anyone other than yourself or Mrs. Tomlinson back here?" she asked.

"No, I can't." Guy's impatience grew. "That door," and he pointed at the compounding room's entrance, "is always closed unless *I* happen to be working back here. None of the clerks ever come in here. They have no need to. And you still haven't answered my question. What prompts all this, anyway? What's important enough to justify skulking about in the middle of the night? You mention an 'incident', and that's all you can tell me?"

"We're not skulking, Guy," I said. "But you know the drill."

"Well, in this case, I *don't* know the drill, Bill. Somebody's been in here, and it looks like they helped themselves to a dangerous chemical. My God, man, I don't think I can impress on you enough just how lethal this stuff can be. I mean, it makes rattlesnake venom look like weak tea."

"We understand that, sir," Estelle said patiently. "We appreciate your cooperation."

"And that's it?"

"That's it. At the moment. We're asking your cooperation and discretion in this."

Guy looked across at me, then back at Estelle. "And if it turns out that I had a moment of brain fade and just shelved the chemical incorrectly?"

"Then I hope you'll tell us immediately," Estelle said. "And if you should find it, please let us know *before* you touch the bottle, sir."

"Because?"

"Because we'll be looking for fingerprints, sir." She handed him one of her cards, but he waved it off.

"For heaven's sakes, I know where you live, work, and even play," he said.

"Yes, sir," she said, holding the card out until he took it with considerable impatience. "If something comes up, or you remember something else, please feel free to call that cell number any time, rather than going through dispatch."

Guy Trombley scrutinized the card, slowly shaking his head. "Is this involving something going on over at the school?"

"We certainly hope not, sir."

He huffed a sigh. "Well, I hope to God not. Teenagers today are a new breed to me." I saw his jaw set a fraction, and his gaze wandered toward the front of the store. I supposed he was already indicting his counter help.

"We'll get back with you, Guy," I offered. "Give us some time."

Chapter Twenty-two

I left the undersheriff at her office just as the clock flipped to one a.m. She didn't need me hanging around, pretending I was still sheriff. And maybe with no distractions she'd be able to break away for home, where Irma Sedillos, the ever-patient *nana*, was tending the roost.

With a full cup of coffee from the Handiway, I headed south again. As I passed the county road that led toward Borracho Springs, I looked for Deputy Jackie Taber's county unit, but didn't see it. That didn't surprise me. She would find a discreet spot and blend with the night shadows, hiding even the bright white paint of her Bronco.

A few minutes later, I followed the winding driveway through the scrub and the cacti to Herb Torrance's H-Bar-T. The lights were on in the house, and the Chrysler was parked in the circular drive with Herb's older Chevy pickup pulled in behind it.

A pair of cats streaked across the yard and disappeared through the fence. By the time I'd parked behind the pickup, Herb had appeared at the door and beckoned. Apparently sleep was eluding him, too.

"Jesus, Bill," he said. "What a goddamn day." Socks the cow dog tried to wedge his head through the rancher's legs, and Herb pushed him back. "Git," he snapped.

"How's the boy?"

"Dale's all right. You know," and he held the door open wide for me, a boot still in the dog's face. "When the sheriff called sayin' that you'd found Patrick, you could have knocked me down with a feather. I guess I'll stop by the hospital in the morning." He looked sharply at me. "He's all right, ain't he?"

"We don't know yet, Herb. Someone did for him, that's for sure. It looks like a skull fracture, with some bleeding on the brain." I shook my head wearily. "And you can save your drive to town. They airlifted him to Albuquerque."

"Son of a bitch." He reached out and took my cup, and I followed him into the kitchen. "Torrez said you found him over to Borracho Springs."

"Yep. We need to locate his folks," I said. "I thought you could help me with that."

"Well, now, I think I can. Now I don't have the phone number or nothing like that, but I know they work for the Martin farms over to Hatch. They were seasonal for 'em, but they went to full time here not long ago. Got their papers and such." He poured my coffee carefully. "You want me to call 'em?"

"Actually, I think Estelle or Bobby should, Herb. They have all the details and can answer any questions that Pat's folks might have. I'll pass on the information about the Martins to them, and they can make it official."

"I'm with ya on that," Herb said, and the relief in his voice was obvious. "His folks will sure want to know." He heaved a great sigh. "Well, shit." He took a long pull of the coffee, looking out into the distance. "This is sure as hell a fix, ain't it."

"We'll do what we can, Herb. We have a description, we know exactly when the thieves crossed the border with the truck, and we have a guess about where they might be headed. That's a start."

"I suppose," he said. "Naranjo be any help, you think?"

"We'll see." There was no point in sounding mindlessly optimistic. How efficient the Mexican police would be was anyone's guess, and Herb knew that. He also knew that our various agencies couldn't just charge cross the border, taking the Mexican law into our own hands. The political line in the dirt didn't mean diddly damn to the coyotes, cacti, or creosote bush, but the humans who lived along both sides of the border knew that the line sure as hell complicated *their* lives.

Even in their rural district, Captain Tomás Naranjo and his officers lived with a nightmare of drug cartel violence that made our incident seem like an unimportant blip on the statistical chart. But he'd do what he could, deft, politic, even subtle when he needed to be. The captain possessed an interesting sense of justice that wasn't necessarily driven by the letter of the law—either Mexican law or ours. That's what I was depending on in this case.

"You know…" Herb took his time lighting a cigarette. He regarded the blue heeler, who had settled in the living room, near the door. "I don't give a shit about the truck."

"I understand that."

"I want those sons-a-bitches behind bars, Bill. Or buried out in the desert somewheres. Whoever hammered that boy? You know, Pat's a good kid. A *good* kid. Been good for my Dale. Kind of steady, you know? Anything I can do to help, well, you just speak up."

"You know I will."

"Fill up?" He reached for my cup again, and I obliged. "Where are you headed at this hour, anyways?"

"I wanted to chat with Victor," I replied.

Herb's laugh turned into a racking cough, and he had to wipe his eyes. "Good luck with that," he managed. "He can be just about the most god-damned unpleasant son-of-a-bitch I know."

"Just misunderstood," I said, and Herb laughed again.

"He don't think much of cops."

"Victor has his reasons."

"Suppose he does. His son and all." Herb didn't delve into that miserable night several years before when Victor's eldest son, Carlos, had been killed, but even long before that, Victor had perfected his impression of a miserable, short-tempered saloon keeper.

I left the Torrance ranch, and for a few miles the night was dark and quiet. Sidewinder personality or not, Victor enjoyed a thriving business at his Broken Spur saloon. I counted eight vehicles in the parking lot, and for Posadas County during the wee hours of the morning, that qualified as hopping.

Victor's Cadillac—one of those older models that looked as if someone had chopped off the hindquarters with a cleaver—was parked behind the back kitchen door and the double-wide trailer where the saloon owner lived with his youngest son. Victor Junior worked in the kitchen of the Broken Spur, trying hard both to do as he was told and stay out of his father's way.

I shut off the SUV and headed for the back door of the kitchen, knowing damn well that my entrance there would prompt acid comments from Victor. Pulling open the door, I saw his son at the sink, doing something with carrots. His father stood in front of the huge gas stove, watching eggs fry in pools of sizzling butter. He glanced at me as I entered.

"We got a front door," Victor said almost affably. "You lookin' for handouts or what?"

"Those eggs look tempting." He flipped them expertly, then reached out with the stainless steel spatula and chopped a series of rows through a pile of hash browns. At the same time he reached up and pulled a plate off the rack. Four strips of bacon joined the eggs and potatoes, and he slid the loaded plate on the prep table.

"Order up," he said, and Victor Junior jumped to deliver the goods.

Victor wiped his hands thoughtfully. He turned and looked at the clock, his expression not lost on me. Minutes before closing, he didn't want interruptions.

"Somebody tried to kill Patrick Gabaldon," I said. "They took Herb's truck and trailer, bashed Pat in the head, cut his throat, and then headed for Mexico. They dumped the boy in an arroyo over at Borracho Springs."

Without comment, Victor scraped the grill. The frown on his broad, homely face deepened, and he racked the big spatula with more force than necessary. "Christine said you were looking for him earlier."

"He's been lying out there for hours, Victor, and he sure as hell didn't need to be. They airlifted him to Albuquerque."

He wiped his hands on his apron again. "What do you want?"

"For one thing, I need to know if you or anyone here saw Patrick earlier. We're trying to nail down some of the details here. We don't know if Pat picked up a couple of hitch-hikers, or what. We think that the actual assault happened up on the mesa. Up on Herb's grazing allotment."

"How'd you get mixed up in all this?"

"I cut the permit for moving the cattle, Victor. That's what Patrick was doing when he was attacked. But we're all mixed up in it."

"What's he say?"

"Patrick, you mean? He can't talk yet," I said. "Look, this is a simple thing, Victor. You either saw him, or you didn't. That's all I want to know."

He took his time turning off the stove as if it were a ceremony demanding serious attention. "I get along by minding my own business," he said finally.

"Oh, for Christ's sakes, Victor." His son had returned to the kitchen and looked apprehensive. "That's what Patrick was doing, too. He maybe thought he was doing a good deed by picking up a couple hitchhikers. They tried to kill him, they stole Herb's rig, and they drove it to Mexico."

"Then you need to talk to your buddy down there."

"Naranjo will do what he can. Look…" and I moved over so that I could lean my hip against the prep table, my arms folded. I knew there was no point in trying to bully Victor, or threaten him. But for all his attitude, he was an intelligent man. "All I want to know is if you saw Patrick earlier in the day. Goddamn it, it's not like you're a priest giving away the secrets of confession."

Victor surprised me by laughing—not much of one, mind you, but enough to show some gold.

"So what's your stake in all this?" he asked. "You're not sheriff anymore, last I looked."

I regarded him in silence for a moment. "Nope, I'm not sheriff anymore."

"Still runnin' around in the middle of the night, though." He glanced at the clock again, a not-so-subtle hint.

"We all have our demons, Victor."

"Yeah, well." He turned to his son. "Tell

Christine that we're closin' up. Shag all the freeloaders out." I hadn't budged, and as his son left the kitchen, Victor dropped the spatula into the sink. He headed for the back door, and included me in a nod of invitation. The outside air was crisp and clean, and I could smell the rich kitchen effluvia on Victor's clothing.

"Come here," he said, and I followed him to the east corner of the building and then around to the parking lot. "I was helping some asshole at the diesel pump," he said. "And no…I don't know what time it was. Sometime this afternoon. There were two guys hitch-hiking right over there," and he pointed west, toward the intersection with Herb Torrance's county road a mile away. "The Gabaldon kid came out of the side road in the ranch rig, and picked 'em up. Right over there." He pointed to a spot almost directly across the highway.

"Could you see their faces? Would you recognize them again?"

"No, I wouldn't recognize them again. Just two guys with backpacks. One taller than the other."

"What were they wearing?"

"Clothes."

"Caps? Anything distinctive?"

"I told you. Why should I notice? Just two guys." He pulled a ragged pack of unfiltered cigarettes out of his trouser pocket, grubbed one out, and lit it. "He picked 'em up, and they drove off toward town. You know, if the kid had pulled in here to buy some diesel, maybe I woulda seen 'em. But he don't do that. Old man Torrance would rather drive all the way to town than buy it here."

I wasn't about to be suckered into that argument. "If you remember anything else, I'd appreciate your letting me know, Victor. This is a help."

Victor didn't care to know that he'd been helpful, of course. Two more quick sucks on the cigarette and he snapped it out into the dark.

"The sheriff or undersheriff might want to talk with you again," I said to his retreating back, and he stopped abruptly.

"You make sure that don't happen," he said. "Then we're about even."

Chapter Twenty-three

My headlights picked up the door shield of Deputy Jackie Taber's unit, parked behind the sign for Borracho Canyon. She'd come out of the shadows and would give travelers of the night a turn. Some of the lingering customers of the Broken Spur would redouble their efforts not to wander.

The deputy had seen me coming—maybe it was my snail's pace. As I approached she clicked on the roof rack for a turn, and I pulled off onto the shoulder. She wasn't parked such that door-to-door was possible, but by the time I'd stopped, she was climbing out.

"Good morning, sir." She leaned both elbows on the door of my truck and watched an oncoming pickup roar by. "Quiet night."

"And I'm glad of that," I said. "I've had all the excitement I can stand."

"Neat trick with the phone, sir. Tom was telling me how you found the Gabaldon kid."

"Well, he got lucky. Look, I was just talking with Victor. He says that Pat picked up a couple of hitch-hikers just west of the saloon this afternoon—yesterday afternoon. No description other than that it was two men with backpacks. Maybe little by little we'll pry some more out of him, but for right now, that's all he'll say."

"That's a start. The undersheriff wanted me to pass along some information to you, sir." She held up three fingers. "First of all, Sheriff Torrez, Tony Abeyta, and I are going to take this place apart in the morning to see what else we can find."

"I don't expect you'll find much," I said.

"Probably not. But who knows how lucky we might get. If you want to join us here, that would be welcome."

"I'd just be in the way. You need sharp eyes, my friend."

"Your choice, sir. Number two, the dumpster party is on, and the undersheriff said you'd want to know about that. She said that if you wanted, she'd meet you behind the Don Juan at six."

"*Behind* the Don Juan? At six, I plan to be *in* the Don Juan, stuffing my face. This is nuts."

Jackie held up both shoulders in a long, slow-motion shrug. "Don't shoot the messenger, sir. Nuts or not, that's what's going down."

I nodded at her hand. "What's third?"

She waggled the finger. "Just a point of information. Estelle said that you'd want to know that Norma Scott?" She waited a couple seconds for the name to register. "The late Norma Scott? She's Phil Borman's sister."

"Shit."

"The undersheriff said you'd want to know. She said that she would have called you direct, but she knew you were probably out with Herb, and she didn't want to interrupt."

"Estelle's at home now?"

"I suppose so, sir."

I sighed. "Anything I need to do for you? Coffee? Hamburger?"

"I'm fine, sir."

"Then I'll mosey," I said. "If we're having a party for breakfast, I need to clean up and change into something more fashionable."

Jackie laughed and stepped away from my truck. "Somehow I had the misfortune to be the one tagged to help out at Borracho. You enjoy, sir."

"We'll get even," I said.

"I'm sure you will, sir."

I resumed my amble northeast, now with nothing to look for except some coherence for my thoughts. With the jog from Estelle, I remembered Norma Scott. The wife of Wes Scott, one of the maintenance men for the school district, Norma had not died quietly at home, but in the middle of the produce aisle at the supermarket.

I knew why Estelle wanted to search the dumpsters, but it was a real long shot, longer even than searching the Borracho Springs parking lot in hopes that the thugs might have dropped something besides Patrick Gabaldon. When someone has something they want to get rid of, odds are good that into the dumpster it goes…either that or tossed out along the roadside. A third option might see the goods stowed in a closet for safekeeping, but I understood the undersheriff's logic. The obvious thing to do first was look in the most likely places. And we could do that without sweating warrants or tipping our hand. Still, the targets were tiny: a tiny chemical bottle, maybe a plastic spoon or a tongue depressor, maybe a little plastic baggie.

In this instance, Lloyd Parsons, the village's sanitation department supervisor, would be amused at our request—as long as *he* didn't have to do the rummaging.

The undersheriff sure as hell didn't need me for this stunt, but she would know perfectly well that I would want to see the investigation through. By the time I'd driven home, showered, and put on some old clothes, it would be time to brew a pot of coffee and face the day.

I did just that, and at a quarter of six, my

phone rang. The undersheriff sounded bright, perky, and well rested.

"Sir, how about if I swing by and pick you up?"

"Who told you that I had any desire at all to go dumpster-diving?" I growled. "Damned dumbest thing I've ever heard of." Before she had time to judge whether or not I was kidding, I added, "That would be good, sweetheart. The front door is open. And when we're done, you owe me the breakfast of all breakfasts."

"Absolutely, and congratulations again, sir. No word on Patrick's condition yet, but we're adding another chapter in your legends book."

"Stop it," I snapped. "Any prints off the phone?"

"A couple of good ones."

"Let's hope they're not Patrick's."

"Exactly, sir. ETA about two minutes."

Friday was one of three trash pick-up days when the big refuse trucks of Southwest Compax Services rumbled through the alleys of Posadas, flipping dumpsters. If something had been discarded anywhere in town or in the outlying areas, another ten hours would see all the trash at the landfill northeast of town. Picking through the tangled heap at the landfill wouldn't be a delightful way to spend the day. One dumpster at a time was easier, more efficient, and probably more productive.

By the time I'd refilled my cup and turned off the coffee maker, I heard a single siren yelp out in my driveway as the undersheriff announced her arrival. Such urgency was uncharacteristic on Estelle Reyes-Guzman's part, and I didn't keep her waiting.

As I settled into the passenger seat of her Crown Victoria, I saw that she was dressed in battered blue jeans and a well worn sweatshirt. "When Jackie told me about this, I hoped that all along you were kidding," I said. "After all, I could be out in the canyon, tripping over roots and bashing myself on rocks. Who do you have working?"

"There are six of us," she said.

"Do you know how many dumpsters there are in this burg?" Of course she did.

She accelerated the county car out onto Guadalupe. "Lloyd gave us a map. We have thirty-three in the village itself, and another twenty-eight outlying. I don't think we'll have to search them all."

"Christ," I muttered. The whole thing made me feel tired, and it wasn't from lack of sleep. "And what if someone got smart and used gloves when they handled the bottle?"

"Then we have the weapon but not the prints. That would be a major success in itself. If they weren't clever enough to wear gloves, then we have both."

In another two minutes, we swung into the fenced area behind the Don Juan, where three green dumpsters waited. So too did Tom Pasquale and Linda Real, both looking as if they'd abandoned a painting project so they could attend this party—spattered jeans and old shirts, looking like a couple of physically fit vagrants.

Deputy Pasquale had the first dumpster's dual lids flopped back, and he was peering inside. When he saw us drive up, he shook his head in amused wonder. "Fun times," he said, as we got out of the car. "This is when we find all the dead dogs, cats, babies, and stuff."

"I'll remember that the next time I order a burrito." I surveyed the first dumpster's aromatic contents warily. We'd drawn the long straw for the easy task with this selection, since most of the refuse that was expelled from the back of the restaurant was neatly bagged or boxed.

"We can tip it, I think," Pasquale said, and sure enough, he, Linda, and Estelle were up to the task, like a trio of eager dumpster bears on the way to dinner. They were more gentle than bears would be, and the container went over with a loud, reverberating *bung*. That's when Fernando Aragon appeared at the back door of the restaurant, wiping his hands on his apron. He watched silently for a moment as Tom, Linda, and Estelle dragged the large, intact bags to one side, exposing the jumbled inner contents.

"If you guys can't afford to pay for breakfast, just say so," he said soberly.

"We appreciate that," I said. I hadn't partaken yet, figuring that someone had to look like the supervisor of this outfit. "What are you doing up so early?"

"I work here," Fernando said, eyebrow raising. "If we open at six, *somebody* has to do the prepping. What are you looking for?"

"If I knew…" I said.

Fernando couldn't resist the attraction, and stepped over to where I stood. He looked me up and down critically. "You look like you need a good night's sleep."

"Indeed I do," I said affably. "But this is so much fun."

"You're not looking in the bags?" He pointed at the big black sacks.

"We think it's loose," I said. "Whatever it is that we're looking for. We might save ourselves a little time and effort by not undoing all your good work."

"*Hijole,*" Fernando muttered under his breath. "You choose a bad day, you know. They pick up on Monday, Wednesday, and Friday. So you got a lot to look through before they come around this morning."

"Right. But it would have been tossed in sometime since Thursday noon," I said.

The restaurant owner sighed with resignation. "Well…you want help?"

"No. You have far better things to do," I said. "We're fine, Fernando."

"You still think something happened to Mr. Payton?" I was impressed that he'd made the connection without prompting.

Other than death? I amended, but I kept the thought to myself. "Yes."

He nodded. "Coffee's on whenever you need some," he said, and reached out to pat my arm as he walked past. He went back inside the restaurant, careful not to let the screen door slam behind him.

For another half hour, we waded our way through a day and a half in the life of the Don Juan de Oñate restaurant. I knew from her determined expression that Estelle had conjured up her own scenario for what had happened on Thursday. I hadn't, but maybe that was because I wanted us to find some innocent reason for George Payton's death, not food or wine spiked with lethal chemicals.

A similar scene was in progress at several other sites around the village—in the alleys that served George's small home on 1228 Ridgemont, in the Borman's neighborhood, even behind Guy

Trombley's pharmacy. They found exactly what we did…lots of garbage, none of it incriminating. No deadly little bottle with the DeMur Industries label, no plastic spoon, no ah-stick used to mix the brew.

It's always nice to hope for a simple resolution, but when a criminal doesn't *want* to be caught—when he doesn't send rude notes to the cops taunting them, when he doesn't leave behind incriminating, obvious clues, when he has no intention of striking a second time, or most simple of all, when there are no witnesses—crimes often remain unsolved, something most taxpayers don't want to hear.

In another hour, we'd finished behind the restaurant. All our digging and sorting had produced nothing.

The two dumpsters behind the county building on Bustos featured an entirely different ambiance, including an interesting mix of bagged governmental detritus, rather than old lettuce and platter scrapings. Somebody spent a lot of time feeding paper shredders. Even though I'd been caught in the middle of county bureaucracy for a fair span of time, I'd never actually appreciated the amount of just plain *stuff* that pooped out the back of the county office buildings every day, headed for the landfill.

By the time we finished there, the sun was

painfully harsh on the metal surfaces. I hadn't had breakfast yet, and none of the young eager beavers around me showed any signs of weakening. I had privately reached the conclusion that of all the interesting wild chases I'd been on with the undersheriff—and most of them had paid off in one way or another—this one took top honors as being the most useless. That in itself was depressing, since I wanted answers about George Payton's death as much as anyone.

At least Estelle, Tom, and Linda were perfecting their technique. The dumpster was eased over, the lids folded back out of the way, and then the trash was eased only as far forward as necessary to examine all the way to the bottom of the container.

About finished with the second dumpster behind the county building, Tom Pasquale straightened up, holding what appeared to be a perfectly good deep throat document stapler. As he turned it this way and that, the sun winked off the metallic inventory sticker on the bottom. "From the assessor's office," the deputy said. He clicked it several times, pulled open the back, and checked the innards. "Anybody want it?"

"Jack Lauerson might," I said, and Tom handed the gadget to me. "It must have slipped off one of the desks somehow and landed in the trash." The bags went back in the dumpster and I watched the trio clean up before tipping the last container back into place.

I looked at my watch. "Look, I need to eat," I said. "Watching all you bears cleaning out the dumpsters is making me hungry. Breakfast is on me." Linda Real wrinkled her nose, looking at her gloved hands.

"Yuck," she said. "Shower sounds better."

"That too," I agreed, although as a bona fide sidewalk supervisor, I'd done nothing to work up a sweat or attract aroma. "What's the deal now?" I asked Estelle, even though I knew perfectly well what the deal was. Her dogged determination wouldn't be appeased by a token effort, one that left any dumpsters unturned.

"It's 8:55," she said. "There are a couple places I'd like to check before we wrap it up." She pulled a folded paper out of her pocket and consulted it. "I didn't assign the dumpster out on County Road 19 just beyond the Hocking place."

"You know," I reflected, "if the killer is driving around with a little bag of trash tossed behind his car seat, we're wasting a lot of time."

"Yes, sir," Estelle agreed. "And that's just as much a possibility as tossing the trash in one of these." She nodded at the dumpsters. "But in a few minutes, the trucks are going to collect all this, and

the only chance to search goes out the window."
She started to say something else, but her phone
chirped.

"Reyes-Guzman," she said, and then glanced
at me as she listened. "Good morning, sir." Silence
followed for a moment, and then she asked, "What
time was that, sir?" A lengthy dissertation followed,
and Estelle closed her eyes—whether out of frustration or fatigue I couldn't tell. "And you're absolutely
sure, sir?" she asked at last. Apparently the caller
was. "We'll be over in about five minutes, then,"
she said. "Thank you, sir. I appreciate this." Something in her tone said that she didn't. Snapping the
phone closed, she looked askance at me.

"Unbelievable," she said.

"Go ahead…I'm gullible."

The undersheriff laughed, but without much
humor. "The histamine diphosphate is back on
the shelf."

Chapter Twenty-four

Despite Trombley's astounding discovery, Estelle Reyes-Guzman was not ready to abandon her dumpster project altogether. I understood her persistence, unproductive as the search had been. Trombley may have made yet another mistake, or the contents of the original bottle could have been transferred into another—all sorts of bizarre scenarios were possible. Tom and Linda were sent out to the county to continue the checks, and other teams, all reporting nothing but garbage, continued from one site to another.

Linda made a face at me when I mentioned that I sure wished that I could be with them every dumpster of the way. But sacrifices have to be made. Estelle asked me to ride along with her the few blocks to Trombley's pharmacy to check the pharmacist's discovery. One block into the trip, Estelle held up both hands, ignoring the steering wheel.

"Why?" she said. I hoped that it was a rhetorical question, since I didn't have any inkling *why.*

"We may well be dealing with a quirk of human nature here," I said, sounding more judicious than I actually felt. "Guy Trombley isn't going to relish admitting that someone could just waltz into the drug store and swipe drugs off the shelf. It's just like Fernando Aragon and his chile. You think *he's* going to admit using canned ingredients? And Victor Sanchez doesn't want his customers thinking that he talks with he cops. Silly ego is what it all is, sweetheart. And when both this case and Patrick's come to trial, these guys can all keep each other company on the witness stand.

"There's that," Estelle agreed. "You often talk about forks in the road during an investigation."

"We're at one," I said, not sure which of several forks she might be referring to.

She swung the car into the alley behind the pharmacy. The single dumpster was neatly closed, not a sign of refuse on the ground. The back door of the pharmacy was tightly closed.

"If Mr. Trombley *found* the histamine misplaced on the shelf, that's one thing. But he wouldn't put it back in the wrong place. I can't imagine him misplacing something like that, as organized as he is. I mean, except for a trifle of dust, those shelves are arranged in perfect order. There's no reason to make a mistake. But on the other hand, if the thief tiptoed back into the drug store to *return* the bottle, that's way too clever. Too calculating."

"Maybe one and the same," I said. "A clever calculator."

Estelle shook her head. "But that bothers me, sir. If the thief crept in to return the bottle, he would have put it back where he got it, would he not? Why would he put it somewhere else, where it's certain to draw attention?"

"That's the way we Monday quarterback it, sweetheart. He might have run out of time and just put it down in the first spot. A quick dart in and out, figuring that old man Trombley would just shake his head and wonder why he misplaced his inventory."

She drove around the store from the alley and turned into the small parking lot out front. Two other vehicles were parked there, including Trombley's silver Cadillac. By the time we got out of the county car, Trombley stood in the pharmacy's doorway, waiting.

"You're out bright and early," he said affably. "Your deputy Mears and another guy were here earlier, sorting through the dumpster. You're going to have to start paying those guys a living wage. I would have mentioned all this to Mears, but I got busy, and then they had already left before I found the bottle."

"We appreciate the prompt call," Estelle said.

"Well, I'm going to have to apologize." The pharmacist held the door for both of us and then followed us inside. The gal at the front register—I should have remembered her name, but didn't—smiled warmly.

"We're going to be in the back for a while, Gwen," Trombley said, and the nickname activated my snoozing memory—Gweneth Barnes, a recent graduate of Posadas High School and the youngest daughter of Lester Barnes, the county highway department supervisor.

"How are you doing this morning, Miss Barnes?" I asked as I passed the register. I wondered if, at age eighteen or whatever, she was in the first year of a fifty-year career behind that counter.

"Hi," she replied, and her smile brightened. Estelle had paused inside the front door to examine the racks that featured various pamphlets, flyers, the *Posadas Register*, and two of the metro dailies. The undersheriff dallied a bit, eyes roaming around a store that she'd seen a hundred times before.

"Gwen, you've been putting in the hours," Estelle said, and the girl shrugged agreement. "Are you working every day now?"

"Sure am," she said brightly.

"Without Gwen, my world would come to a

stop," Trombley laughed. He waited for us at the back of the store, obviously impatient.

"Did you work all day yesterday as well?" Estelle asked the girl.

"Yes, ma'am. I worked all week."

"Nine to five?"

Gweneth nodded. "Just half days on Saturdays, though." Guy Trombley had returned down the aisle, as if to be close at hand should the interrogation of his young clerk turn serious.

"Now, let me show you what I mean," Trombley said, as Estelle turned her attention toward the rear of the store. We followed him back, past the bandages, laxatives, vitamins and whatnot. "I'm beginning to feel a little foolish," he said over his shoulder. "You know, you didn't mention when you were here earlier that all this had to do with George Payton's death." He stopped by the padded bench where customers could plop down to wait for their prescriptions. A small rack off to one side included magazines that were now closer to historical documents, as well as another selection of those ubiquitous folders touting area attractions that the Chamber of Commerce circulated.

"What's the deal, anyway?" Trombley asked, regarding us both critically.

"I'm not at liberty to say at this point," Estelle said, and her tone had taken on an edge that even

Guy Trombley understood, reluctant as he might be to admit to a woman's authority.

"No, I suppose not." He shrugged and opened the door to a narrow hallway leading to the back of the store, then turned left into the compounding room. Sure enough, the small, dark bottle nestled in centered perfection in its assigned spot, label turned outward. Trombley started to reach for it again, but Estelle touched his arm. "I already touched it," he offered.

"This isn't where you found it," she said, and it wasn't a question.

"No...no, of course not." Guy would remember perfectly well that Estelle had taken meticulous photographs of the vacant spot, complete with the ring of dust visible on the shelf. "Now, I came in here not twenty minutes ago, and the bottle of histamine diphosphate was sitting right here." He touched the front corner two shelves above, just inside the doorway, a small spot next to a white cardboard box. "Sitting right here. Completely out of order. No wonder I didn't see it."

"Did you inadvertently leave it there after using it last time?" Estelle asked.

I saw a little flush travel up Trombley's neck. "Come now. Why would I do that," he snapped. "In the first place, as I told you earlier, the last time I compounded histolatum was nearly six months ago. Sometime along the way, I would have noticed that the bottle was out of place and returned it. Second, when I *do* compound, I work in that area over there," and he pointed at the far end of the small room. The Formica countertops were spotless, with one area that was completely enclosed. The pharmacist would have to work with his arms inside rubber access gloves, much like a mechanic's sandblaster booth.

"Why would I formulate *there,* and then return the bottle *here,*" and he rapped the shelf, "when where it belongs is even closer, down *there.*"

"Good point," I said.

"I just don't understand any of this," Trombley said. "Now you're saying that someone first took the histamine, and then, when they finished with it, *returned* it to the pharmacy—good heavens, why would anyone do such a thing? Why not just throw it away?" His eyebrows lifted at his own brainstorm. "That's why the dumpsters, then."

"It's the 'how' that's interesting," I said. "It's not like this store is left untended."

The flush shot up Trombley's neck again. "Of course it's not left untended," he snapped. "I'm here, or Harriet is, or Gwen, out front. There are two other girls who work for me as well, part-time."

"I need to take the bottle of histamine with me

for a short time," Estelle said. "I hope that won't put you out."

"Of course not," Trombley said. "I'll dial in and get another, just in case. I don't expect a call for it, but you never know." He reached out toward the bottle, but Estelle beat him to it.

"I'll get it, sir." If he was surprised to see that she already had an evidence bag with her, he didn't say anything, watching in silence as she first filled out the short label and then nudged the bottle into the bag with the tip of her pen. Next in hand was the small digital camera, and she snapped several shots of the spot where the bottle had been stashed upon its return. I ambled out of the compounding room, admiring the view of mops and buckets by the back door.

I could see that it wasn't closed tightly, and as if reading my mind, Trombley said, "The door to the alley is always locked, if that's what you're thinking."

I rested my boot on the bottom corner and pushed a bit, and the door slid open. "Most of the time it's locked, anyway," I said. The pharmacist had reached his own fork in the road, where he could either continue to bluster his way through this, or give in and join us. Apparently he chose the latter, because he let out a long sigh and leaned against the wall.

"God damn it," he murmured fervently. "What the hell is going on, Bill?"

"I honestly don't know, Guy. I wish I could just present all the answers on a silver platter for you, but I can't."

He turned as Estelle emerged from the compounding room. "My prints will be on that container, obviously. Thanks to this business, the FBI has them on file, along with a dozen other agencies and bureaus. It'll be easy to make a comparison. I'd be interested to know what *other* prints you find."

"Yes, sir," Estelle agreed, and Guy Trombley laughed at her reticence.

"You haven't asked me how I found out you were looking into George Payton's death," he said.

"That's true, sir." Estelle didn't add the obvious question.

"One of the lab techs over at the hospital told me when I called on another matter," he said. "I hope she won't get in trouble for that."

"I don't think so, as long as it went no further than you, sir."

"I'm sure it didn't. I'm sure it won't."

"Good. I need to talk with Gweneth, if that's all right with you, sir," Estelle said. *Or even if it isn't,* I thought.

"I'm sure that she has had nothing to do with

any of this," Guy said quickly, sounding like a protective parent.

"No doubt not," Estelle replied. "Is Mrs. Tomlinson working today?"

"She'll be in right after lunch. You want to talk with her too?"

"Yes, sir."

"And then there's me," Guy Trombley said. "What else can I tell you that I haven't already?"

Estelle took a deep breath, looking down at the evidence bag. "I'd like you to take a moment and write down a list of every single customer you can remember from Wednesday through this morning."

"Well, hell."

"Yes, sir."

"You're serious?"

"Yes, sir. Right up to when you telephoned us a few minutes ago."

"Do you have any idea how many customers we serve every day?"

"A goodly number, I'm certain."

"Indeed, *goodly*. A *lot*, is what the number is, Undersheriff Guzman." I did some mental computing and decided that, if the pharmacist was trying to find time to duck out for coffee and donuts, or a quick nine at the grubby Posadas links, then even ten customers would seem like a burden.

Guy Trombley was not exactly running a big-box store pharmacy here.

"We appreciate your cooperation," Estelle said.

"You'll let me know?" he said as we walked out into the store proper.

"Of course," I said. "When we know, you'll know." I patted his bony shoulder.

"Okay, then. Gwen," he said to his clerk, "these folks would like a few minutes of your time. That all right with you?"

The girl's eyes opened a little wider. "Oh, sure."

"You can use my office, if you like," Guy said. "It's that little room right across the hall from the pharmacy."

"Outside is fine," Estelle said pleasantly.

"Let me know, then," he said. "Gwen, I'll take care of things. Just go ahead." It sounded as if maintaining that last bit of control was important to him.

Chapter Twenty-five

Listening to someone with a sharp memory is always a treat. Gwen Barnes was able to cruise through the humdrum memories of the previous Wednesday and Thursday, replaying the events of her days. I saw that, given not very much time in this job, she'd be the sort of employee who would greet each customer by name, probably remember what drugs they were taking, and always remember to ask how the grandkids were doing—and then the real trick, listen to the answers.

I knew most of the names that Gwen recited, and in her own eager way, the young woman seemed perfectly willing to divulge what she shouldn't…the reason for each customer's visit. She didn't need to scour through the computer records to recall most of her day. As expected, the customers painted a cross-section of Posadas. Students dropped in for a candy bar or two, maybe hoping that Guy Trombley had relented and started carrying tobacco products in his pharmacy. The elderly chased blood pressure, blood sugar, and cholesterol. The high-school football coach came in with a purchase order for a dozen three-inch elastic bandages, and I reminded myself to cut out the Posadas Tigers game schedule from the paper. Late Thursday afternoon, Honor Gallegos had dropped off the usual twenty-five copies of the *Posadas Register,* tucking them neatly into the folding stand just inside the door.

Earlier this Friday morning, Maggie Payton had stopped by and purchased a newspaper, at the same time dropping off another supply of the brochures that touted her agency and current real estate bargains. I happened to be looking Estelle's way when Gwen recited that bit of information and didn't see as much as an extra blink of interest. My self-control wasn't so finely honed.

"What time was she here?" I asked.

"Just about first thing," Gwen said. "That's when she always comes in."

"Which reminds me that I'm supposed to have lunch with her and Phil today," I said to Estelle, hoping that the creative fabrication might deflect Gwen's curiosity.

"And Mr. Borman came in with Mr. Trombley," Gwen added helpfully. "He keeps the stock of antacids rotating."

"Real estate will do that to you," I said. The

day after George's death, both of the Bormans were trying to live life as usual, I guess. Routine could be soothing.

"Was Mr. Trombley here when Mrs. Payton came in?" Estelle asked.

"No. He hadn't come back yet." She lowered her voice as if her boss might be able to hear her through the pharmacy's cinderblock walls. "He opens up the store at eight, brings the cash drawer and stuff out of the safe for me, and then he goes for coffee and donuts with his group over at the SuperMart. He's always back by nine or a little before, though."

"And Mrs. Tomlinson doesn't come in until nine or so?" I asked.

"Most of the time," Gwen replied.

For another ten minutes, we chatted with Gwen, and a few more names were added to the list. We went back inside, and Guy Trombley held up a hand in salute.

"Anything more we can do, you just say so," he called. He ambled out from behind the register, hands massaging as if he'd just lathered on hand cream. He nodded toward the rear of the store, obviously wanting us to follow. Once out of earshot from Gwen, he relaxed with one elbow propped on the edge of the prescription counter. "You know, I had a chat with Phil Borman this morning that was a little upsetting." He puffed out his cheeks and shook his head as if the memory was painful. "A few of us meet every morning over at the SuperMart, and Phil and I had a private moment. Sad time for them."

"A *rough* time," I said, and Trombley waited as if expecting me to add more to my noncommittal response.

"He says it looked like a full-fledged homicide investigation over at George's place," Trombley prompted. When neither Estelle nor I replied, the pharmacist persisted. "Well? Was it? *Is* it? Is that what all this interest in the histamine is all about? How's that all tied in?"

I thought of several undiplomatic replies as I counted to ten, but the undersheriff could read my mind, and cut me off.

"Sir, I hope you'll give us a chance to do our jobs," Estelle said. "I know this is a hard time for people who knew and respected Mr. Payton."

"If this is homicide," Trombley said, "then it affects us all."

"Indeed it does," I said. "Homicide or not, as a matter of fact."

"This investigation isn't community property." Estelle's tone was both pleasant and patient. "If there was a problem, it's not going to be resolved over coffee at the SuperMart."

Trombley seemed to relax a bit, and flashed a smile of genuine amusement. "Well, now, you never know. We cover a lot of ground every morning. If there's anything I can do to help…"

"You've already been of great assistance," Estelle said. "I appreciate both your and Gwen's cooperation, sir."

An impossibly elderly woman entered the store—probably at least ten years older than myself—and Guy greeted her with an outstretched hand into which she placed a prescription order. "George was a good friend of mine," he added over his shoulder. "Let me know." He turned his attention to Eva Sandoval and her prescription needs. We made our exit after a "Bye, guys," from Gwen.

"So," I said as we settled into Estelle's car. I could see her mental wheels turning, her dark face sober as her dark, bottomless eyes searched the Posadas horizon. After a minute, she turned and regarded me.

"I'd like to know what you think," she said.

"Well, I'm flattered," I replied. "This is one time I don't *want* to think."

"But I can hear the gears working."

"Smoking from disuse and under-oiling. You know, when Miss Gwen said that Phil Borman came back to the pharmacy this morning with

Trombley, I couldn't help thinking how easy it would be to just duck into the back, maybe with the excuse that he was using the restroom. He reaches around the corner and puts the bottle back on the shelf."

"Yes. That's a logical scenario." Somehow, she managed to make it sound as if the suggestion *wasn't* logical.

"He had a talk with Trombley earlier," I added. "What do you think the odds are that Trombley let it slip that we were investigating the use of histamine?"

"A hundred percent," she readily agreed. "And word of dumpsters being searched spreads faster than wildfire. I have to wonder who else was within earshot when that discussion between Mr. Borman and Mr. Trombley took place at the supermarket."

"The entire coffee and donut group," I said. "All of them. And do you suppose that Trombley would mention to Phil about seeing police officers rooting through the dumpster behind his store, just in case there might be someone who didn't already know?"

"A hundred percent chance of that."

I nodded. "So let's just suppose. Borman knows we're looking. There are a dozen ways to get rid of the bottle, but he chooses to go cute. Return the bottle knowing that the only person that would implicate is Guy Trombley." I hesitated.

"And you know," I said slowly, "if we put the light on Trombley, the whole thing is pretty easy. He's not above suspicion, you know. Think about that. He has the drug right on his shelf, he knows all there is to know about its actions."

"We have nothing that even hints that Guy Trombley was at Mr. Payton's home," Estelle said. "Phil Borman found the body, remember. That's what he says. He could have stopped by any time after Ricardo Mondragon left the house. There's the opportunity."

"True enough. But there could easily be some little link that we're missing with Trombley."

Estelle frowned and thumped the steering wheel thoughtfully. "Now why would Trombley do that, sir? What reason would he have to want to kill a man whose days were limited anyway?"

"I have no idea. But stranger things have happened. I..." A pickup truck pulled in beside us, and I looked up to see Herb Torrance's worn, wrinkled face peering down at us. Trying to talk with my neck craned wasn't going to work, and I hauled my carcass out of the car. "Herb, what's the news?" From the passenger seat, Socks regarded me with disinterest. How soon they forget, I thought.

"Morning to you. Look, I was able to get a hold of Pat Gabaldon's folks, and I guess the Sheriff's dispatcher did, too. They're on their way to the city. The hospital says that Patrick come through surgery okay."

"He's in good hands," I said.

"You heard from the Mexicans yet?"

I glanced at my watch. Hell, we hadn't even managed breakfast yet, let alone had the chance to follow up on international relations. "Naranjo said he'd call me when he knew something," I said. "That's all I can tell you. We can't just go charging down there, Herb."

"Yeah, I know that." He lit a cigarette. "Just hopin', is all. I was thinkin' of drivin' down and havin' a word with Domingo. I've met him a time or two, and we get on all right."

"Do me a favor?"

"Sure thing," Herb said.

"Don't do that. Not right now."

"Well, I was thinkin'…"

"I know. You're concerned, and so are we. You want to find out who whupped up on Pat, and so do we. You want your rig returned." I leaned back and surveyed the dented, faded truck's flank. "I didn't think this thing was still on the road."

"Almost isn't."

"Well, give us a little time," I said. "I trust Naranjo. He'll do what he can." I saw the muscle in Herb's cheek twitch with impatience. "And think about this, Herb. The officer at the border said that the driver of your rig mentioned Domingo's ranch. That doesn't mean that's where they were really headed. It might just be a convenient ruse. Everybody down there knows the Domingo ranch. It'd be like someone headed northbound across the border telling one of our guards that they were headed for the Torrance H-Bar-T. Everybody knows where that is, too."

The corner of Herb's mouth wrinkled with amusement. "Yup," he said.

"Give us a little time," I said. There was no point in making promises, but it sounded good. "We'll work this out."

"Those sons-a-bitches ought to just end up as buzzard feed out in the desert somewheres," Herb said. "That's what ought to happen."

"And it sometimes does, especially south of the border." I reached out and tapped his shoulder with an index finger. "Don't you go getting involved in something like that."

Herb let out a great sigh, half air and half smoke. "Hell of a thing." He ducked his head so he could see past me to Estelle, sitting in the county car. She'd been on the phone while we gabbed, not wasting a moment. "You two up to any good?"

"Maybe," I said. "Maybe."

"You still workin' that deal with George? Something going on with that?"

"I guess." I didn't ask Herb how *he* happened to know our business…I'd never seen him at the early morning donut conferences at the grocery store, but maybe he was a new member.

He shook his head ruefully. "Just goes to show," he said. "You put things off 'til tomorrow, and sometimes you ain't got it." He took his time lighting another cigarette. "You know, I was going to buy that piece of property on the mesa."

"From George, you mean?"

He nodded. "It ain't much, but it'd solve a problem or two for us."

"Where the drill rig is?"

"Up behind there. Just kinda that piece up top, there."

"You'd already talked to George about that?"

"A while ago. When he was still gettin' out and about. He said it wasn't going to cost me much. But," and he shrugged philosophically. "Didn't get to it." He reached over and stroked the dog's round head, and then his hand sank to the gear lever. "I guess we thought we had time, you know."

I thumped the door sill. "Isn't that the way it is," I said. "We'll be in touch, Herb. Give my best to Annie."

Estelle watched as I settled into the county car. Herb's truck departed leaving behind a fine, oily potpourri. "He's impatient," I said.

"Of course," the undersheriff replied. She held out her phone. "I wondered if you wanted to join me for lunch."

I laughed. "You need to ask? As long as it's early. We never had breakfast. I'm running on fumes."

"With a guest, though" she added. "I just talked with Kevin Zeigler. And then maybe we should see Jack Lauerson. Give him his stapler back, for one thing. Kevin is in his office now. Grab a bite after that?"

"I'm your captive audience," I said. "What's the deal with Kevin?" Finding County Manager Kevin Zeigler in his office at all was something of a miracle. The county assessor, Jack Lauerson, was equally peripatetic.

"Herb was talking about that piece of land on the mesa?"

"Yes," I replied. "I would guess it's only a few acres. Herb would like to end up with it eventually. Either him or Waddell's outfit." I looked sharply at her as a number of possibilities started to brew in my undernourished mind, but Estelle had already started the car and was pulling out of the pharmacy parking lot for that long, two-and-a-half-block drive to the county building.

Chapter Twenty-six

The county manager was waiting in the hallway outside his spacious office, standing with both hands on his hips as he looked up at a huge, mahogany-framed map of Posadas County, printed in 1923 and now preserved behind glass. I'd examined it many times and had a bare spot on my library wall that was large enough to handle the spectacular six-by-seven foot artifact. I knew that there were nay-sayers who would ask what features or historical treasures Posadas County might include that warranted it. Maybe when they built the new addition to the county building, some architect would rule it out and consign it to the pile of government surplus that was auctioned off once a year.

"Hey, guys." Kevin Zeigler reached out to touch a spot of county that included Herb Torrance's ranch. "I heard what happened."

"Which time?" I asked.

"I heard about what happened to Pat

Gabaldon," he said. "And Herb's son." He turned away from the map and nodded pleasantly at Estelle. "Talk about a turn of rotten luck."

"Indeed." I filed away a mental note for a retirement project—a study of rumor logistics in a small community.

He beckoned as he made for the double door of his office complex. "Come on in." The county manager's digs were toward the far corner, hidden behind the racks of county records, the huge slant-topped cabinets that patrons could use to peruse the mammoth, heavy volumes, and the constant hum of a dozen computers. The place was like a clash of two ages, that of the quill pen and of bits and bytes.

The largest desk in the place belonged to Penny Barnes, Zeigler's secretary. She was sitting with her nose inches from the computer screen, chin resting in a cupped hand, elbow on the keyboard tray. She looked up without turning her head as we passed and smiled as if she knew a private secret. Maybe her daughter, Gweneth of the Pharmacy, had called mom after our departure to spill the latest gossip.

Penny reached out a hand to Estelle, a sisterly sort of connection. "Are you keeping this guy out of trouble?" she asked.

"We try," Estelle replied.

"Oy vay, vee try," I added. Kevin waited

patiently for us to file into his sanctum and then shut the door. Penny never changed position.

"So," he said affably. "Nasty times."

"Yes," I said, taking advantage of an aging leather-covered chair that I knew had belonged to Efrem Martinez, county manager when I'd joined the Sheriff's Department back in the dark ages. Zeigler waited until Estelle had settled in a south-westerny designed thing with sort-of Zia symbols laser cut out of the back and sides, and a cowhide seat. Then he perched on the corner of his desk, both feet off the floor, hands clasped in his lap.

"You wanted to know what the status was of the Payton property behind us, here," he said, and nodded. "I like it when I get simple questions. Unfortunately for us here in the county, the status is simply that the property now will go through probate with the rest of George Payton's estate."

"I could be wrong, but I don't think that he left a will," I said. "He and I talked about it a time or two, and George saw it as a damn nuisance. I don't think he ever got around to it."

Zeigler nodded slowly. "If that's the case, we all wait a little longer. No doubt we'll end up dealing with Maggie Borman." He tried a smile, but it didn't work. "That's going to be an entirely different kettle of fish."

Maybe or maybe not, I thought. I didn't want to hazard a guess. Just when we think we know our neighbors, fate throws a curve ball.

"You and Mr. Payton hadn't firmed anything up? Nothing in writing?" Estelle asked.

"You know," Zeigler sighed, "I talked with George on Monday…no, Tuesday. Tuesday morning. I saw him in the hospital parking lot. He said he was going in to get a flu shot. He was proud that he was driving himself around. He said he wasn't supposed to be out and about by himself." The county manager shrugged. "Go figure. Anyway, he said that he wanted to get the paperwork done on the transfer, and asked if I'd have the county attorney swing his house one of these days so we could get the deal going."

"One of these days," I added, feeling vindicated that I'd pushed Dr. Francis Guzman into taking the first steps for the clinic, not falling into the trap of my usual procrastination. I had paid for a survey of my property, including the four acres that I gave the Guzmans. I sat at their dinner table a good many times, talking and listening them through their dream. I cheerfully admitted that it was all self-serving. If there was anything I could do to keep Francis and Estelle and my two godchildren from moving away to some hinterland, I was ready to do it. Four acres of brush and trees was a cheap enough price to pay.

"And you didn't have a chance to talk with Simmons?" Estelle asked.

Zeigler laughed ruefully. "As you're well aware, Mrs. Reyes-Guzman, the door to the county attorney's office is about thirty feet from mine. The phone's even quicker. E-mail takes a nano-second. After I left George that morning, the first thing that happened was a phone call from the county barns. They informed me that our best road grader blew a piston right through the block." He held up his hands in surrender. "That's ten thousand bucks that has to be found somewhere in the budget. And then one thing leads to another, as I'm sure you're well aware in this business. I saw Paul Simmons yesterday morning, and forgot to mention the paperwork to him. By noon, I guess it was? By noon, it was too late." He regarded Estelle quizzically. "What's the sheriff's department's interest in this, anyway? And I mean beyond planning your own building renovation that this whole project is going to allow."

"Well, there's that, too," Estelle said. "It's just that there are some puzzling things about the whole situation, that's all." Zeigler was a perceptive young man and looked as if he wanted to ask more questions, but he let it go. Estelle had managed to dance around Guy Trombley's curiosity, hadn't divulged anything at all to Gweneth Barnes, hadn't discussed any of the possibilities with Herb Torrance, and certainly not with either Maggie or Phil Borman. She wasn't ready to start now, even with the county manager, a man she clearly trusted.

Kevin Zeigler didn't say anything but after a moment turned and looked at me as if I might have something to add. Maybe he was curious why a New Mexico livestock inspector would have an interest in the case.

"You've known Mr. Payton for a long time, haven't you?" he asked, his voice subdued. He slid off the corner of the desk, moved around it, and slumped down in his fancy black leather ergonomic swivel chair, leaning forward to rest his elbows on the planning calendar.

"For decades," I replied. "And as a matter of fact, in the missed opportunities department, yesterday I was supposed to have lunch with George. I got hung up when a horse stomped Herb's boy and couldn't keep the date."

"I sorry to hear that," Zeigler said. He adjusted his fashionable granny glasses carefully. "I heard that Mr. Payton suffered a heart attack. That's not the case, then? There's more to it than that, is that what you're saying?"

I glanced at Estelle, not knowing how far she

wanted to go fielding specifics about the case. Kevin Zeigler had been county manager for less than three years, a transplant from Socorro. I knew him well enough—or thought I did. During that time, I'd come to my own conclusions about the young county executive's sense of discretion. Even so, his office, like any in the county building, hosted a fair amount of small talk and gossip. Estelle obvious shared my conclusions, since her response was immediate.

"We think there are some issues," she said. "We want to make very sure, is all."

"Ah," Zeigler nodded. "I suppose so. Nothing is as simple as it seems at the get-go."

"That's exactly right."

"Whatever I can do to help clear things up," Zeigler said, and I liked him all the more.

"We're just getting started," Estelle said. "Give us a few days. Once things are cleared up…" That was as far as she was prepared to go in discussing the case, and Zeigler was astute enough realize it. He settled back in his chair, staring at the mass of paperwork awaiting his attention.

"'I ain't going to pay no goddamn lawyers,'" Zeigler said, growling a fair imitation of George Payton's crusty baritone. "That's what Mr. Payton told me. That's why I offered to have Simmons work up the paperwork for him. But that prompts an obvious question."

"And that is?" I asked.

"Mr. Payton's daughter is a realtor. It would seem logical to me that he'd just have her take care of the transfer."

I laughed. "Sometimes being a relative works, and sometimes it doesn't," I said. "Maggie Payton is a wonderful lady, Kevin. But she and her dad were about this far apart in personality," and I held my hands out, spread wide.

"And she might not approve of his giving the property away," Zeigler added. "We were ready to pay fair market value for it, you know. It's not as if we were trying to cheat Mr. Payton out of anything. But he wouldn't hear of it. Once he decided to transfer the property for a dollar, that was that. No more discussion."

"I'm sure she knew that," I said. "That may be why she didn't pressure him."

"How much was the county going to offer?" Estelle asked.

"Eighty-five," the county manager said without hesitation. "That's what we'd penciled in. Just for the lot that borders our current county building property."

"What was the current assessment on it?"

Zeigler frowned. "You'd have to ask Jack Lauerson to be exact, but the figure I remember is about sixty."

I whistled. "Well, it's location, location, location," he said. "That's what drives value in these things. The property is right downtown, an obvious addition to the county holdings. In fact, the expansion hinges on that property, so it jacks the value up even more. George could have held out and negotiated us up even more. In fact, if that property was on the open market, I'd expect it to go for close to a hundred. Maybe more."

"It's my understanding that George owned a lot of properties around the county," I said.

"And some outside, I'm discovering," Zeigler said. "What's that guy's name." He leaned over and pawed through a mound of papers on the left side of his desk. "There's a rancher up in Newton who wants us to extend a spur from County Road 14 to a piece of his property."

"Waddell?" I offered.

"That's it. Miles Waddell. He's trying to pre-empt some development by the BLM over that way. It's looking like the feds are going to develop something with the caves, as I'm sure you're aware. Waddell called me a couple weeks ago and said that he was planning to trade a couple of pieces out of county to Mr. Payton for some little piece over that way."

"I saw his drill rig," I said.

"A little premature with that," Zeigler said.

"Anyway, there it is." He glanced up at the clock. "I just saw Jack walk past, so if you're needing to see him, this is a good time."

"It would be," Estelle said, and pushed herself out of the chair. "Are you going to be free for lunch?"

"I wish," Zeigler said. "I need to head out to the county maintenance yard to see how much more money they're going to need." He smiled ruefully. "It never ends. You guys let me know if there's anything else I can do to help."

With the old chair molded around my backside, I was perfectly comfortable, but I could see that Estelle was edgy, so we left the county manager to fight his own fires. A visit to the assessor would add some intriguing parts to the puzzle. It was apparent that George Payton had been a little busier than I ever would have suspected.

Chapter Twenty-seven

Why anyone would want Assessor Jack Lauerson's job, I didn't know. *Tax* is a four-letter word to most folks, myself included. I loved my ancient, sprawling *hacienda* on Guadalupe Drive, with its too many rooms, sunken library with flagstone floors, all graced with a patio shaded by immense cottonwoods and dense brush that I was going to trim someday. But I cringed every year when Jack's office sent my tax notice.

By giving Francis and Estelle Guzman the rear four acres of my spread for their new clinic, I'd cut my tax liability a bit…but the annual assessment would still hurt. I felt a little sympathy for the assessor, though. Jack Lauerson must have developed hide tougher than an aging steer. I'd rather deal with armed felons or bovines afflicted with mad cow disease. I couldn't imagine that the assessor saw many folks who stopped by his office door just to say, "My God, Jack…you did such a *great* job assessing my house! Thanks a lot! Can I buy you lunch?"

Jack Lauerson's secretary, a gal who had been in my youngest son's high-school class and thirty years later still looked like the teenager who'd almost stolen the boy's heart, beamed at me from behind a mountain of papers.

"Hi, Sheriff!" she chirped, a year behind the loop when it came to titles. "What's up? Hi, Estelle. Are you keeping this guy on the straight and narrow?" Was I really that wayward, I wondered.

"I'm trying," Estelle said. And I was trying to remember the young lady's name. The plaque on the desk said *Wanda* something, but I couldn't read the last name. And if my memory served me even a little bit, that last name was the third or fourth for the young lady. "Is Jack available?"

Wanda swiveled her chair to scan the crowded office. One of the other three clerks raised an arm and pointed a finger, and at the same time I spied Jack Lauerson kneeling by a huge file—one of those enormous things with banks of four-foot wide, shallow drawers that stores maps spread out flat and unfolded.

"Caught him," I said. "May we come around?"

"Of course you can." Wanda beamed again. Estelle skirted the counter, dodged desks and cabinets and drafting tables, but I paused at the secretary's desk. "We found this orphan out in the dumpster," I said, handing her the big stapler. "Thought you might want it."

Her face crinkled up in astonishment and disbelief. "The *dumpster!* My *God.* I *wondered* where that went."

"Must have slipped into a trash can," I said.

"Well, stranger things have happened," Wanda said, and she turned the stapler this way and that. "My gosh." She didn't ask why we'd been rummaging through dumpsters. "Thanks, sir." I nodded and followed Estelle, arriving at Jack Lauerson's elbow without trashing half of Posadas County's records.

Hands deep in the third drawer from the bottom, the assessor looked up at us over the tops of his half glasses as we approached. Small-town folks often wear several hats, and Lauerson was no exception. He'd found the time to coach the high-school varsity girl's volleyball squad to four state championships, making him the odd combination of hero in one life, villain in another. The fit and trim coach could probably outrun most enraged taxpayers, but I knew he didn't depend on that. It was hard to stay mad at Jack Lauerson for very long. He'd scratched his head in puzzlement over property values for so long that his hair was thinning to a few strands, combed straight back, stuck to his skull with some kind of shiny gunk.

"You guys have the look," he said. He extracted a hand from the file, letting a sheaf of maps fall back into place, and shook hands first with Estelle and then with me. His grip was firm and brief, and he took a second to pat the maps back into place before he stood up without a single crack or creak of bones. He nudged the drawer closed with the pointed toe of his boot.

"We need some information, if you have a minute," the undersheriff said.

Lauerson held out both arms to include the entire, cavernous office complex. "All is public information under this roof," he said. "You're welcome to it all, either solo or with a tour guide." He looked at the Seth Thomas on the wall. "Is this a quick thing, or a long, involved search for deeply buried secrets, sheriff?" He smiled helpfully, apparently willing to go either route.

"We'll need a guide," I said quickly, fearful that Estelle might want to wander off, rooting and burrowing on her own, the hours flying by until we'd missed supper as well. Months from now, they might find our two dusty skeletons over behind one of the files.

Lauerson settled back against the corner of a desk, crossed his arms, and cocked his head at us, ready to listen. "So," he prompted. "I saw you two across the hall with Kevin. Somebody's world is ending, is it?"

"Sir, you have an organized listing of county properties, I would assume," Estelle said.

Lauerson laughed good-naturedly. "Of course. Now, some would argue the 'organized' thing. *I* think it's organized. But yes. We live in a world of lists, Sheriff. That's what we do."

"If a taxpayer owns more than one piece of property, are those properties listed all together somehow?"

"You mean can we access information about each piece of property by the name of the owner? Of course." He nodded slowly. "Actually, property is listed and mapped in a variety of ways. Over in the county clerk's office, they have those wonderful old binders with the deed legends and whatnot? Our mission is a bit different over here. But we do have a master listing that's always updated. Each time there's a property transfer of any kind that's recorded across the hall or a building permit that's issued, our lists are updated." He smiled self-deprecatingly. "Most of the time. We've been known to slip up on occasion." Cocking his head, he regarded Estelle with interest. "What was it you were looking for, exactly? Do I get to know?"

"Suppose I wanted to inventory George

Payton's real estate holdings in the county. How hard is that to do?" she asked.

"Not hard at all," Lauerson said. "Somebody told me this morning that George passed away. That's a shame. He used to come in and grump at me from time to time. More as a way to pass the time of day than anything serious." He pushed himself away from the desk. "You know, I had that thought this morning when I heard about his passing. When his estate is probated, all the records will be scrutinized. Lots of changes. Lots and lots of changes." He crooked a finger at us. "Come."

A young man at a drafting table looked up as we passed and flashed a smile of welcome. "Don't mind the mess," Lauerson said when we reached the mountain under which his own desk was buried. His clutter made Kevin Zeigler's workspace look downright antiseptic. A vast collection of neatly rolled maps and documents was stacked strategically to avoid slumps and avalanches. A small area around his computer remained clear, and the assessor sat down and pulled himself up to the keyboard. In a moment, lists appeared. At least I thought they were lists. The print was so fine it could have been text for a new Biblical translation.

"Here's how they're listed," he said, and scrolled down. "Let's get to the P's here. Padilla, Padilla, Padilla…there's a lot of them. Patterson,

Payne, Payton comma Bruce, no relation, Payton comma George. Wowser." The screen suddenly created a black chunk of text, with a whole field of listings. "All these are George's," Lauerson said, running his pencil eraser down the screen.

I bent down on one side of the assessor, Estelle on the other. Lauerson scooted his chair back and rose. "Here, sit."

"Go ahead sir," Estelle prompted, and I did so, then read the entries—legal descriptions of property with all the range-township mumbo-jumbo, acreage to three decimal places, and zoning classifications of the properties. The final five columns compiled the five most recent annual valuations.

Jack reached past my shoulder and touched the last column, where the figures were bold-faced. "These are current assessed valuations," he said. "This is what went out to every property owner on the last statement, half due in December, second half in the spring."

"A guy sort of has to know," I mumbled, cruising down through the numbers. The problem was that if I was interested in a piece of property, I thought of it as "that little patch out past the Torrance ranch, just off County Road 43." But these were all legal descriptions, down to the last dotted 'i' and crossed 't'. "How do I tell what's what?" I asked.

"Well, you find a translator," Lauerson laughed. "What are you looking for in particular?" He scanned down the highlighted brick of entries. "This tells us that he owns fourteen parcels in Posadas County. It's none of my business, but I happen to know that he owns property outside of the county as well. I know that he traded with Miles Waddell for some property up in Grant County, for instance."

"May I have a copy of that?" Estelle asked quickly. "This whole listing?"

"Certainly you may." Lauerson reached past me again and tapped computer keys. In a moment, the laser printer beside his desk came to life.

The undersheriff had never actually said what it was that she was tracking, but I had my own curiosities.

"George owned a little chunk of prairie out by Herb Torrance's ranch," I said. "Just north of Herb's house, on top of that little mesa there." Lauerson reached out and scrolled the screen a bit, then jotted a number or two down on a scratch pad.

"That would be 1453," he said, and touched the screen with the tip of his pencil. "And actually, he owns three parcels out that way. Here's the listing with the legal. It shows 11.325 acres. He paid $17.90 last year in property taxes on that piece you're talking about."

"Eighteen bucks," I remarked.

"It's unimproved range land, no utilities, no easy access to the county road, no nuttin' except a great view. Now, when the BLM does some development with the cave property across the county road, he may have something. One guy I know is positive that some of the cave complex extends under that mesa. Up on top might be a killer location for a visitors' center or something like that."

"Like Carlsbad Caverns," I said.

"Exactly. I heard some scuttlebutt that the BLM was planning to trade the land that they own across the road to the Park Service."

"Interesting," I said. "I wonder how those properties got chopped up so that we're left with an eleven-acre parcel out there in the boonies, unrelated to anything else."

"Well, records will tell you, if you want to research hard enough," Lauerson replied. "Over the years, these things get divided, given away, forgotten, you name it. You could research the deed and have a better idea of the history. Now, 99 percent of the time, it has to do with either water or access to something. Neither one of those applies to this little mesa top, though. I couldn't even guess why George bought it originally."

"Because it was there," I offered. "Maybe he liked the view."

"Most likely that's exactly right." He laughed. "What's the old saw…'they ain't makin' no more land, pardner.'" He beckoned toward one of the huge filing cabinets. "Is that the only one you're interested in? He owns this little chunk down here, too," and he high-lighted 1456. "That's a little more than seven acres."

Estelle said reached out and indicated 1463, farther down the column. She had done a pretty good job of letting me run wild over her investigation so far. "I'm curious about the lot right behind this building," she said. "Right behind the county building. The one that fronts the alley and then wraps around behind the old bank."

"Okay," Jack said, and he jotted numbers on his scratch paper. "Let's look at the ones out west first." Confronting the massive file cabinets, he pulled open the fifth drawer from the top. Flipping through the corners of the stack of maps, he found the one he sought and slipped it carefully out of the drawer, then carried it to the nearest sloped drafting table.

Before I had a chance to bring the thing into focus, he thumped a portion with his index finger. "This is Herb Torrance's ranch—actually, let me correct that. This is the portion of Herb's ranch where his residence is located. See County Road 14 right here?" I nodded, following the thin blue line down to its intersection with the state high-way. Lauerson slipped the sharp blue pencil from his pocket and used it as a pointer. "That black symbol is his residence. And the various permanent outbuildings."

The pencil pointer moved over to one of the blue lines. "This is the property boundary of Herb's ranch. To the south is a block of land owned by George Payton that runs out to the county road. That's 1456. In fact, if I'm not mistaken, one of the windmills that Herb uses is right there." He touched the map gently.

"On George's land."

"That's correct," he nodded.

"How many acres is that plot?"

He cocked his head, reading the legend under the neatly printed name. "Seven point two one five, more or less."

"A little seven-acre postage stamp," I said. "Now what the hell is the point of *that?*" I meant it as a rhetorical question, since it was obvious that George Payton had collected and bartered land like some folks collect and trade postage stamps. But Lauerson was a walking, breathing property gazet-teer, and he was eager to share what he knew.

"Oh," he said, "always water out here. A good well, access to the county road? A great home site, for one thing. I mean, seven acres is ideal for that.

Just a good investment. I remember how he got that one, too. In fact both of you probably do, too. George bought the property in a deal with old Reuben Fuentes, years ago." He turned to smile at Estelle. "Your infamous uncle, if I'm not mistaken."

"My great uncle," she corrected. The relationship was actually more complicated than that, since Reuben had been Estelle's adoptive mother's uncle—making him a *step*-great-uncle. "He liked land, too."

"Sure. Now this particular piece…I always wondered why Herb Torrance didn't acquire the land when Reuben passed on. But he didn't. George Payton jumped on it. I know that Herb uses the well, and I don't know what kind of deal he had worked out with George. You'd have to ask him."

"And the mesa parcel?"

"Those eleven acres are high and dry." He traced the outline with his pencil. "Herb might have use of them for pasturage, I suppose. The parcel joins his land at the east end."

I turned to Estelle, tapping the map just north of the mesa parcel. "Waddell's drill rig is parked right here."

"That's BLM land," the assessor said. "Waddell has grazing leases with them all through that area. He's doing some range improvement, would be my guess."

"Interesting place to do it," I said.

"No comment," Lauerson quipped. "You didn't ask about them, but Payton had two other parcels a little to the north, too." He stepped to the file and removed another map. "One parcel is 56.48 acres, the other is…" and he hesitated while he found the legend, "it's 108.225 acres, more or less."

"So about a hundred and sixty or so."

"Yep. The larger one was part of the exchange deal with the Forest Service ten years ago or so. They wanted some land that George had up on Cat Mesa, so they cut a trade for this."

"That's another, what, about a mile on up the county road from Herb's place?"

"More like two," Lauerson said. "But in the same general neighborhood."

"And all those parcels…they're still in George's name?" Estelle asked.

"As far as I know," Lauerson said. "If he's sold one or more parcels here recently, then there hasn't been time for the information to make it over from the County Clerk's office."

"But that's an instant transfer of information, is it not? When the deed is transferred in their files, it shows up on yours? All on computer?"

"Essentially correct." He looked at the under-sheriff and raised an eyebrow as if to say, "what's next?"

"And the courthouse property?"

"Another map," he said good-naturedly. From another filing cabinet two stalls down he searched for a few seconds and slipped out a sheet. "A really irregular-shaped piece, as I recall. It used to include the old Nolan Pet Shop, remember that? It burned way back when?"

"Back when there were enough people living in Posadas that someone could actually make a living selling goldfish and gerbils," I said.

"Well," Lauerson said, "it's this narrow little parcel that runs down the side of the old bank's rear parking lot, and then right over to the property boundary with the county building. The village had great plans when the bank moved into its new place behind Pershing Park. The city council had visions of an office complex that adjoined the county building. That never happened, and now we want to expand."

The property lines were a jumble. "What's that little piece assessed for?" I asked.

"Just a second." Lauerson crossed to his desk and consulted the computer. In a moment he returned with a scrap of paper that he handed to me.

"This is current?" I asked, forwarding the paper to Estelle. "Sixty-two thousand bucks is a fair chunk of change for a postage stamp."

"Well," and he shrugged. "I could argue that it's on the *low* side for a piece of property right downtown, right next to the county complex, right in the path of the planned expansion that's in the works."

"That's not necessarily the market value, though."

He laughed abruptly. "God, no. Not likely. Depends on who wants it and who's selling it. The average right now for downtown properties is roughly a 150 to 200 percent of the valuation. Where this one goes is anyone's guess. When they floated a bond issue to fund the additions and renovations, this little piece of land is what makes it possible. So it's a seller's market."

"I never had the impression that George sold much," I said. "He *collected* a lot. Anyway, he was planning to *give* this property to the county. His contribution to the project. He's told me that a dozen times."

"I heard he was going to do that. That would help Kevin's budget."

"If it happens," I added. "Deals may change now."

"Well, that's true. They hadn't moved to finalize that generous offer before he…before he died?"

"No, they hadn't. And it was just a matter of

days, too. Kevin had the county attorney working on it."

"Ouch. Somebody is going to have a good time straightening it all out," Lauerson added. "It'll fall in Maggie's lap, I suppose."

"That's what she's good at," I said. I turned and looked at Estelle. "What do you think?"

"I have a favor to ask," she said. "I know it's a bother, but you have records for fourteen properties owned by George Payton. That's the whole list in Posadas County?"

"You'd like some copies?" the assessor guessed.

"I really would. You don't have a way of telling what he might own in surrounding counties? Grant, Luna, Catron?"

"Ah, no. You'd have to contact the county offices in each one. I could do it via e-mail for you, but you can do it just as quickly yourself. Let me fetch what material we have for you." Less than fifteen minutes later, we had not only the list, but a neat little stack of plats. Lauerson tapped the pile into order, ranked by ascending file number, clipped the lot together, and slid them into a shiny blue folder with the Posadas County seal on the cover.

"Absolutely wonderful," Estelle said. "Will you make time so we can buy you lunch?"

I was delighted but astounded to hear her say that, since as far as I'd ever been able to tell, she had the daily caloric intake of an anorexic gnat and was deaf to my occasional whimpers of gastronomic suffering.

Jack Lauerson glanced at the clock again, held up a finger, and walked quickly back to his desk. He shuffled through half a dozen Post-it notes that had accumulated, frowning at one of them, and then nodded. "Never turn down a free meal," he said. His waistline looked as if his idea of lunch was half a tuna sandwich on whole wheat with ice tea as a chaser. What a trio of extremes we made.

As we walked out of the office, Lauerson held the door for Estelle. "How are the plans for the new clinic coming along?"

"Always a few kinks," she said. "But fine. I think."

He laughed. "Bill, wait 'til you see what *that* place does to property values in that part of town. Your neighbors will be delighted with you."

Chapter Twenty-eight

The number of meals that I'd eaten at the Don Juan de Oñate over the decades was enough to earn me plenty of frequent eater perks…admittedly along with an impressive waistline. The choice seemed simple enough to me. Did I want to be able to tie my shoes without grunting with the effort, or did I want to be able to sigh with something close to ecstasy when I took the first mouthful?

Besides, this was important. Estelle Reyes-Guzman had suggested lunch, and that in itself was an occasion that demanded nurturing. How she kept going on her caloric intake was a mystery to me. In my world, salads and herbal tea were only of use to pass the time until the main course arrived. Second, I was sure that assessor Jack Lauerson knew a good deal more than he would casually offer in an office where a dozen ears might overhear. Third, what better tribute to George Payton could there be? I wasn't one to mope around in a church, surrounded by teary people in black, nor one to pick at one of the five meat loaves out in the kitchen brought by sympathetic neighbors.

I led the way toward my customary booth in the back of the restaurant. JanaLynn Torrez appeared with a cheerful smile of greeting and three tall glasses of ice water with lemon. She was pretty enough that when she walked by, more than one customer had missed his mouth with a loaded fork, but she'd never married…not that at the ripe old age of thirty-one all options were lost.

JanaLynn knew that this was the time to hone appetites, not wallow in regrets. She raised a pretty black eyebrow at Jack Lauerson. I guessed that the Don Juan wasn't a customary haunt for him. The best thing in my day was a bountiful lunch followed by a nap, but maybe that didn't fit the assessor's work schedule. I could see him pulling a pathetic little brown bag of dry sandwich out of his desk drawer come noon, his work pace never slackening. Maybe on occasion, for a real treat, he bartered sandwich halves with Kevin Zeigler.

"What are you going to have, Mr. Lauerson? I already know what this guy wants." She leaned against me, bumping me with her hip.

"What's good?" he asked, confirming my suspicions.

"Well, a menu might help." JanaLynn stepped

over to one of the server islands, pulled a menu out of the rack, and handed it to Jack. "I get so used to folks knowing what they want that I sometimes forget." She grinned down at me.

Lauerson frowned at the vast selection. He looked skeptical, as if he were about to skate on really thin ice. "I'll try a couple of the beef enchiladas, I guess."

"Red or green?"

Our official state question prompted a cautious pause. "Is the green really hot?"

JanaLynn made a face to defuse his anxieties. "It's not bad. Not like yesterday, when it melted out the bottom of one of the stainless steel pans." She reached out a hand and made contact with Jack's left shoulder. "I'm kidding. It's really good."

"I'll try that, then."

"Smothered?"

"Sure. Why not."

"Comin' right up." She gathered the menu, slipped it under her arm, and held up both hands to demonstrate the size of a football. I nodded, feeling no pangs of remorse at being so predictable. "How about you?" she said to Estelle. When the undersheriff ordered a chicken taco salad, it surprised the hell out of me. It's a great dish, with lots of savory roast chicken, fresh beans and other wonderful secrets in a large taco shell bowl. Add the quacamole, salsa, and sour cream, and it's a decent snack. I knew that Estelle was thinking overtime, and some actual food was going to help fuel the process.

Jack Lauerson watched JanaLynn's retreating figure. "You always order the same thing?" he asked me.

"Of course not. I had the enchiladas once. In the spring of 1982, I think."

He laughed, still watching as JanaLynn reached up to clip the ticket on the kitchen's Lazy Fernando. I said nothing to interrupt the assessor's day dreams. After two previous tries at matrimony, Lauerson was enjoying bachelorhood again...or not.

"Isn't she related to the sheriff somehow?" he asked after a moment.

"JanaLynn is Robert's youngest sister," I said. "One of many sisters, in fact."

He turned back toward the kitchen, but Jana-Lynn had disappeared. "She's attractive," he said.

"Indeed she is," I agreed, and watched as Lauerson pulled his cell phone out of his pocket, glanced at it, and then switched it off, a brave, relaxed thing for a government bureaucrat to do.

"So..." He leaned back, hooking one arm over the back of the booth, and sighed with obvious contentment, enjoying the break in scenery from filing cabinets, light green walls, and patrons whose standard expression was a frown. "Losing old friends is tough."

I nodded. "Especially when you reach the age that you no longer buy green bananas. All us geezers sit around making bets about who's going next. Not a real healthy outlook."

"Mr. Payton was how old?"

"Seventy-seven," I replied. "And not a particularly hale or hearty seventy-seven, either. He'd been living on a third of a heart for a long time."

"Maggie's going to have her hands full," he said. The familiarity in his tone, the way he tossed Maggie Payton Borman's name into the conversation, surprised me a bit.

"The properties, you mean?" Estelle asked.

He nodded and pulled his arm down. "Of course, that's what she does for a living, so she's used to it. Didn't she get married or something here not long ago?" I heard a wistful note in his tone, although the steady, unexciting assessor didn't seem to be the type-A Maggie Borman's type…then again, neither did her current husband.

"She married Phil Borman," I said, wondering how someone like the county assessor, in the hub of activity in such a small community, wouldn't know that.

"That's right," he said. "He's a Realtor too." He straightened up, pulling back from the table to make room for JanaLynn as she arrived with two enormous platters.

"Be careful," she said. "They're really hot." With her hands now free, she pointed her right hand pistol-like at me. "You'd like coffee with cream. How about you, Mr. Lauerson?"

"Ah, I guess the water's fine."

"You got it. I'll be right back with your salad," she said to Estelle, and in a handful of seconds, she was.

The next several minutes were spent in silent bliss…at least for me. I noticed that Jack Lauerson had to spend as much time dabbing at his leaking nose and perspiring forehead as he did eating.

"I should eat here more often," he said. "This is *really* good."

Estelle Reyes-Guzman had been delicately sorting through her salad, ushering various green things to one side so she could pick out the chunks of perfect chicken. She paused with one properly loaded piece on her fork. "Have you talked recently with Kevin about the county building property?"

"You mean about George's piece? You know, Kevin and I cross paths a dozen times most days." The assessor's office made sure that money flowed in to the county coffers, and Zeigler spent it. "But now we have something of an issue, don't we," Lauerson added.

"But the transfer of that property hadn't been formalized?" Estelle asked.

"Ah, no, as a matter of fact. The last I heard, Mr. Payton was going to transfer the property to the county for a dollar. But that's Kevin's bailiwick. I know that he was going to have Paul Simmons handle it."

"When would you hear about it being finalized?"

"A deed transfer would be filed with the county clerk, and then I'd hear about it," the assessor said. "You ought to catch Stacey Roybal. She's the clerk, and the one with the paperwork." He prepared another mouthful. "But I see *her* all the time, too, and she never said anything one way or another."

"That's what Kevin said," Estelle agreed. "Mr. Payton's property here in town has *not* been transferred yet to the county."

"As far as I know, that's how it stands." He dabbed his nose again and lowered his voice. "What do you want to bet that now Maggie isn't going to give away the property for a buck? We had no written agreement with George, you know. And it wasn't even a handshake kind of contract."

"No bet," I said. I liked Maggie Payton well enough, but I had no idea how altruistic she might be. Handle a $100,000 sale, and she might garner a $6,000 commission. Own the property outright, with none of her own money invested in it, and the whole hundred grand was hers—assuming that her father had left his holdings to her in his will… assuming he had left a will. If he hadn't, the state would run the whole mess through probate in its own good time, and all of George Payton's estate would go to his only daughter, minus the various blood-lettings and pounds of flesh that the feds and the state would require.

Lauerson looked across at Estelle. "You know," he said, "It's incomprehensible to me that George wouldn't have at least talked with his daughter about what he wanted to do. I mean, I realize that he was a brusque old guy. But why hide something like that?"

"Because he didn't want to have to argue with her?" Estelle said. "It's not so much a question of hiding as it is just doing things his way. No haggling, no negotiations, no nothing."

The assessor wagged his fork at me. "Did George know that you gave the Guzmans those acres behind your house?"

"Sure," I replied. "We talked about it once or twice. That's what gave him the idea." I knew what Estelle meant. I had told my four adult children that I was giving my land away, but as a point of interest only, and damn near after the fact. I hadn't asked for permission or help in the process. I had asked neither sons nor daughters what they thought, or if they agreed with my decision. To my way of thinking, it wasn't any of their business. The property was mine, and I disposed of it. End of story. I could see crusty old George Payton doing the same thing.

Lauerson stretched back away from an empty platter. "Did you see Maggie yesterday?"

"Sure."

"She's taking it all right? Her dad's death, I mean?"

"I think so," I said, and let it go at that. We had no way of knowing what was going through Maggie Payton Borman's mind.

"What's the department's interest in George's land, anyway?" Lauerson asked. It had taken him longer to echo Kevin Zeigler's question than I expected.

I considered several options for an answer, but not surprisingly, Estelle Reyes-Guzman beat me to it.

"Whenever there's an unattended death, we want to be as thorough as possible," she said.

"There's some question about the circumstances? I hadn't heard that."

"Yes," she replied. JanaLynn approached and favored us all with a wide smile.

"Dessert for anyone?" she asked. "We have an amazing triple fudge thingee that'll make you reconsider that afternoon nap." That sounded terrific to me, but Lauerson groaned protest, and I knew that Estelle wouldn't indulge.

"I really need to get back to work," the assessor said. He started to reach for his wallet, but I clamped his arm.

"Mine," I said. "It's not often we get to enjoy the company of such distinguished company." By the time I'd settled the modest ticket with Jana-Lynn, Jack Lauerson was outside, exercising his back to help it support the added weight in his gut. Estelle waited for me in the small foyer.

"Tom Mears should have the histamine jar processed for prints," she said as I approached. "And Patrick's cell phone. I need to see what he came up with, and I have a couple of other stops to make. Do you want to shake down lunch?"

"Well, sure. Where are we headed?"

She hesitated. "I'd like *you* to talk with Herb Torrance again, sir. There are some questions that are nagging at me, especially after talking with Jack Lauerson. If you'd do that," and she pulled her small notebook out of her pocket, "it would free me up for a couple of errands."

"Perfect," I said. "That'll give me time to think great thoughts."

Chapter Twenty-nine

County records showed that George Payton owned property on both sides of Herb Torrance's H-Bar-T ranch. Maybe George had some insider information about the future.

When Claudio Martinez, the elderly sheepherder, had first felt the rush of cool air pouring out from the jumble of rocks in 1966, he had been intrigued. What he'd found hadn't rivaled Carlsbad, or the weird and wonderful serpentine complex of Lechugilla discovered just a few years ago. But, I'd been told, in this new find, a brave soul could squirm through limestone passages for many hundreds of yards, even reach an ice cave that one Realtor said reminded him of the ice caves in the Malpais National Monument southwest of Grants.

Over the years, the Bureau of Land Management had acquired several pieces of property along County 14. Inevitably, enough explorers tried their hand at spelunking Martinez's Tube that the feds became concerned. The spread of trash and SUV tracks marked the entrance, making it fair game for anybody and too likely that someone might crawl in to the labyrinth and not crawl back out. In recent months, the BLM had found some funding to begin their master planning process and had initiated some serious exploring on their land paralleling County Road 14, just across the road from the Torrance ranch.

None of this was a big-dollar operation, and as far as I could see, didn't promise much for the near future other than an improved fence and a small sign. Of course, the only cave I was interested in exploring was my own dark adobe. Crawling through rat shit and bat guano or among sharp-tailed bugs or sleepy rattlesnakes didn't appeal to me one bit.

"It's curious that Herb didn't buy the Payton property a long time ago," Estelle said as she handed me a reminder note. "The property south of his ranch includes a good working well, for one thing. I'm not sure about the value of the mesa top north of his place."

"He's had use of the well for years," I said, "and what acreage there is around it. If he had an agreement with George that didn't cost a penny, why pursue buying the land? There's not a whole lot of money in ranching these days."

Estelle's brow furrowed. "If Herb depends on

that water well, I would think he'd do something to make the arrangement permanent and legal."

"Well, from his standpoint, the arrangement *was* permanent and legal, sweetheart. An old friend told him to go ahead and use the property and water his livestock, and he did. That's what it amounts to."

"With George Payton so frail lately, it's interesting that Mr. Torrance hadn't made other arrangements," she said. "I would think that some long-term planning would put his mind at ease. It would be good insurance."

"Git to it tomorrow," I said, imitating Herb's measured drawl. "I'm sure Herb knew that he *should* do something. But you have to remember what that requires. He has to call up George, and they'd talk. Herb might get around to mentioning that he'd like to make an offer on the property. George might say, 'Well, now, let's talk about that. Why don't you swing on by next time you're in town.' You can see how it goes, sweetheart. Neither one of them were the sort to say, 'Let's set a date for nine on Wednesday morning.'"

Estelle sighed. "Ay," she whispered. I wasn't surprised that boot-on-the-lower-fence rail small talk, the straw-in-the-teeth sort of thing, was such a frustration to her, but it was the rule in this case.

"Not everyone is as goddamn efficient as I

am," I chuckled. "The minute you and your hubby decided to take the property off my hands, it *still* took a month to move that measly four acres of mine from my deed to yours. And most of that month was because I didn't get my carcass into gear. So what's your theory?"

"I need to know what was in the works," she said. "The single question keeps nagging at me in all of this...*why now?*" She glanced across at me. "Something always is the trigger. Something precipitates, something motivates." Her light accent touched each of the syllables, *pre-cip-i-tates, mo-ti-vates,* turning them into music for my dull ears. "If it's not a crime of passion," she added, "then it's one of planning and opportunity."

"George wasn't exactly a moving target," I said.

"That's the whole point," Estelle said.

So, armed with the undersheriff's concerns, I headed south once again, fortified with another cup of coffee to fight off the nap urge. The sun didn't help as it roasted through the windshield. A phone call caught Herb just as he was walking from house to truck, and we agreed to meet at the intersection with the state highway.

My SUV's tires slapped the tar strip announcing the bridge across the Guijarro arroyo, and as if bumped into life, my phone warbled its high, thin alert. I wasn't driving in a rush, but I took my time finding the phone, making sure that I didn't have the damn thing upside down, or fumble it off into space.

"Ah, my good friend." The gentle voice was serene. Of course, Captain Tomás Naranjo could sound like that as his finger tightened on the trigger of his pump shotgun, too. "Are you aware of what is going on?"

"I'm on my way down to meet with Herb Torrance, Tomás. Other than that, I'm not sure what kind of progress we're making."

"I have spoken with the sheriff, and he suggested that I talk to you as well."

"I appreciate that."

The Mexican state policeman chuckled. "I would have called you first, but protocol, you know."

"I'm in your debt."

"You will be interested to know," Naranjo continued, "that we have recovered the truck and trailer. So it's fortunate I located you. You will have good news for Mr. Torrance."

"I'm glad to hear that. Who had it?"

"There is a certain small shop in Villa de Oposura that we have been watching, *señor.*" He paused, giving way to his habit of searching out the most politic way of phrasing things. "They have the habit of removing certain desirable parts that are then easily marketed."

"A chop shop," I said.

"Ah, yes. That is the colorful term. The vehicle is undamaged, I am happy to report. They had not started the chopping, so to speak. The owner of the shop was eager to give us a description of the two young people who sold them the vehicle."

I bet they were eager, I thought. "A boy and his girlfriend?"

"Ah, no. Two young men. It is amazing how a wig can change things, ¿*no?* There was the impression that they were both in college, perhaps."

"How did they know that? About the wig, I mean?"

"Well, apparently the two desperados were inordinately proud of their accomplishment at the border crossing," Naranjo said. "And pride loosened the tongue. But the interesting thing," and I could hear paperwork rustling in the background, "is that this is not their first accomplishment in this line of employment."

"That doesn't surprise me, I guess."

"I have here a description of another vehicle that they delivered to the same shop, less than forty-eight hours before. A certain Dodge Ram three-quarter ton *extended* cab truck, a most impressive beast. I relayed the license number to the sheriff, but I understand that it was taken from a shopping mall parking lot in Las Cruces. Or so our two industrious friends claimed."

An enormous RV had been growing in my rearview mirror, and now roared past me, its occupants impatient to be somewhere else.

"I know nothing about the incident except that the vehicle originally had been left unlocked, with the keys in the ignition, while its owners went shopping," Naranjo said.

"That makes it easy. No witnesses?"

"I don't know, Bill. That is something...how do you say...beyond my jurisdiction. But Sheriff Torrez was most interested, and said that he would talk to authorities in Las Cruces."

"Wonderful work, Tomás. We appreciate it. What time did our two geniuses leave Oposura—with payment in cash, I presume?"

"Now, that is curious," Naranjo said. "They delivered the truck to the shop early this morning, not yesterday. They received payment upon delivery of the truck and then left promptly. The shop owner assures me that he warned the two young men that traveling in this part of the country with so much cash in hand might not be wise."

"We can always hope," I said.

"Another point of interest," Naranjo said. "The village of Tres Santos was mentioned in passing, giving the impression that the two young men were planning to return to the United States by that route. Retracing their steps, so to speak. Unless they were simply mentioning it as a diversion." The word rolled off his tongue with elegance.

"Not east to the crossing at Juarez, then," I mused.

"I would guess not. A certain arrogance in that decision, what with the current interest of law enforcement agencies. But perhaps they considered it safer in other ways. By now..." he hesitated. "I would guess that they have already crossed back into the United States. They certainly have had enough time."

The Broken Spur saloon came into view, and I slowed, scanning the vehicles in the parking lot. One car, two pickups, all local. Midafternoon was a slow time in the bar business.

"Tomás, I appreciate the heads-up. I'll get with the sheriff and see what he's found out. I don't know if this is a couple of college kids pulling a quick one, or what. They had it easy the first time. The second time got messy."

"Perhaps so. The ugly assault on the young man—Gabaldon, is it?—that is more than a college prank."

"Indeed it is. We'll do what we can to cut these two careers short."

Naranjo chuckled. "I have the impression, after talking with the shop owner, that our two young men aren't looking over their shoulders. They are too smart for the rest of us."

"Let's hope they keep thinking that way," I said. "We'll work on that. Thanks, Tomás. I'll be in touch."

"We must do lunch, you know. It has been too long, my friend."

"Absolutely." I switched off and slowed for the turn onto County Road 14. True to his work, Herb was headed southbound from the ranch, and he'd timed it just right.

Bumping over the cattleguard, I pulled off into the gravel and waited. Herb's pickup ground to a stop. At first, the rancher cranked down the window and lit a cigarette, but when I climbed down out of my SUV, he turned and said something to Socks, then stiffly worked his way out of the truck. His bandy legs didn't work so well any more.

"Hello again." He eyed the manila folder that I placed on the SUV's broad hood.

"I was just headin' to Cruces for a bit," he said. "Dale's doin' okay. Comin' home tomorrow, most likely. That's what they say, anyway."

"Well, that's good news," I said.

"Patrick's folks made it to Albuquerque. I

talked to them some," Herb added. "They said that he come out of the surgery all right."

"Is he conscious yet?"

"Nope." Herb shook his head and glared at the gravel. "So," he said slowly, as if having a hard time controlling his temper, "you got some news from down south, or what?"

"That wasn't the reason for my call, Herb, but as a matter of fact, I just got off the phone with Naranjo. They have your truck and trailer."

Herb eyed me as if he didn't understand English.

"Delivered to a chop shop in Oposura," I added.

"Well, hell. Anything left of it?"

"No damage whatsoever. Mexican bureaucracy and paperwork being what they are, you'll probably be able to pick it up by spring." The rancher looked heavenward.

"That's something, anyways."

I tapped the folder on the hood of the SUV. "We've been caught up in a few other things at the same time. You know how that goes." I pulled one of the maps out of the folder. It was the section of George Payton's land that included the windmill just south of Herb's spread. "We need to ask you a couple of things about some of the properties around here."

"Don't know what I can tell you," Herb said, but he pulled a pair of variety-store reading glasses from his shirt pocket. Those adjusted, he supported himself with both hands on the hood and examined the map. "Okay, now," he said. "That's right out here." I reached across and touched the spot marked as the windmill. "Right," Herb said. "You lookin' to buy a water well now?"

"I wanted to ask what sort of arrangement you had worked out with George on that piece."

"You mean about me usin' that mill?"

"For the water, yes."

Herb looked askance at me, then took his time to grind out the cigarette butt in the gravel. I could see that he wanted to snap, *"Why is that any of your business?"* But he didn't.

"George just passed on yesterday," he said, *and here you are already.* He didn't have to add the latter. We'd known each other long enough that he was aware of my aversion to prying into other people's business. If we belonged in this conversation—either the Sheriff's Department or the State's Livestock Board—then Herb could figure out for himself that we were on the trail of something.

"That's what prompts my question," I said. "According to the assessor's map, this is about seven acres surrounding a producing well. That must be important to you, as the nearest neighbor."

"'Course it's important. Christ almighty, you know this country."

"Did you have a formal agreement of some sort with George?"

Herb looked at me as if I had gone simple. "Well, I guess formal enough. Nothin' in writing, if that's what you're gettin' at."

"Meaning that he said 'go ahead and use it,' and you did?"

"That's about it." He dug out another cigarette and snapped the lighter.

"Had you talked with George recently?"

"Sure."

"Did you two talk about the possibility of your buying this property?" The blunt question pulled the aging rancher up short. When Herb looked as if he was going to settle into ruminating too long about that, I added, "We're trying to determine the status of several of George's properties." I knew that sounded lame. When a person dies, the status of property is hardly the province of law enforcement agencies. "That guy collected acreage like some folks collect stamps, and his estate is kind of complicated."

"He sure did that," Herb agreed, and I could see him opening up.

"You had talked with him about this parcel? About actually acquiring it?"

"Well, look," the rancher said. "Last month,

I took a rifle over to George's so he could see it. I wanted to see if he could tell me when it was made." Herb took a deep drag on his cigarette. "An old Winchester that belonged to my dad. I was always going to do that, and one day here not too long ago, Dale was out shooting the '86, and the subject come up. He said he'd like to have it someday. I told the boy that the rifle wasn't never to be sold. He said he'd never do that. Then the both of us got to wondering more about it. So I took it over to George's. Wasn't much about guns that he didn't know."

"That's for sure," I agreed.

"Well, he looked up the serial number in one of his books, and sure enough, it was made right at 1927." He looked off into the distance. "My dad bought that rifle brand-new from the old mercantile in Deming when he was twenty-one years old. He told me once it cost him two months' pay."

"Still worth that," I said, and Herb hacked out one of his short, rasping laughs.

"God damn if that isn't what George said, too. Little different wage scale now, though."

That's the way it goes with conversations, and I maneuvered to bring us back to the present.

"At that time you talked about the property as well, then."

Herb nodded. "One thing led to another, and

we talked some about that land. George said he was thinkin' of cleanin' some things up, and that he'd sell that land to me for a dollar," Herb said. "He said if he was ten years younger, he'd try to trade me out of that Winchester. Maybe swap for the land. Now, I wasn't about to do that, then or now. You know, my father shot that rifle for sixty years. I wasn't about to part with it, especially with Dale wantin' it. I told George that I'd pay a fair enough price for the land, though." He bent down and regarded the map once more. "I offered him a thousand an acre and figured that was fair. I kinda depend on that water."

"He took the offer?"

Herb coughed another little chuckle. "Nope. He said I'd used the land all these years, that I'd fixed up the windmill and maintained it, fixed the fences… anyways, he said no. Pay him a buck, and that'd be it. Wouldn't talk about havin' it any other way."

"And did you do that?"

"Not then, no. Maybe I should have, you know. But I wanted him to think on it some. I felt like that would be takin' advantage, don't you know. He said he'd dig out the abstract, and we'd settle up." He smiled ruefully.

"You hadn't talked with him about the land since then? He hadn't called you? You didn't go over to see him again?"

"Nope. Got busy. You know how that goes."

I shuffled papers for a moment, and selected the photocopy that included the land on top of the mesa. "And this piece?"

Herb cocked his head sideways, regarding the small map. "Don't need that more'n what a dollar would buy." He traced the boundary line with a bent finger. "That's the rimrock right behind my place. Nice view, and that's about it. No water. Damn near no grass. Now, I know that Waddell wants it. He's got some development in mind for right down here," and he tapped the north side of the mesa, where I had seen the drill rig. "You know," and his face wrinkled up in a grimace as he turned to stare up at the cloudless sky. "I'm tryin' to recall how George got ahold of that piece of property on top, there. I think it comes out to about eleven acres. Anyways, I was thinkin' of cuttin' a deal with George on that, just so I didn't end up with a damn parkin' lot or something lookin' down from the rimrock through my bedroom window."

"Had you mentioned it to George?" I turned a bit as an aging sedan headed by on the highway, a 1980s Chevy sedan that had once been dark blue but now bore faded patches on hood, roof, and trunk where the sun had fried the paint.

"Nope. But the mood he was in last month, I damn sure coulda got it cheap." He straightened up with a popping of joints. "It's a damn shame how this country gets all chopped up. Give us another fifty years, and a fella will really think he's got somethin' when he signs for a quarter-acre lot."

I wasn't about to argue that, but my attention followed the Chevy sedan. Now, a profiling cop would peg the big old sedan as a drug runner's delight, running a little heavy in the rear, with all that trunk space and those nice nooks and crannies along the enormous undercarriage. But I knew the car, and I knew the driver, headed from his parish in Regál to another in María. No doubt he had visited his Mexican parish in Tres Santos, too, but border agents didn't have to worry. Father Bertrand Anselmo would have no drugs in that old boat.

The Chevy went by slowly enough that I could see two additional passengers. Any other day, that wouldn't have been unusual, either. Father Anselmo ferried parishioners on a regular basis. Herb Torrance said something else, but I was no longer paying attention. The left turn signal of the Chevy flashed and the car pulled into the Broken Spur Saloon. From that distance, Anselmo's car was not much more than a dark dash, but I could tell the difference between pausing to drop someone off and nosing in to park.

Chapter Thirty

There was one thing wrong with what I was doing—I was no longer sheriff of Posada County… or undersheriff, or sergeant, or even a rookie deputy. As a livestock inspector, I was sworn to enforce any law, policy, or state edict that applied to the raising, marking, selling, or transferring of livestock.

But I wasn't ready to quibble over minor points. As I drove toward the Broken Spur Saloon, I searched the electronic phone directory, then punched the right button, pleased that the last time I'd looked the number up in a hard copy directory, I'd added it to the electronic gadget, too. In a moment, Christine Prescott's cheerful voice answered.

"Christine, this is Bill Gastner. I need to talk with Victor ASAP."

"He's in the kitchen, sir."

"Tell him to pick up." She didn't argue, and when Victor came on the line—he took his sweet time doing so—I had slowed with the parking lot less than five hundred yards ahead. It appeared that Anselmo and his two passengers had gone inside.

"What?" Mr. Cheerful would be balancing the phone receiver between shoulder and ear as he worked the grill.

"Victor, Father Anselmo just entered your place with a couple of guys. Take a look through your kitchen door and tell me if they're the same two that you saw yesterday. The two that Patrick Gabaldon picked up."

"How am I supposed to know that?"

"You saw them, Victor. Now go look."

"What's it to you, anyway?"

"God damn it, Victor, don't be an ass. Go look."

The phone whacked against something, and in the background I could hear the hissing, clanking ambiance of the Broken Spur's kitchen. Victor's tone wasn't quite so grouchy or antagonistic when he came back on the line. "Two young men. Yeah, they could be the ones."

"Victor, listen to me. *Are* they the two that Patrick picked up?"

"I think so. Right now, all they're doing is sittin' at the bar, looking at the menu. What am I supposed to do about it?"

"Absolutely nothing. Just give 'em whatever

they want. I'll be there in a few minutes." And I'd feel like an absolute jackass if we were wrong in this.

Victor started to say something else charming, but I disconnected, punching the autodial for the Posadas County Sheriff's Department. As the phone rang, I drove into the west end of the parking lot, then around the building to park behind Victor's Cadillac.

"Posadas County Sheriff's Department, Sutherland."

"Brent, I need whoever you've got down here at the Broken Spur. Silent approach. We may have the two men who attacked Patrick Gabaldon."

"Yes, sir. Deputy Pasquale is at Moore. He's closest."

"That'll work. No siren. Make sure he understands that. If this is a wild goose chase, I'll be the first to let you know."

"Are you inside the building right now, sir?"

"No. I'm in my truck."

"You should probably stay there, sir."

"I probably should." Brent Sutherland was such an earnest kid.

Victor appeared at the back door, his eyes narrowing as I approached.

"It's them. I'm sure of it."

I nodded my appreciation at his unembellished

statement of fact. "Just be patient," I said. "I need a couple of minutes, so go back and engage them in conversation." Victor was ready to nix that idea—there were limits to his cooperation, after all. But I walked around the west side of the building without giving him the chance. There were no windows on that side except the two opaque single panes in the restrooms, high up on the wall. Anselmo's Chevy was the first vehicle in line, so if the men were sitting at the bar, I was entirely out of their view.

From two strides away, I could smell the old crate. The door locks were down except for the driver's, and that was pure Anselmo. He wouldn't even consider locking his car, since he owned nothing worth stealing. The inside of the car was an amazing clutter, with the seats threadbare, oozing stuffing in half a dozen places. What interested me most were the two backpacks on the rear seat.

Glancing toward the Spur, I opened the driver's door, rewarded with a loud squawk of sagging hinges, and reached around to pop the lock. As I did so, I could imagine Judge Lester Hobart's dour expression as he mentioned the issue of illegal search and seizure. But I wasn't sheriff and I wasn't seizing anything, so I felt no qualms.

Both backpacks were the generic sort of rigs that students use. I unzipped the top of the first and found clothing, one of those cardboard cylinders of potato chips, a small toiletry kit, and various other odds and ends. The large front pocket contained a fat bag of Mexican hard candy and two inhalers of prescription asthma medication. A plastic liter water bottle was shoved into a side pocket.

The second pack was equally uninteresting, until I opened the front pocket. A blonde wig was stowed neatly in a plastic bag. Along with it was a potpourri of gum, tissue, lip balm, and curiously, a wrinkled, drab book. I pulled it out and saw that it was a generically bound stage script for *The Andersonville Trials,* and, my curiosity tweaked, I flipped it open. The role of Wirz was highlighted in yellow. "And what do we make of this?" I whispered to myself. "In spare moments between heists he's studying his lines?"

The two weren't so foolish as to stow large sums of cash in the backpacks, nor any weapons. I tucked things back into place and straightened up, closing the car door gently.

Nothing incriminating, except the wig— which certainly didn't mean that this was the very blonde over whom the Mexican *agente* had drooled at the border crossing. No money, no weapon.

What I had was Victor's word, and he didn't indict others lightly. These were the two men he'd seen Pat Gabaldon pick up on the state highway.

They might *be* that, all right. But they might have had nothing to do with the cowboy's misadventure. Sure enough. And one of them might have left nice, clear fingerprints on Pat's cell phone before heaving it off into the trees. For the moment, that possibility was enough for me.

I walked quickly back to the kitchen door. Before going inside, I took a moment to check that the pudgy Smith and Wesson was still where it always was, just to the right of the small of my back, concealed by my short jacket and not buried under an overhanging belly.

Victor was busy at the stove, and the aroma of burgers, onions, and other wonderful things was strong. He ignored me. I ripped a single page out of my small pocket notebook, and printed a note in block letters, taking my time. Victor Junior came out of the pantry with a tray of hamburger buns, and I folded the note and handed it to him. "Will you give this to Father Anselmo for me? You don't need to tell him who it's from."

Victor Junior took the note and glanced over at his father.

"Just do it," Victor said without turning around.

"Just give this to Father?" the young man asked. This time, Victor turned and glared at him venomously.

"And ask Christine to come into the kitchen," I added. My messenger shrugged and headed out through the swinging door.

I waited without giving in to the temptation of looking through the little triangle of glass in the swinging door.

"You got people coming?" Victor asked. He flipped the three burgers and then lifted the basket of fries out of the grease.

"Eventually," I said. Christine entered the kitchen and favored me with a wide smile.

"Hey, sir. I didn't know you were back here."

"Christine, I need to talk with the two men who are with Father Anselmo. They don't need to know who I am, all right?"

"Sir?"

"Don't call me sheriff, or anything else. Stay on the opposite side of the bar from them."

She looked uneasy. "Sure, sir. They're just grabbing a burger before heading on down the road. They're hitching to Las Cruces. Father Bert is buying them some lunch." She glanced at the clock. "Very late lunch."

"That's good," I said. "You have some coffee?"

"Sure thing."

"I'll be out in a minute. Remember what I said." I watched her leave the kitchen, passing Junior in the doorway. He nodded at me and finished it off with a shrug. I turned to Victor. "I don't want any ruckus," I said. "I want to make sure of that. Nobody gets hurt." He didn't reply, but pointed at the rack of buns. His son unzipped the first package and handed it to his father.

I walked through the swinging doors and down the length of the bar, nodding at two state highway employees who sat at a two-top by the juke box, and a young couple I didn't know just inside the door. Father Bertrand Anselmo sat at the bar, right where an alcoholic shouldn't have been, both rms resting on the polished surface. A cup of coffee nestled between his hands. To his right were the two hikers, and they didn't even glance my way as I passed behind them.

As I did so, I touched Anselmo's shoulder.

"Well, hello there," he said brightly, turning to extend his hand. A big, bear-like guy with full beard that his Roman collar, Bertrand Anselmo would have looked at home in the seventeenth century. Always in black, his clothing was threadbare and his shoes on their last mile. "How have you been?"

"Just fine, Father." How's your day going?"

"Buying a couple of wayfarers the best burgers on the planet," he said. "They're headed on back from south of the border to college in Cruces." He leaned forward and spread one hand. "Richard Zimmerman and…"

"Rory," one of the boys said.

"Rory Hobbs," Anselmo finished. "This is an old friend of mine, Bill Gastner."

Well done, I thought. Zimmerman had a grip like a dead fish, but Hobbs shook my hand with vigor and interest.

"Down here?" Christine asked. She held up the coffee.

"Right at the end, there," I said. That put me where I could see the two men without leaning past Anselmo. I settled on the stool and added two tubs of creamer to the coffee. By the time I'd done that, Christine had returned with three baskets of burgers.

I regarded the two travelers as I sipped the coffee. Slumped as they were, it was hard to judge height, but Zimmerman was the larger of the two, with long black hair pulled back in a pony tail. His baseball cap, with a logo I couldn't read, was settled backward on his head. His bony features looked as if he needed more than a few burgers.

Rory Hobbs reminded me of one of those perfect child stars now grown into a young man without losing any of the magic. Large, luminous eyes looked through a thick, dark forest of lashes. A good, strong chin and finely sculpted, small ears were partially hidden by his copper-streaked brown hair—the kid was a publicist's dream. As he leaned forward to sink perfect teeth into the burger, his expression of pleasure showed a hint of dimples.

"So, how's Mexico these days?" I asked. "Lots of bad news out of that place."

"I tell you," Hobbs said, chewing industriously, "I could live there. I mean, it costs just about *nothing,* you know?"

"So I've heard." I eyes him critically. His eating slowed as he realized that he was under scrutiny. I remembered Naranjo's assessment. This was a young man entirely at ease. Deciding to try a tack that might prompt a little discomfiture, I asked, "Why do I think that I've seen you before?"

"Really?" Only mild interest slowed the food, and Zimmerman shot him a look that said something like, "*you, not me.*"

"Did you go down to Cruces for any of the college plays this past year?" Father Anselmo asked. "We have something of a celebrity on our hands, Bill. This young man tells me that he's a drama major."

I snapped my fingers, surprising even myself with how easy it was to invent plausible nonsense from a single dim memory. "The Shakespeare Festival this past summer. I saw the excerpts contest. You were in that, if I'm not mistaken." I hadn't seen the contest, but I'd read about it—two teams of five actors each, chosen at random from a roster of drama students, given only the time when the other team was on stage to prepare. "They gave you only ten minutes or so for each performance, the winner to be the last team standing, am I right?"

"Last man standing. I like that," Hobbs grinned. "That's how it was."

"Did you make it down for any of the festival?" I asked the priest, and he shook his head.

"So…am I right?" I pursued. "You were in the short scenes?"

"I confess," Hobbs said. "And maybe you saw the performance of *Midsummer Night's Dream?*"

"Didn't see that," I said, and smiled at him. If it was a trap, it was a clever one. "I was going to catch the Scottish play, but I missed that, too. So…what did you do for the contest? I don't remember?"

"Ah." He leaned far back and stared at the ceiling. "All kinds of stuff. And in a couple of things, I think we faked out the judges." He smiled, altogether fetching.

"Well, it was remarkable," I said. "What's coming up? Anything interesting?"

He took a chunk out of the burger. "Heavy stuff," he said. "I'm trying out for a couple of things."

"Can I be nosy?"

He shot me another assessing look. "Like, one of the profs wants to do *The Andersonville Trials*. I thought I'd try for that."

I held up both hands, framing his face with my fingers. "I see Wirz," I said. His delicate eyebrows shot up. "A maligned commandant of a Civil War prison camp would be a challenging role." But what I really saw was that, replacing the dark hair with a light wig, the kid's visage could easily fool anyone.

"You're a history buff?" Hobbs asked.

"Oh, boy!" Anselmo said, well aware of my hobby of tracking down tidbits of frontier legend. For a moment, I thought that he'd forgotten my note.

"Western military history," I said quickly. "My one hobby, I'm afraid."

"So you know the play, then."

"Certainly do. Wirz was an interesting, conflicted character. Even tragic in some ways. You're going to have a ball with that role."

"That's if I get the part."

"Oh, no doubt about hat." I grinned at Zimmerman, who didn't seem to mind being left out of the conversation. "And what's your story, son?"

He tucked the remains of the burger wrapper into the bottom of the baket. "I'm just in one of the pre-med programs."

"*Just?*" I said. "Since when did medicine become a *just?* That's a handful, son. Congratulations. I'm surprised that either one of you found time to break away from school for a trip to Mexico."

"Sometimes you just have to get away," Hobbs said easily. "The opportunity comes along…" and he finished with a shrug.

"You're smart to recognize it." I held my coffee mug while Christine refilled it. I cut her off at half. The trouble with this conversation was that I was enjoying the hell out of it, and enjoying the company of the two college kids. That conflicted with the sour thought that, if they were indeed the ones who assaulted Pat Gabaldon, they were carrying thousands of dollars in cash—and still were about to allow a parish priest without an extra two cents to his name to pick up the tab for lunch. They'd laugh about that, no doubt.

Victor Sanchez came out of the kitchen and stood with his hands on his hips, regarding us all as if it was an hour after closing and we should all vanish.

"What do you do, sir?" Hobbs asked pleasantly.

"I'm retired," I said. "Sort of. I work for the Livestock Board." I waggled a finger. "Count brands, that sort of thing."

"You haven't always done that," he said.

"Nope." The young couple by the door rose from their table, the girl making just enough of a detour to hand the ticket and a twenty-dollar bill to Christine over the bar. Neither blonde nor pretty, she wouldn't have drawn an agent's attention. She nodded at us, and then the couple left the saloon. That left the two highway department employees, and us. As the door closed behind the young couple, I heard another car swing off the highway, braking hard.

Sipping coffee with one hand, I pulled my phone out of my shirt pocket, looking at it as if it had just announced an incoming call by vibrating. I pushed the autodial.

"Hello?" I said, and dispatcher Brent Sutherland came on the line.

"Sutherland."

"Hey, you found me," I said, and if that confused the dispatcher, he didn't let on. "Where's Tom at?" In the background I could hear radio traffic.

"He's in the Broken Spur parking lot, sir," Sutherland replied.

"Tell him to hang tight."

"The sheriff just left the airport, so. ETA is forty at least."

"Okay. I'll be in touch." I folded the phone and put it back in my pocket. Christine came out of the kitchen, where she'd followed Victor, and as the door swung behind her, I caught a glimpse of Deputy Tom Pasquale. Forcing a confrontation was pointless, since we had all the time in the world and all the *space* in the world once outside. Rory

Hobbs and Richard Zimmerman had no vehicle of their own. They had nowhere to run.

As if sensing an escalating tension, Zimmerman looked down the bar, perhaps wondering where the pretty barmaid had gone. Victor came out of the kitchen, ignored us, and went over to the table where the two laborers were just finishing up. He gathered their burger baskets and nodded at the ticket. The two men conferred over the payment, then tossed down a few bucks, rose, and left the Spur.

Holding the two baskets, Victor paused and nodded at Father Anselmo. "Come back to the kitchen for a minute," he said. "I gotta talk to you."

"Well, sure," the priest said. He rose and almost as an afterthought said to the two young men, "Give me a second. Then we'll head on up to the interstate."

"You got it," Hobbs said. Zimmerman rubbed the palms of his hands on his trousers. I guess that his radar was more finely tuned than his partner's. He might not have even known why his nerves were twanging, but Rory Hobbs was oblivious.

Now, with everyone out of harm's way and just the three of us in the bar, I saw no reason to put off the inevitable. I rose to my feet and beckoned toward the kitchen door, hoping that Deputy Pasquale was paying attention. Both young men followed my gaze, and none of us heard the front door behind us.

"Gentlemen, put your hands on the bar in front of you," the voice commanded, and it startled even me. I pushed away from the bar, right hand flying back to the butt of my revolver. Pasquale had moved with stealth belying his size, and his automatic was drawn. "Right now. I want to see four hands."

Zimmerman gasped something incoherent and half-turned, his face drained of color. Hobbs rose slowly, an unreadable expression on his handsome features. He looked at me then, and his eyes were chilling. "You old bastard," he whispered.

"Don't be stupid," I snapped. "Hands on the bar, spread the feet."

Facing a drawn gun, and Tom Pasquale's was steady and out of reach five paces away, most folks would turn to gelatin. Zimmerman was well on his way to that state, but Hobbs was calculating. I could see it in those dark eyes, shifting this way and that, playing the numbers.

"There's nowhere you can go," I said. Pasquale stepped forward, closing the distance. "It's over, Rory. It's over. We have good descriptions from the chop shop in Oposura, and from a witness in the parking lot in Cruces where you took the Dodge."

"I don't know what you're talking about," he said.

"Oh, God, Rory," Zimmerman whispered.

"The good news is that you didn't kill Patrick Gabaldon, the cowboy whose truck and trailer you highjacked. I'm sure he's looking forward to meeting you two."

Zimmerman's knees buckled, and he let the bar stool take his weight. Hobbs turned slightly, and in fifty years of paying attention to such things, I have never seen anyone move so fast. With the deputy advancing but still three strides away, Hobbs spun and grabbed his partner in a hammer lock, a blue utility knife appearing in his right hand.

"Back off!" he screamed at Pasquale. The razor tip of the knife dug into Zimmerman's neck. He hauled his partner to his feet and backed along the bar toward the kitchen. Barstools crashed out of his way. "Back off!" he repeated.

"What's that going to accomplish?" I slipped around the end of the bar into the bartender's aisle. "Let him go, Rory."

"You just back off. I mean it."

"Where do you think you're going to go?"

A thin tendril of blood laced down Zimmerman's neck, and I could see that this time, the small triangular blade was in just the right spot, a thin layer of skin and muscle between it and the young man's carotid.

"Not across the border," I said. "They're

waiting for you. And even if you did make it across, Mexican authorities would be delighted to see you."

"Get the priest out here!" he cried. For the first time, I heard panic in his voice. He jerked upward with his left arm, yanking Zimmerman's head backward.

"Can't do that," I said.

"I'll kill him!" He jerked his partner again, and Zimmerman let out a cry.

"Well, you can go ahead and do that if you want, I suppose," I said. Zimmerman's knees sagged. "I'm not sure what that will accomplish, other than saving the taxpayers a lot of money." I took a step or two down the bar, keeping my hands in sight.

"Drop the weapon," Pasquale ordered, but Hobbs ignored him, eyes locked on me. He'd twisted his hold enough that his captive provided effective cover from the deputy's gun. He was full face to me, though, and maybe could judge that I wasn't the one to put a bullet between those expressive eyes.

Behind him, the swinging door to the kitchen drifted open, silent and smooth. Victor appeared, face glowering.

If he felt the air change or heard a soft foot tread, I wasn't sure, but Rory Hobbs turned ever so slightly to his right, arm still locked around Zimmerman's chin, blade still digging into flesh.

Victor struck with precision, the pan hitting Hobbs squarely on the temple before the boy could lift an arm to protect himself. The impact was an ugly, muted thud. Victor hadn't selected an aluminum pan, or a copper one, or even stainless steel. The old-fashioned cast iron caved in Hobb's elegant skull like a gourd hit with a baseball bat. Pasquale moved just about as fast. He grabbed Hobb's right arm even as the kid slid to the floor, twisting the utility knife free. Released, Zimmerman staggered against a bar stool, hand clamped to his neck, then recoiled in horror as he saw Victor's arm draw back again.

Before I could round the end of the bar, the deputy bulldozed Victor to one side, spun the young man around out of harm's way and cuffed his hands behind his back. Zimmerman offered no resistance as I reached across with a bar towel and pressed it against the small incision on his neck.

"Back off," Pasquale snapped as Victor stepped toward the crumpled figure on the floor. The dark pool of blood was spreading inexorably across the wooden floor from Rory Hobbs' skull.

"Get him off my floor," Victor ordered.

"I said, *back off!*" Pasquale roared. "I mean it, Victor. Drop that pan."

"My Lord," Anselmo said. He'd swung open the kitchen door and now strode forward, catching Victor by the arm.

The deputy bent down, eyes still locked on Victor, and touched two fingers to the side of Rory Hobbs' neck. After a few seconds, Thomas looked up at me and shook his head.

Chapter Thirty-one

Concentrating on the *what,* and not the *why,* I wrote my way through a lengthy deposition, taking my time so that I included every detail, from the utility knife to the old-fashioned leather-covered lead slapper that Rory Hobbs had carried concealed in his hip pocket. There was no point in dwelling on the *why* of it. Over the years, I had seen a fascinating number of people who, certainly knowing better, had done astonishingly stupid, self-destructive things.

The late Rory Hobbs and his incarcerated-without-bail partner Richard Zimmerman were certainly in that category. Hobbs had gone from promising actor to dead; Zimmerman had traveled his own slippery slope from pre-med studies to charges that included conspiracy, aggravated assault, grand larceny auto theft, international trafficking, and even cruelty to animals.

Of course, most of those charges would vanish

in the cluttered haze of the legal process, but the certainty was that Richard Zimmerman would spend many years behind bars. If lawyers were clever, civil suits on behalf of Pat Gabaldon would hammer Zimmerman and Hobbs' family for years to come.

In short, two lives wasted, and all because one of the two young men—it was still not clear which one—happened to glance into the cab of a fancy truck and saw the keys dangling from the ignition. Of course, Zimmerman said that it was Hobbs who had hatched the scheme, but he wasn't a half-bad actor himself.

The pre-med student had been smart enough to hurl Patrick's phone when it rang and scared the crap out of him—but not smart enough to think about prints.

At five minutes after seven that evening, I became conscious of a figure standing silently in the doorway, watching me. I relaxed back from Estelle Reyes-Guzman's computer, clasped my hands behind my head, and smiled at the undersheriff.

"You look right at home, sir," she said. "How's it coming?"

"Ah. Well, there's a tendency to wax eloquent, but that's what the 'delete' key is for."

"I faxed a photo of Zimmerman and Hobbs to Captain Naranjo. The descriptions fit, and we should be getting confirmation from his witnesses here in a little bit."

"By next week, maybe."

"And I thought you would like to know…the district attorney is not going to press any charges against Victor."

I grunted approval. "If he did, I'd rewrite this deposition," I said. "Hobbs was threatening great bodily harm during the commission of a felony, and besides that, Victor had no way of knowing whether or not Hobbs would turn his whacko attentions toward Christine or Father Anselmo."

"Besides, he's Victor," Estelle said.

"That's right. He's Victor. He doesn't cringe behind the nearest table. There's a certain element of frontier justice at work here, sweetheart. I *did* tell Victor that he needs to find a good lawyer, though. I'm willing to bet that Hobbs' family won't see it our way. So I'm being extra careful here. Then again, they'll be busy in a blizzard of other legal paper."

"I wondered if in a few minutes you'd be ready for a break."

"Absolutely. I'm ready for food, is what I am. This is what you get for sending me out on errands," I laughed. "'*Go ask Herb some questions,*' you say. And see?"

"Yes, sir. I knew that Herb would talk with you more easily than he does with me. That's all."

"Nonsense." I knew damn well that she was right.

"And we made some important progress," Estelle added. "I'll be in the conference room when you're ready."

Ten minutes later, I saved, printed, and filed my deposition, complete with the notary seal that Gayle Torrez affixed for me. My six-page version of events would go into the hopper with all the others, and Zimmerman's fate would churn out the other end. It was out of my hands, with the exception of testimony eventually in court.

Expecting a short ride either to Estelle's home or to the Don Juan, my home-away-from-home, I was surprised when we pulled into the small parking lot of the Town and Country Liquor Store.

Formerly the Town and Country SuperMart and before that the Posadas Ball and Pin Bowling Center, the liquor store was not the destination I had in mind. Both Estelle and Francis enjoyed a glass of wine now and then, but I'd never actually seen Estelle buy any—and certainly not while on duty in a county car. The way the day was shaping up, though, I was thinking that a good stout belt of something high octane might be the drug of choice. We pulled into the parking lot of the liquor store, and before getting out of the car she took a moment to retrieve a small plastic evidence bag tucked in her briefcase.

She held up the bag so that I could see the store receipt inside. The tiny blue print recorded the purchase of a 1.5-liter bottle of Tucker's Aussie, one of the strong, cheap Australian merlots of which George Payton had been fond…and a near full bottle of which had been on his kitchen table.

"That receipt was in the trash under the sink," I guessed. "In the bag that the bottle came in."

"Yes, sir." She ran her fingers thoughtfully along the zip closure. "A fresh bottle of Tucker's merlot was on the table, minus a single glassful that had been poured and then spilled when Mr. Payton collapsed. We found an empty bottle in the trash as well…along with the bag and this."

"All right."

"Tom Mears found George Payton's prints on both wine bottles, sir."

"As I would expect he would." I gazed at her, waiting.

"And no one else's." Estelle turned the evidence bag this way and that. "No one. Not a clerk at Town and County, not a distributor…no one."

"A glass wine bottle is about the world's best surface for prints," I said. "So it was wiped clean. That's what you're telling me?"

"Yes. Tom Mears found a faint smudge or two,

but nothing else. Nothing of use. You said that Mr. Payton almost always had wine with his lunch?"

"Every time that I've eaten with him. Yes. Before and during. He always had a dose before the food. 'Gotta wake up the taste buds,' he would say." I could see George's gnarled, arthritic hands holding the eight ounce tumbler in a two-handed grip. I'd seen him chug down the merlot the way most people can chug tap water.

"That may have been when he finished the first bottle, then," Estelle said. "He…or someone… poured a second glass from a fresh bottle, and that was what was spilled during the attack."

"Without a doubt," I said. "He'd drink that first glass, and have about thirty seconds before he'd have to waddle off to…" I stopped in mid-sentence.

"Waddle off?"

"He'd go to the bathroom," I said. "He had the beginnings of prostate cancer. Slow growing, Perrone told him. Not to mention that George wasn't a good prospect for surgery. He wasn't supposed to drink alcohol. Or smoke. Maybe you can imagine what a six- or eight-ounce tumbler of red wine loaded with tannic acid would do to a cranky prostate and irritated bladder."

Estelle smiled sympathetically. "Uncle Reuben was always muttering about his *próstata*."

"Well, it gets your attention, let me tell you," I said. "But what's the fun of giving in to the doctor's orders, George would say. He just stayed close to a bathroom. But it's predictable as hell. You drink, you pee. That's just the way it is."

She held up the receipt. "I find it hard to believe that he went out to buy a bottle of wine when he knew that the food was on its way over from the Don Juan. Would he do that? Would he drive himself?"

"*I* was supposed to buy it," I said. "When we talked Thursday morning, he asked me to pick up a bottle on the way over. He knew he didn't have enough for lunch."

"But you didn't buy the wine."

"No, I didn't. I got hung up at Herb's. I did talk to George briefly, and he didn't want to wait. *He* cancelled the luncheon date, not me. He didn't mention the wine then, or that he was asking someone else to fetch a bottle. He wouldn't ask Ricardo Mondragon to do it. But no… I don't think *he'd* go out to get it himself. He'd just make the one glass last."

"So," Estelle mused regarding the receipt thoughtfully. "At 11:47 a.m." She held up the baggie, her thumb marking the cash register's daytime imprint.

"If the computer's clock is accurate." I nodded

at the store's front door. "Blake would remember if George came in," I said. "Well, he might," I amended.

Blake Pierson had tended the little bar at the bowling alley in the 1970s, then worked at the supermarket, tending *its* small liquor department, then managed the current iteration. His knowledge of things alcoholic was encyclopedic. I knew him well not because I drank—nobody got rich off my intake—but because the largest percentage of crimes involved lubrication before their commission, wearing the badge meant talking with the source of the sauce from time to time.

I followed Estelle inside, struck as always by the odd, cloying aroma of the store. The merchandise didn't ooze through the glass of the shelved bottles. It oozed from the pores of those who drank too much and then returned to the store for a refill. The potpourri of wine and spirits thickened over the years, permeating the very skeleton of the building itself.

Pierson, a stumpy little guy who favored plaid flannel shirts any time of year, was studying a multipage computer print-out as we entered. "Ohhhh," he shuddered. "I didn't do it." He folded the print-out carefully, patting it flat on the counter. From somewhere amid the racks of red wine, a rail-thin elderly man appeared clutching a liter-and-a-half bottle, and Pierson reached out across the counter to tilt the bottle just far enough that he could scan the bar-code with the little hand wand. "Thirteen thirty-eight, Pop," he said, and made change from the twenty with economical motions, counting the change out like a rapid-fire auctioneer. "You come back and see us," he said. He slipped the bottle into double paper bags and handed the cargo to the aging customer. Pop Mendoza ambled past us with a curt nod of greeting, headed for the door.

"How's it goin'?" Pierson asked, and leaned on the counter.

Estelle had removed the receipt from the evidence bag, and she placed it on the counter. Pierson framed it with both hands without touching it and closed one eye as if peering through a spy-glass.

"Right over there," he said, and pointed over the top of the cash register. "The Aussie end cap display. We sell a lot of that. Good shelf life when it's uncorked, robust, lots of fruit. Good, honest stuff, and cheaper than it should be."

"Sir, did George Payton come in sometime during the last day or two to buy a bottle of this?"

"Oh," Pierson groaned, and when he exhaled I could smell the afterlife of something robust, with lots of fruit. He touched the date on the receipt as if assuming we hadn't noticed its presence. "Damn,

I was so sorry to hear of Georgie." He frowned and shook his head. "What a guy, you know?"

"Yes, sir," Estelle said. "He was in?"

"Oh, gosh, no." Pierson bent down and rested stout forearms on the glass counter, pushing the receipt back toward Estelle. "I haven't actually *seen* Georgie in a couple of months. I asked Maggie the other day how he was doing, and she said he was real frail. Just real frail."

"When was that?"

He tapped the receipt. "Guess it *was* yesterday. Yesterday morning." He squinted one eye at the receipt again. "This says 11:47 a.m."

"So, yesterday morning," Estelle repeated.

"The one bottle, right there," Pierson said, and straightened up. "Probably for Georgie. 'Course, I don't *know* that for sure. She strikes me as a *martini* type, you know." He held thumb and forefinger together as if pinching the slender stem of a glass. "So I'm guessing it was for Georgie. Phil...you know Phil comes in and buys that from time to time for his father-in-law, too. But he's a beer man. Phil, I mean." He puffed out his cheeks. "I could be nosy," he added, and looked quizzically at the undersheriff.

"Whenever there's an unattended death," Estelle said easily, giving him the stock answer. "We like to tie up all the loose ends."

"Well, sure you do. What else? Mornin', Evie," he called to the woman who had entered and was angling off toward the single section of grocery items.

Estelle picked up the receipt. "This was Maggie Payton, though," she repeated. "You're sure of that?"

"Well, as sure as I am of anything these days," Pierson laughed. "That's a cash sale, so we don't have a card receipt with a signature. But she was here yesterday morning, and I remember her buying the Aussie." He grinned, showing a diminishing supply of teeth. "You could ask her, right? Don't go tattling on me, now. I'd hate to have her as an enemy."

"Not to worry," Estelle said pleasantly. "Thanks, sir." She held the receipt so he could see it. "This time is accurate?"

"Right on the dot," he laughed. "Lookit," he said, and held out the tail end of the register tape. He twisted around and eyed the Coors clock behind him. "Right on the money. To the minute." Estelle nodded appreciatively.

The walk back outside to the car seemed like about fifteen miles, all of it uphill.

Chapter Thirty-two

The neat brick ranch house on East Fairview Lane was manicured to the hilt, ready for a magazine photo-shoot. Neither Phil nor Maggie Borman would call their place a "house," of course. That word was taboo in their circle. The Bormans' *home* cried out to me that the owners would rather be somewhere else...nothing about the place said *Posadas County* to me.

Only heavy, diligent watering could produce such a verdant yard, coupled with endless mowing, aerating, fertilizing, and fussing. The lawn would make a golf course envious. I had no doubt that the Bormans had a water treatment system, since Posadas water was hard enough to break with a hammer. On top of that, the soil held enough alkali that the upward leaching deposited white ghosts on the surface when the water evaporated.

I knew the Bormans' aging yardman, a sober guy who rarely spoke and even more rarely smiled.

His customer list included several similar owners, and I guess he had the touch that assured business. The busy Bormans' perfect lawn, perfect cosmos and chrysanthemums, perfect token cacti, perfect everything—all flourished.

It made my yard seem like a bramble pile… but then again, I considered my yard an *authentic* bramble pile, and that saved me a lot of time and energy. I had no desire to be reminded by a perfect green lawn that I had at one time lived somewhere else, or that I wanted Posadas to somehow morph into something it wasn't. The thought occurred to me that if I *had* hired Maggie Payton Borman to handle my real estate deal with the Guzmans, she would doubtless have had a fit about my brambles, perhaps even arguing me into doing something about them. Well, by and large, the bulldozers had taken care of that.

The Bormans' driveway was empty, the front drapes pulled against the afternoon sun. Estelle slowed the county car, but drove past without stopping. "Nice place," I said. "So southwesterny." Estelle didn't reply, not acknowledging my cynicism. "You know, it nags at me," I added.

"What does, sir?"

"Gweneth Barnes said that Phil Borman came into the pharmacy with Guy Trombley first thing this morning."

"Yes, she said that."

"Phil could have palmed that little bottle easily enough. Suppose he went back to the restroom, way in the back of the store, past the prescription counter, out behind Trombley's office. If the door to the compounding room was open, or even just unlocked, he could have just reached around and put the bottle back on the shelf. It would only take an instant. Clumsy as I am, *I* could even do that."

"Yes, he could have done that, sir."

I regarded her with interest. "And that's just part of it."

"An interesting part, though."

"Why did Phil come to the pharmacy in the first place? He just had coffee and donuts with Guy and the town fathers. Why not just head back to the realty office and go to work?"

"He needed to buy something…a bottle of aspirin, a tube of lip balm—who knows."

"The cash register knows," I said. "But Gwen didn't say that he *did* buy anything. She said he used antacids all the time, but she didn't actually say that he *bought* any. He came back with Guy because he knew that he'd be able to find the opportunity to return the histamine bottle. He either some-how heard on the grapevine that we're looking for something related to George's death, or he put two and two together all by himself. *Somebody* assumed that you'd never figure out that George's death was anything other than a natural event, but when they heard that you had suspicions, there was no time to waste getting rid of that little bottle."

"That's possible, *padrino*."

"You don't think that he did? That would explain why the bottle ended up out of place, at the end of the shelf. It was a spot easy to reach in a hurry. Just reach around the corner. You wouldn't even have to look."

"Assuming he'd spent time back there and knew the layout of the room."

"A single casual visit would have accomplished that part of it," I insisted.

"It's interesting that it would be so easy for him to do that," Estelle said. "For anyone to do it. Mr. Trombley does not run a tight ship."

"Bet that the ship will tighten just a bit?" I laughed. "And there's this. With his sister's illness, Phil would have known about histamine diphosphate."

Estelle tipped her head sideways at that notion. "That's not necessarily true, sir. It may be *likely*, if he was close enough to his sister to discuss her treatment with her. But…"

"But?"

Estelle glanced at the dash clock. "He didn't

purchase the wine, sir. Unless Mr. Pierson is imagining things, but I don't think that even he could confuse Maggie with Phil."

"Well, maybe she *did* buy it," I insisted. "Pierson wouldn't be wrong about that. But then, she might have given the wine to Phil to deliver. Maybe she got busy. Remember, Phil was the one who found George after lunch. He might have actually gone over there a few minutes earlier. There would have been opportunity. In fact," and I held up a hand. We were galloping too fast toward an indictment with all this painful stuff. "In fact, yes, Phil could have brought the wine over to the house. And then left. And then someone else came into that kitchen and helped George Payton with his histamine tonic."

"Perhaps so." She pulled the car out onto Bustos and turned east, toward what passed as the downtown of Posadas. "We already know what Maggie told me yesterday. She had not seen her father Thursday morning—she was busy with business. She claims that Phil called with the bad news about her father right *after* he dialed 911. And as anyone would expect, she dropped everything and dashed right over. If all that were the case, we wouldn't have found the bag from Town and Country Liquor, with the receipt inside, in Mr. Payton's kitchen trash under the sink. If Maggie was telling the truth, the bottle of wine would still be in her car, or at her house." She thumped the steering wheel. "If she bought the wine and then gave it to Phil to deliver, then *Phil* is lying."

"We need a decent, readable fingerprint," I said. "This is goddamn frustrating."

"Yes, sir," Estelle agreed readily. "In this case, we may have to settle for the lack of one."

"The wine bottle, you mean?"

"Yes. If that were an innocent bottle, there would be clear prints of the person who purchased it, almost certainly...unless that person always handled it by that crinkly foil wrapper around the screw cap—but who does that? You take off the foil, and when the bottle is opened, one hand holds the bottle while the other turns the cap and breaks the seal. When it's poured, at least one hand clamps the bottle. There's all kinds of smooth, shiny surface for a perfect set of prints. It's just impossible to handle it without leaving a record, sir."

"An 'innocent bottle.' What a concept."

"There's just no reason to wipe it off," Estelle said. "Just no reason at all. Unless the handler *knew* that there was a question of incriminating prints." She eased the car to a stop in front of the small, neat Posadas Realty building. "I want to talk with them both."

Through the large front window with its lace

curtain trim, I could see Phil Borman standing by the receptionist's desk, telephone to his ear. His Lexus SUV was parked in the narrow driveway between the realty and the empty building next door, but I didn't see Maggie's fancy Cadillac sedan. If one judged by vehicles alone, then the real estate business was booming.

Nine o'clock was but minutes away and the realty office staff had long since gone home. Phil appeared to be alone, and when he turned and saw the county car, he stepped closer to the window. His bland face offered nothing but greeting when he recognized us, and he beckoned us inside.

Whether it was just his gregarious nature or whether he actually had something to tell us, I couldn't imagine. Estelle left the car running, but before she got out, dialed her cell phone.

"Brent," she said to the young dispatcher who responded, "who do we have on the road?" She listened for a few seconds. "Will you have her swing by 1228 Ridgemont for me? I need to know if Maggie Borman is over there. Have him call me." Estelle had her little notebook open, and in response to a question, she added, "Negative contact, Brent. Just the information. Mrs. Borman is driving a metallic gray Cadillac CTS, license Paul Robert Edward One. Thanks, Brent. Make sure Jackie uses the phone, not the radio. I'll be out of the car for a few minutes at the Borman Realty on Bustos. Bill Gastner is still with me."

"Do you want me to wait here?" I asked, and the undersheriff shot me a sideways glance of amusement as she snapped the phone closed.

"You're my backup, sir," she said. "My moral support. Even if you keep trying to avoid the logic here."

"I'm *not* trying to avoid anything, sweetheart. I'm just trying…to avoid it."

By the time we were out of the car and on the sidewalk, Phil Borman had opened the front door of the office and greeted us pleasantly. "Another thirty seconds and you would have missed me," he said. "You know, if it isn't one thing, it's another. Just about the time we could really stand some peace and quiet, we're up to our necks in all kinds of things. These twelve-hour days are killing me."

"Real estate is hopping, eh?" I said.

"Well, *hopping* is relative, I suppose. But fits and spurts. Just enough that we can't ignore the place for a few days, which is what we *should* do. Come on in." He stopped and looked up and down the street. "I assume you were stopping by here?"

"We were," Estelle said agreeably and shut the front door behind us, the chimes jangling an irritating, cheerful greeting.

"Come on back," Phil said. "Coffee? I can make some in a jiffy."

"No, thanks, sir." Estelle was always faster on the draw than I was, but I deferred. Hell, a nice cup would have been welcome, since the promised dinner hadn't materialized. Borman slumped down in the big leather chair behind his desk and waved us to the comfortable seats where he normally placed his victims. Estelle took one of the guest chairs, but I roamed the back of the office, looking at Phil's art, his diplomas and various licenses. "This whole business with George," he said, and let the thought trail off.

"Sir," Estelle said, "our records show that you called 911 at 12:58 p.m. yesterday to report that your father-in-law had suffered an attack of some kind."

Phil nodded. "The minute I saw him all slumped there, I knew he was gone."

"You called Maggie shortly thereafter?"

"Sure," Phil said. "I told you yesterday. The instant I hung up from 911, I called Maggie and told her that she needed to come over."

"Where was she at that time?"

"I…I have no idea, really. Her cell, you know. But…" he held up a hand while he gathered his thoughts. "I *think* she was with a couple from Lordsburg. She had said earlier that she was going to be tied up with them." He hunched his shoulders. "If not with them, then with any one of a dozen other projects. That's why I went over to George's in the first place. She wasn't going to be able to make it. He hadn't been feeling real perky lately, and like I'd told you, we've been keeping close tabs. For one thing, he ignores his meds about half the time. He won't call Dr. Perrone, and I tell ya…" He smiled in resignation. "He got mad as hell if we meddled." Phil cleared his throat and glowered a pretty good imitation of George Payton. "'I don't need a goddamn nursemaid.'" At that moment, I liked Phil Borman even more.

Phil held out both hands toward Estelle. "Look, I knew he had ordered lunch from the Don Juan, and he said that they were going to deliver for him. I figured to help him clean up afterward. That's all. Maggie suggested that, too, but I had already planned to do it." He looked quizzically at the undersheriff. "That's what I told you yesterday." He frowned as Estelle opened her cell phone. Its vibration had alerted her, and she didn't apologize for the intrusion.

"Reyes-Guzman." She listened for about the count of five, and then said, "Thanks, Jackie. That's all I need." She folded the phone back into her jacket pocket.

"Had Mr. Payton mentioned to you that Bill

Gastner was planning to have lunch with him yesterday?" she asked.

"Yep. He told me about that a day or two ago. And then yesterday Bill got busy and had to cancel."

I felt as if I'd become invisible, but resisted the temptation to dive into the conversation.

"When did Mr. Payton tell you that?"

Phil hesitated. "Well, *he* didn't. He called Maggie and told her. Look, she knew that she was about to get busy, so she offered me. You know, to get his lunch, but George said that it was all taken care of. I mean, I would have done it gladly. So she didn't have to worry about it."

"And when was that call?"

"Good God, I don't remember. All I know is that at one point in a zoo of a morning, Maggie was on the phone with her dad. She stuck her head into my office and reminded me to go over and pick up the casserole dish after lunch." He closed his eyes, trying to remember. "Late morning, I suppose."

How did it become so important to pick up a food delivery dish, I thought, thinking of the usual, casual routine.

"Did George ask you to pick up some wine for him?" Estelle asked.

"No," Phil replied, showing no surprise at the question. "But it wouldn't have surprised me if he had. He goes through that stuff like water. Maybe he asked Maggie, but she didn't say anything to me about that." He leaned forward and rested both hands on his desk, fingers intertwined. "I don't get this."

"We realize that this is a painful process for you, but bear with me." She studied her small notebook. "Did your father-n-law ever talk to you about any allergies he might have had? Serious ones, like to medications, that sort of thing?"

"Allergies?" He laughed weakly. "That would be the last thing George needed. No, he never mentioned that. How's that related to all this? You think that he had an allergic attack or something?"

"He may have," Estelle said. "It will be a number of days before we have the toxicology reports back, but it's an avenue we're exploring."

"Wow," Phil said in wonder. "Now *that's* a curveball. Allergic to what, I wonder? All I know about is cats. He's always grousing about the neighborhood cats in his yard, but I don't think that had anything to do with allergies. They use his yard as a kitty litter box, and he said nothing stinks worse than a cat." He pointed his fingers like a handgun. "He always said the damn things made his trigger finger itch."

"It's just an avenue to explore," Estelle said. "Are you expecting Maggie back here in the office this evening?"

"No. She was going over to her dad's place for a few minutes, and then over to the house. I was going to take her out to dinner." He grimaced. "God, about time, too. Christ." He rubbed his face in exasperation. "Try to relax a little. We've got an appointment with Salazar tomorrow for the services. George didn't want anything done, but Maggie and I both decided that we had to do something. Some kind of simple memorial."

Just a little something to make George's ghost furious, I thought. I changed the subject. "Had George ever talked to you about his properties? It was my impression that he had land all over the county." Estelle didn't fire one of her dark looks my way, so I knew the questions wasn't out of order.

The question caught Phil by surprise, and for a second or two he looked at me as if I were a stranger. "His property," Phil muttered as he pulled his thoughts together. "What a mess *that* is going to be. But yes, he does. Little stuff, I think. A few acres here, a few there. But we haven't pursued it with the county. You know, he even owns that little nuisance lot behind the county building itself." He waved a hand in dismissal. I had never thought of property worth seventy or eighty grand as a nuisance, but then again, I wasn't in real estate.

"But no," Phil continued, "we never talked about that. I mean George and I didn't. Now,

Maggie mentioned his land holdings now and then," and he smiled. "With some frustration, too, I might add. You might talk to her about that if you need more information."

"Probably not," I said easily. We still knew nothing about a possible will. Among her other challenges in cleaning up after her father, Maggie Payton Borman would have something to look for over at George's house.

Chapter Thirty-three

Maggie's Cadillac was parked at the curb of 1228 Ridgemont, and we pulled in behind the fancy little hotrod. The front door stood open, the storm door propped wide by a ceramic flower pot. If Maggie heard our approach, she didn't acknowledge it.

I stepped up on the little concrete entry step and rapped on the door jamb.

"In the living room," Maggie greeted, but her voice sounded flat, even dejected, and I felt a pang of sympathy. I stood to one side to let Estelle pass. To my surprise, George's daughter was sitting on the center cushion of the old sofa in the tiny living room, her hands clasped together between her knees, looking like a little kid who had run out of toys or joys. She didn't rise to greet us. The Maggie Payton Borman who bubbled effusively to customers all day long, who appeared to revel in the upside of life, whose glass was always half full rather than half empty—that Maggie had ticked to a stop.

The undersheriff took two steps through the door and halted, a habit so predictable that I was prepared for it and didn't run her down from behind. She surveyed the room for a few seconds, inventorying. The only changes I could see, beyond a general tidying and dusting, was that the sad bouquet of plastic flowers had been removed from the piano top, and the wool blanket that had adorned the sofa was gone.

Maggie rose wearily. She had reason to be exhausted, beyond the demands of housecleaning, which eventually would be done by someone else anyway.

"Bill and Estelle," she said, and held out both hands toward me. "I confess I'm not feeling like much of a hostess."

"That's okay," I said. "I understand how it goes."

"And how are you?" Maggie said, holding out a hand to Estelle, but she didn't wait for the undersheriff to answer. "I'm hearing some disturbing things," Maggie added. "I don't know what to think."

"Disturbing in what way, Mrs. Borman?" Estelle asked. Of course Guy Trombley would have talked with his assistant, Harriet Tomlinson. That didn't surprise me, nor that Harriet had chatted at the first opportunity with Maggie Borman.

"I'm hearing that there was some sort of complication with dad's death," Maggie said. "Some kind of reaction?" Her eyes hardened a bit. "I'm not sure why I should have to hear this from a friend."

"Nor I," Estelle said. "Mrs. Borman, did your father ask you to purchase some wine for him yesterday morning?"

Maggie Borman's lips started to part, but then clamped shut for just an instant as she took the time to engage brain before mouth. I had never thought of her as *calculating* before this—maybe I had been kidding myself. Now there was caution, a certain wariness in her eyes.

"The *wine?* That's what it was? The *wine?*"

"It appears that your father had just finished one bottle, then opened a second and poured a glassful. That was the one that was spilled on the kitchen table and floor."

"Oh, my word," Maggie Borman murmured. She backed up an awkward step or two and sat down abruptly on the sofa. "Do you think…"

Estelle allowed her a moment, then prompted, "Do we think what, Mrs. Borman?"

"The wine, I mean. Dad just won't do without it, but when he drinks it by the *tumbler,* for heaven's sakes, he gets so *breathy.*" Interesting, I thought, how long it took us to switch habits, in this case from present tense to past. Maggie waved a hand in front of her mouth as if trying to force more air down the pipes. "And on top of his meds…"

"Did you purchase the wine for him?" Estelle asked again.

"I…I suppose I did. I had to open it for him. His hands are *so* arthritic. A corkscrew is just too much for him."

"What time was that? When you bought the wine and brought it over here?"

"Oh," Maggie said, and looked at her watch, as if she might have marked the time on the dial for future reference. "I stopped on my way to work this morning, so I suppose…" She cocked her head this way and that. "It would have been shortly after eight, I suppose."

"At Town and Country?"

"Yes, but," and Maggie clamped her hands together against her chest. "do you really think it was the *wine?* I mean, he liked the same old thing."

"After you purchased the wine, you brought it over here?"

Maggie nodded immediately. "I did. Dad said that you were going to join him." She smiled affectionately at me. "He was *so* looking forward to that."

"Wish I'd kept the date," I said. "But you know how things go, Maggie."

"Oh, I do," she said. "And then later, he called to say that you'd gotten tied up somehow but that the Don Juan was delivering for him. So that was all right."

"You asked Phil to run by and check on your dad?"

"I told him he should if he got the chance. And I would, too, if things cleared up." She heaved a great sigh. "It's so sad, the elderly. That's what I think. I see dad sitting at that table," and she turned to gaze toward the kitchen, "eating all by himself."

"Your dad always enjoyed his own company," I said, although I knew that's a concept that many people find hard to accept.

"I suppose so," Maggie said, and pushed up out of the sofa. "The wine." She shook her head. "There are blood tests for that sort of thing, I suppose."

"Sure," I said. "They take a while. We won't have a full panel of toxicology reports back for days—maybe weeks."

"Will you keep me posted?" She frowned one of those *you won't make that mistake again, will you?* expressions at both of us.

"Rest assured," Estelle said, and the two words might have sounded comforting to Maggie but sure as hell didn't to me.

Maggie reached out a hand and rested it on my

forearm. "And Bill, when you have time, I wanted to sit down with you and talk about all of Dad's hardware." She sighed. "I have no idea what those guns are all worth, or who would be interested. And if there's anything *you* would want…"

"That's very kind of you, but I can't think of a thing, Maggie. Got a lot of good memories, and that's enough."

"Well, if there is something, I'm sure dad would have wanted you to have it. If you could help me with some of the appraising, I'd be grateful."

"Whatever I can do," I said and glanced at Estelle to see if she had more on her mind. But she had flipped her notebook closed and checked her watch.

"Did your father leave a will?" she asked. "That will make it so much easier."

"Oh, my," Maggie said, shaking her head in exaggerated exasperation. "If I had a dollar for each time we talked about *that.*" She held up both hands in surrender. "Promises, promises."

"So he didn't?"

"Not to my knowledge. But then…" Maggie surveyed the living room. "Who knows? He would never talk about it. I don't even know what lawyer he used…if any."

"Did he ever talk about the deal he had going with Herb Torrance?"

She waved a hand airily at my question.

"Oh, dad and his *land.*" She sat down on the sofa again. "All of that's going to have to wait until after probate, unless we find some paperwork. You know, I talked with Miles Waddell just last week. He's been trying to get dad to sell him that little wedge of property on top of the mesa out that way, out where the BLM is toying around with the cave project." She rolled her eyes. "We'll all be old and feeble by the time *that* breaks ground, but Miles really wanted to move on it. You know, I'm not sure that Dad really liked him, that's the trouble. He'd rather give land away to someone he likes than sell to someone he doesn't…I don't see what difference it all makes. A sale is a sale. And dad certainly had no use for any of it."

"Like stamp collecting," I offered, and Maggie laughed agreement. She rose to see us to the door, and as we passed through, nudged the ceramic pot with the toe of a well-polished shoe.

"It's getting chilly these evenings," she said. "I just had to start airing out the cigars. My, how that odor clings."

We settled into the car and the doors thudded shut. Estelle finished her meticulous notations in her log, her head shaking from side to side the whole time as if she disapproved of each word and number that she wrote.

"She lied," I said, although Estelle wouldn't have missed the obvious. "God damn it, she lied."

"And she's a flight risk."

"Oh, I don't think so," I responded, but I knew the undersheriff was right and that anything else was wishful thinking. In fact, I'd been guilty of wishful thinking about Maggie's innocence all day.

Estelle snapped her log closed. "She's middle-aged, used to the pretty good life, and facing the certainty of prison," she said. "If she can run, she will."

"I can predict all kinds of problems, though," I said. "For one thing, you don't have a single print of Maggie's...not on the wine bottle, not on the histamine bottle, not on the glasses. Other than a lapse of memory about *when* she bought the wine and took it to her father's house..."

"That's all true."

"You have testimony that Maggie was in the pharmacy, along with a fair collection of other people, but not that she was caught out in the back, in the compounding room where the histamine was kept. No one saw her at her father's place, before, during, or after. You know the mess a good defense attorney is going to make of this case?"

"But," Estelle said, and started the car.

"But what? Yes, I agree she has motive as much anyone. Maybe more. It makes my gut ache, but

I see that. It looks like George was giving away property hand over fist, and obviously she gains if she can stop the flow." I thumped the dash with the heel of my hand. "Nickel, dime, nickel dime. A few hundred grand maybe, at the most."

The undersheriff lifted her shoulders, and I knew what that meant. "Yes," I said, "We both have seen folks murdered for a good deal less." I huffed a sigh. "We have the means. I'm *not* sure we have the opportunity. And without something firm there, a defense attorney will make hash."

"If Maggie stopped by her father's place at noon, just as he was sitting down to eat, that's opportunity."

"Ah, but," I said. "She would need to have the histamine in her possession well before yesterday... she'd have no way to know for sure when this supposed opportunity would present itself."

"Exactly so, *padrino*. Exactly so. Guy Trombley said that the last time he compounded histolatum was in May, for Phil's sister. Then she died. Let's suppose that somehow, Maggie found the opportunity to take the chemical. Guy wouldn't even know it was gone. Sir, he *didn't* know it was gone when we first checked with him. It came as a complete surprise."

"You're saying that Maggie might have been wandering around for who knows how many goddamn months, the stuff in her purse, waiting for an opportunity?"

"So to speak. Or working up courage, hoping something would change her mind. Maybe she *did* argue with her father against giving away the property. Maybe she did. And maybe her father stone-walled her. Yesterday, the opportunity presented itself. Her dad calls asking her to pick up some wine, and with the news that you've canceled out on lunch. She goes over to Ridgemont, and sure enough, the old man sees a fresh bottle of wine, chugs the remains of the old bottle, and then heads for the bathroom. She opens the new one, pours, and spikes. Even time to wipe the bottle."

"Could have, maybe, maybe," I said. "I'd still bet on the defense attorney."

"She's a sales professional," she said, enunciating each syllable. "And that's why I think she'll run, given the chance, sir. She cuts deals. That's what she does for a living. But right now, she doesn't know how little we have. As soon as it's clear that we're not just chasing a red wine allergy, as soon as she knows that we have her trapped in a lie, she'll be ready to cut a deal."

"You think so."

"Yes, I do. I'm certain that we have enough for a grand jury indictment. That gives us all the time we need to find something more concrete than a cash register receipt that calls her a liar."

"That's for sure."

"We have Ricardo Mondragon," Estelle added. She pulled out her little notebook and ruffled pages, finally holding one out for me to see. "'*It was on the table. I asked him if I could throw it away... I didn't see no new bottle.*' She closed the notebook. "If Maggie had taken the fresh bottle to her father's house earlier in the morning, why wouldn't it be there? She said that she opened it for him. Who would put an *open* bottle away in a cupboard somewhere? It would be standing on the table...which is exactly where we found it."

I settled deeper into the seat and stared out through the windshield at nothing much. "Now what?" I asked, although I knew the answer as well as the undersheriff.

"I'll talk with Schroeder and see what he says."

"I know what he'll say."

"And then an arrest warrant. She'll be held pending grand jury action."

The process sounded so cut and dried. Maggie Payton Borman's life would come to a halt, the legal process more drawn out and painful than what she'd inflicted on her unsuspecting father.

I hoped that Estelle was wrong about one

thing. Maggie could run and spend the rest of her life running, leaving the law behind. Whether that would be a worse fate, only she could decide, since all the memories would go with her.

There was nothing further I could accomplish that night. To the north, the state laboratory clanked its test tubes and watched the drip down the chromatography strips…that's all I could remember from my own college chemistry class, but I had no doubt that the eager young chemists would find whatever could be found. At the same time, surgeons did their best to patch Pat Gabaldon back together again. We had no idea when he'd be able to tell us his version of events, but the news of nailing his assailants might speed his recuperation.

I didn't take much satisfaction that the wheels of justice were still turning in George Payton's case, however slowly. For the first time in probably too long, I wasn't even hungry. Instead of to the Don Juan de Oñate restaurant, or to the Guzman's for something homey in good company, I went home, deep into my dark, quiet burrow.

In a moment of silliness, I even contemplated calling my oldest daughter, Camille. I wouldn't discuss the Payton case with her, of course—she'd make the connection in a flash and call me worse than silly. No, Camille wasn't going to poison me so that she could heist the family wealth.

Instead, I took my time making the perfect mug of coffee, enjoying the aroma of freshly ground Sumatran beans. Leaning comfortably against the kitchen counter, I waited for the drip gadget to finish its work, then took the mug down into my sunken living room/library. One of the joys of being both an insomniac and a reader is that the clock never mattered. I perused the shelves, looking for just the right break from reality. Eventually, I pulled Trulock's *In the Hands of Providence* from one of the upper shelves, a book I'd read half a dozen times and unearthed some new tidbit each time. Settling into the massive leather recliner, I buried myself in Joshua Chamberlain's Civil War.

Three mugs of Sumatran later, as troops tried to find a way to storm up through the eastern woodlands without being cut to pieces by cannon and musket fire, the battle lost its focus for me. I ended up reading the same paragraph three times, then surrendered, letting my head sag back into the leather.

I awakened once when the furnace came on, closed the book and placed it on the slate table. With hands folded over my belly, I relaxed back again. What the hell. Bed was where I made it, like the old *tejón* that Estelle affectionately nicknamed me—an old badger who likes things his way.

With a jolt that twanged the arthritic spurs here and there throughout my skeleton, I awakened to the telephone. It was the landline, that black thing that hung on the wall in the kitchen. For several rings, I listened to it, holding up my wrist so that I could see the time. With a curse, I hauled my carcass out of the chair, barking my shin on the recliner mechanism. Whoever it was waited patiently, and I lifted the receiver after the eighth ring.

"Gastner." The clock over the stove agreed. It was just coming up on midnight.

No one on the other end spoke, and for an instant I thought it was one of those robots that call, offering extended vehicle warranties or the command *'don't be alarmed,'* from account services, whoever they were, warning that my credit card was doomed if I didn't subscribe to their service, whatever that might be. But the vocal robots didn't work at midnight. In a moment I heard an exchange of distant voices.

"Gastner," I said again, and the circuit switched off. "Well hell," I grumbled, and leaned back against the kitchen counter, regarding the coffee maker. But ten pound weights hung from my eyelids.

The next day was going to be a whirlwind of activities, including conferences with District

Attorney Schroeder, maybe even Judge Hobart. Estelle would map out a game plan to deal with Maggie Borman, and I wouldn't want to sleep through that. Gambling that my eyelids would slam shut the rest of the way, I made my way to the bedroom and eased onto the down comforter, too tired to bother undressing. There'd be plenty of time come morning for a shower and all those ceremonies that begin a new day.

When the stupid phone rang again, it jerked me so hard that my neck twanged with whiplash. The clock read 5:10, the room still so dark that the three-inch clock numerals could be read without trifocals. In a moment, I found the side table, and then the phone.

"Gastner." I relaxed back, eyes closed, phone tight to my ear. The connection was silent—no voice, nothing in the background, not even the click of circuits or automatic dialers. Thinking it a repeat of the midnight call, I was about to hang up. But then a voice broke the silence, and it was almost a whisper.

Chapter Thirty-four

"What's going to happen?"

I lay motionless, letting the words sink in, giving my foggy brain time to spool up. There was no point in sputtering a bunch of noise. I knew the voice, and I could guess the mix of emotions behind it.

"Are you awake?"

"Yes, I'm awake," I replied.

"I need to talk to you," Maggie Payton Borman said. "Can I do that?"

"Here we are."

The line was quiet for so long that I could have gotten up, put on the coffee, and returned to bed. But I remained quiet in the companionable silence, concentrating on listening for background noises, wondering where Maggie was, what she was doing.

"She's not going to give up, is she."

I could have asked for an explanation, for a

repetition, but that wasn't necessary. I knew exactly what—and who—Maggie meant.

"No, she's not," I said. I didn't add that Undersheriff Estelle Reyes-Guzman would be conferring with the district attorney later this morning. The phone went silent as Maggie gave me plenty of time to be forthcoming, but I outwaited her.

"Did you know just how ill Dad was?" she asked.

"I think I did."

"His prostate cancer had metastasized, Bill. More than we had thought. Dr. Perrone said that he should be on morphine, but dad refused. Did you know that?"

"No." I could not imagine crusty, garrulous old George doubled over, whimpering with agony. I heard a long, shuddering sigh from his daughter.

"You know, that wasn't his greatest fear, Bill. Not the pain."

"I don't think your father was afraid of anything," I said.

"Oh, he was. He was." Maggie laughed, but it was a sad sound, a hopeless little chuckle. She lowered her voice and the growled imitation of George Payton was pretty accurate. "'I'm going to end up in goddamn diapers,' he'd say."

"It's not easy," I said.

"The past two weeks have been really hard, Bill. Just awful."

I didn't know what I was supposed to say. I would have understood if George had selected a favorite gun from his diminishing collection and put an end to the agony. But that would have been *his* choice, a choice that he was free to make. Evidence didn't suggest that George had dosed his own wine with histamine diphosphate, and he never would have chosen that route anyway.

"Will you tell me what you think?"

"What I think doesn't matter at this point."

"I need to know, Bill. I *want* to know what you think."

"What I think. Well, on several occasions, your father said what mattered to him most was cleaning up his mess. Not leaving a tangle behind that someone else—no doubt you—would have to clean up."

"He talked with you about that sort of thing?"

"Oh, yes. Two old geezers, gumming away. He might not have been especially demonstrative about it, but he cared about you, Maggie. He was proud of you. He didn't want to leave something behind that someone else would have to unsnarl."

"That's dad," Maggie agreed. "Very neat, very organized in some ways."

"Yep. He had a lot of different properties, as you are well aware. He was in the process of giving them all away…well, I don't know that. He was in the process of giving *some* of them away. To Herb Torrance, to the county, maybe others."

"And you think…"

"Yes. I do." Hell, why not. We'd jumped into the deep water. "You're used to making a profit, Maggie. That's what you do. If your father left a will behind, I have no doubt that he left his estate to you, not that it's any of my business."

"He didn't leave a will. That's one of the things he kept saying that he was *going* to do."

"Well, regardless. What do I think? I think that you convinced yourself that if bringing on the inevitable would stop the loss of property from his estate, even if you had to wait for probate, then there you go."

"You agree with her, then." *Her.*

"You're referring to the undersheriff, I suppose."

"You know I am."

"Using her name is difficult for you?"

Silence greeted that remark. "No," Maggie said, sounding like a little kid. "I feel hunted. I can't sleep, I can't tend to business, I can't imagine what's going to happen now. Everything I worked for…"

"A bunch of choices," I said. "Where are you now?"

"I'm…" and she hesitated. "Are you going to call in? Do you have one of those pager things that alerts the department?"

"I'm retired," I said. "You've got the edge. Where are you, Maggie?"

"I can't do this," she said, as if talking to someone else.

"Is Phil there with you?"

She laughed. "Dear Phil. No, he's not. He's home, sound asleep. I don't know how he does it. Are you recording this now?"

"No."

"You'll testify, though."

"Yes."

"Will you tell me how these things work?"

"These *things* take time," I said. "If the district attorney wants to go the grand jury route, you'll be notified. The target of the investigation always is. You have the opportunity to testify on your own behalf during a grand jury hearing if you wish. You aren't required to. You aren't even required to attend. If the grand jury indicts you, you'll be taken into custody, the judge will set bail, and a trial date will be set. That could be early next year. These things don't exactly move at the goddamn speed of light."

"My God," she whispered. "They really think I did this?"

"They don't have to think anything, Maggie. All a grand jury does is determine that sufficient question, sufficient evidence, exists to warrant a trial. They decide whether or not a petit jury will hear the case to decide innocence or guilt. That's my version of Justice System 101." I reached out, turned on the bedside light, and found my glasses. The little cell phone, with all its nifty features that Estelle had programmed for me, that I'd learned to carry most of the time, rested out on the kitchen counter. The undersheriff was one click away.

"What if they don't think that?"

"Don't think what?" I pulled the blanket up around my shoulders.

"That I killed my father. What if the evidence…"

"Then you're free to continue your life."

"But she'll make sure there's evidence, won't she," Maggie whispered.

"That's her job, Maggie."

"And she's very, very good at it," Maggie added, and I heard more resignation than bitterness. "What do *you* think, Bill?"

I sighed. "Are we going into rewind here? I told you what I think."

"You think I killed my father so he wouldn't

give away his properties? So I could make a profit on them?"

"What I think at this point doesn't matter."

"It matters to me, Bill."

I took a deep breath and pulled the blanket a little more snuggly around my neck. "All right. Yes, that's what I think happened." She started to say something, but interrupted herself. "I think you got too clever, Maggie. That's what I think. Now, why? Well, we humans have this goddamn wonderful capacity not to recognize slippery slopes when we're standing on the brink. We don't remember how momentum works once we stumble over the edge, once we take that one step too far. You thought that we all would just accept on face value that your father had the expected seizure. You didn't give us much credit." *Not us,* I thought. *Her.*

"I can't…" and she stopped again.

"You can't what?"

"This is going to ruin me," she whispered. "Even if…even if they can't prove it. It's going to be in the papers and on television. No matter what the jury says, all the tongues will wag…"

"That goes with the turf, Maggie. But that's why grand juries operate in secret."

"In this town? You've got to be kidding."

"What can I say."

"*That's* not very helpful," she snapped,

sounding for the first time like the hustle-bustle Maggie Borman Payton of old.

"You asked what I think," I said.

"I'm trying to decide what to do," she said, as if I hadn't spoken.

"I hope you'll decide the right thing." In the past hours, I'd had a bellyful of people deciding the *wrong* things.

"And what *is* the right thing? What am I supposed to do now?"

"You're at the office?"

"It doesn't matter where I am."

"Well, wherever you are, go out to your car and drive over to the sheriff's department. Deputy Ernie Wheeler is on graveyard over there, and he's a good guy. Just tell him to call the undersheriff. Tell him that you'll wait in the conference room. It's just across the hall from dispatch."

"Oh, please, Bill," Maggie said, with exaggerated condescension. "I'm not going to turn myself in. I don't care what she thinks she's found."

"So be it. Maybe the first phone call you make after you hang up with me should be to a good lawyer. A very good lawyer."

"Well, obviously." Her short-tempered umbrage turned into a long, painful groan. "I just can't do this."

I didn't know what the *this* was. Maybe she

was sitting with one of her dad's shotguns between her knees, staring down the chokes. Maybe she was trying to remove the child-proof top from a jumbo-sized bottle of tranquilizers. Maybe she had a travel brochure about life in Puerto Vallarta or Buenos Aires. No matter what route she chose, it was going to leave a mess behind, and that would have made old George Payton flush with anger.

"May I ask *you* a question?" I said.

"I know what it is," Maggie Payton Borman said.

"Maybe you do. All right, suppose that I believe that you didn't lace your father's wine with histamine diphosphate. Suppose, despite everything that the evidence shows, that I believe that. There are two people that our MMO mumbo-jumbo fits. Both you and Phil had the means, the motive, and the opportunity, Maggie." I knew that I shouldn't have mentioned the drug, but there it was. If Maggie hadn't known the connection before, she did then.

Silence. As I waited for her to decide what to say, the thought occurred to me that this might have been Maggie's grand scheme in the first place. Poor Phil would never have seen it coming.

"Are you telling me that Phil did this to your father?"

Once again, her voice drifted into the small and forlorn. "Oh, Bill," she whispered.

"Oh, Bill, what?"

"Do you think that Phil…"

"No, actually, I *don't* think that Phil anything, Maggie. I think he did just what he says he did. He went over to your dad's place in the early afternoon to check on him, and maybe clean up some dirty dishes. He found his father-in-law dead. That's what I think."

"His sister used that drug, Bill."

"I know she did. And you know, Maggie, I think we've taken this about as far as I want to take it just now."

"I thought I could count on you, Bill." Now, her tone was soft and accusing, and that sent my blood pressure up into the red zone. She had depended on my friendship with George and my affection for his daughter.

"You can, Maggie." I shrugged off the blanket and let my feet touch the wooden floor. "I'm advising you to call a good lawyer, then go over to the Sheriff's Department and turn yourself in. I can be there in ten minutes. You do that and I'll help you any way I can." Silence. "On the other hand, you go off and do something stupid, well…then you're on your own."

The silence continued for a full minute. I

could hear nothing in the background to tell me where Maggie might be.

"These things are so simple to you, aren't they?" she said finally.

"Simple? No. None of it is simple, Maggie."

"Good night, Bill."

"You still haven't told me where you are, Maggie," I said, but I was talking to a dial tone.

I took the luxury of getting up and shrugging a bathrobe over my rumpled clothes before dialing. The undersheriff's voice was muffled and distant. I don't know why there's something sacred about sleep—waking someone up always seems to prompt those *I'm sorry to disturb you* excuses, with lots of valuable time wasted with apologies.

"Hey there," I said, sounding as cheerful as possible. "You ready for breakfast?" I twisted around and glanced at the clock. Hell, at 5:27 a.m., half the day was gone.

"Good morning, *padrino*," Estelle said, now fully awake. The absence of background noise told me that the rest of the household wasn't.

"And good morning to you. Look, I was just on the phone for half a day with Maggie Borman. I suggested that she make her way over to the sheriff's department and turn herself in."

"She confessed to you?"

"Ah, no. Not in so many words. In fact, I

wouldn't be surprised if she's toying with blaming Phil for the whole thing. I could be wrong."

"She actually said that?"

"No. She sounded like she was ready to imply it."

"Ah…*that's* good stuff for court," Estelle said, and I could hear the amusement in her tone.

"Well, what can I say. Anyway, she wanted to know what I thought, and I tried to tell her without tramping my size elevens all over your investigation."

"Where was she, sir?"

"That's the interesting thing. She wouldn't tell me. I asked, but no dice. I couldn't hear anything in the background, either. Maybe she's sitting there in her Cadillac, ready to head out. That worries me a little." I glanced over at the clock. "The Regál crossing opens at six a.m., but that doesn't seem like her style, somehow. And she doesn't have any family to run to."

"Let me call dispatch," Estelle said. "Shall I pick you up?"

"I'd appreciate it. You talked with Schroeder?"

"I did. He's coming over from Deming, and we're meeting this morning at eight. But he said that we were free to make a move before then, if we have to."

"We're going to have to," I said.

Chapter Thirty-five

One challenge of living in a rural, quiet little niche of the world such as Posadas, New Mexico, is that it's easy to lose track of life on the world stage. Maggie's first assumption was that we all would accept her father's passing as the expected monstrous heart attack that George had been working on for years.

I knew now that when I'd first arrived at the scene and found Maggie staring out the living room window of her father's house that it wasn't the shock of grief that had flummoxed her. It was that damn yellow police line tape across the kitchen door and Undersheriff Estelle Reyes-Guzmans methodical harkening to her intuitions.

Sitting in her swank living room in the house on Posadas' East Fairview Lane, long before she called me at dawn, Maggie had planned all the right moves—at least they must have *seemed* right to her. That's what her cryptic, final "Good bye, Bill" had told me.

The undersheriff had to wait only a couple minutes until I emerged from my badger hole clean and neat, showered and shaved. Deputy Jackie Taber and Sgt. Tom Mears had already scoured Posadas, looking for a new Cadillac bearing the vanity plate *Posadas Real Estate 1*. It wasn't in the village. It wasn't waiting to pass through the border crossing.

Poor Phil Borman had no clue where his wife might be, and he walked in circles in the conference room of the sheriff's department, refusing to go home, looking as if he wanted to vomit.

That's when the electronic tendrils reached out and tapped Maggie Payton Borman on the shoulder. Folks who live in small, quiet, out-of-the-way niches forget how easy that is. No matter how clever you might be, radio or phone signals move at the speed of light.

Because Homeland Security had made obsolete the notion of traveling incognito on anything but a stinky bus, Maggie had been required to produce a photo I.D. to obtain her plane ticket. Thus, in only moments we knew that she had boarded a flight out of El Paso International Airport that hit the clear purple skies promptly at 11:50 p.m. the day before, bound for Houston. Airport security confirmed that the Cadillac had been left in a back row of long-term parking. Phil had been snoring loudly and never knew that she'd gone.

Tracking her that far wasn't a difficult chore. Both Estelle and I had talked face-to-face with Maggie Borman just a few hours before. If she wanted to fly out of the country, the choices of metro airports near at hand were limited—Tucson to the west, Albuquerque to the north, El Paso to the east. El Paso was the closest, and with a number of telephones and computers checking manifests, it didn't take long.

And Estelle had called it exactly right—*if she can run, she will.* Maybe with her own edition of women's intuition, Maggie had read the undersheriff correctly. The door was closing, and if she was to run, then best that she run quickly.

Authorities in Houston confirmed that Maggie Payton Borman had boarded flight 921, bound for London's Heathrow Airport. That particular Boeing 757 had rumbled out onto the runway only eighteen minutes late, at 5:21 a.m., with a painfully sparse manifest of passengers. She had been able to call just before flight attendants gave the word that cell phones should be stowed for takeoff. And just about the time I had stepped into the shower that morning, flight 921 had started its take-off roll.

"She called me from the goddamn airplane

in *Houston*," I said. "I never heard anything in the background. I'll be damned."

"A light load of passengers, and it's easy to tell when the flight attendants start moving around, making final prep," Estelle said.

"Now what?" I asked, and I read Estelle's body language correctly. She had relaxed back in her chair, hands folded over her stomach.

"She's in the can," she said with uncharacteristic slang. "The flight is nonstop to Heathrow, and that's good for at least eight or nine hours from Houston. There's no point in inconveniencing a plane-load of travelers by diverting. There's an air marshal on board, and arrangements have been made to alert him."

"A quick round trip," I said.

Estelle nodded. "Once in Heathrow, she won't even go through customs. The air marshal can take her into custody on the airplane, and it's just a matter of making the return connections. Because she's arrested on board our airplane before it touches down, there's no matter of extradition—and even if there were, English authorities aren't going to want to waste time with her. They'll be delighted to see her off. Wash their hands of her."

"You're bound for Houston?" I asked. "Authorities there might hold her, you know."

"If they do, they do. But no. Jackie's going to

do that. I have an appointment with the D.A., and a bunch of other paperwork to do." She glanced up at the clock. "The preliminary hearing for Zimmerman is in an hour or so."

"Houston cops would make the tag for you, you know," I said. "Jackie doesn't need to go, either."

"She deserves some time away," Estelle said. "It's her turn. Plus, it's good for Mrs. Borman to see a familiar face when she deplanes."

"What can I do for you?"

Estelle smiled and reached out, nudging a pencil toward me. It rolled a few inches on her desk calendar and stopped. "I need a sequel. The deposition you wrote last night was pure art, sir. Now, we need another. On everyone and everything that's happened this week to which you are personally privy." She patted my hand.

"Personally privy," I said. "I like that."

"Absolutely. And be particularly thorough with your last phone conversation with Mrs. Borman. I don't think Phil had anything to do with this nightmare, but your deposition is going to make a difference with the district attorney on that."

I groaned and picked up the pencil, then dropped it in an empty cup. "Not on an empty stomach," I said. "This is going to cost you. A nice green chile breakfast burrito, maybe? Some fuel before I start my memoirs? And good company. We've got the time. Go with me."

"Why, sure," Estelle said, and that surprised the hell out of me.

To receive a free catalog of Poisoned Pen Press titles, please contact us in one of the following ways:

Phone: 1-800-421-3976
Facsimile: 1-480-949-1707
Email: info@poisonedpenpress.com
Website: www.poisonedpenpress.com

Poisoned Pen Press
6962 E. First Ave. Ste. 103
Scottsdale, AZ 85251

LaVergne, TN USA
27 October 2009
162203LV00006B/24/P